'An **enchanting** and heart-lift...
of plants and com...
Sophie Ander...

'A **wonderfully vibrant** story, of community,
family and self-discovery.'
Jasbinder Bilan

'It's **funny, heartfelt** and packed full of magic. A
joyful reminder that magic can be found anywhere –
even in a flat just off the North Circular.'
Abi Elphinstone

'**A magical, cosy, spellbinding treat!**'
Kieran Larwood

'**Magical and empowering**. It was so satisfying to
see how the power of community spirit can triumph
against the odds.'
G M Linton

'An **utterly charming** and hopeful story of
family and community.'
Lizzie Huxley-Jones

'A **comforting read** with a blast of magic and a
touch of the Caribbean! I couldn't put it down.'
Janelle McCurdy

FABER has published children's books since 1929. T. S. Eliot's *Old Possum's Book of Practical Cats* and Ted Hughes' *The Iron Man* were amongst the first. Our catalogue at the time said that 'it is by reading such books that children learn the difference between the shoddy and the genuine'. We still believe in the power of reading to transform children's lives. All our books are chosen with the express intention of growing a love of reading, a thirst for knowledge and to cultivate empathy. We pride ourselves on responsible editing. Last but not least, we believe in kind and inclusive books in which all children feel represented and important.

ABOUT THE AUTHOR

Alexandra Sheppard (she/her) was born in north London, where she still lives with her family. *Oh My Gods* was her first YA novel in 2019. Alex is also the co-author of *Fly High Crew* and *The Day We Saved The Future* in collaboration with the Banjo Brothers and has contributed to *Happy Here*, an anthology of stories from Black British authors and illustrators. Her second YA novel, *Friendship Never Ends*, also published to great acclaim.

ABOUT THE ILLUSTRATOR

Bex Glendining (she/they) is a biracial queer, UK-based illustrator, comic artist and colourist. Bex has worked as an artist on projects such as *Buffy the Vampire Slayer* and *When Life Gives You Mangoes*. When not working they can usually be found building gundams, playing video games with friends or fussing Cookie, their very spoilt tortoiseshell cat.

For my mum,
who believed in me before I believed in myself.

First published in 2024
by Faber & Faber Limited
The Bindery, 51 Hatton Garden
London, EC1N 8HN
faber.co.uk

Typeset by MRules
Printed by CPI Group (UK) Ltd, Croydon CR0 4YY

Text © Alexandra Sheppard, 2024
Illustrations © Bex Glendining, 2024

The right of Alexandra Sheppard and Bex Glendining to be identified
as author and illustrator of this work respectively has been asserted in
accordance with Section 77 of the Copyright, Designs and Patents Act 1988

A CIP record for this book is
available from the British Library

ISBN 978–0–571–37742–8

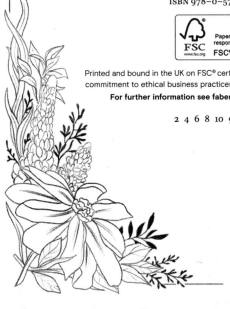

MIX
Paper | Supporting
responsible forestry
FSC
www.fsc.org
FSC® C171272

Printed and bound in the UK on FSC® certified paper in line with our continuing
commitment to ethical business practices, sustainability and the environment.
For further information see faber.co.uk/environmental-policy

2 4 6 8 10 9 7 5 3 1

ALYSSA and the SPELL GARDEN

ALEXANDRA SHEPPARD

ILLUSTRATED BY BEX GLENDINING

faber

Angelica
(for protection)

CHAPTER ONE

The morning Alyssa Charles-Reid's life imploded was a perfectly pleasant one. The sky above her house was a piercing shade of blue, the smell of cut grass hung in the air and the sun's rays toasted the pavement.

'See you in a few weeks, darling!' said Mum as she waved cheerily from the front door.

A bit too cheerily, Alyssa thought. Three weeks was the longest she'd been away from home. It was the longest she'd been away ever. Would Mum miss her?

Alyssa put on a smile and waved goodbye to Mum as she climbed into Dad's car.

It was the start of the summer holidays and Alyssa was preparing for a number of firsts:

Her first solo trip to London.

Her first time meeting Great-Auntie Jasmine.

Her first holiday without her parents, who were dumping her in London with the aforementioned great-aunt for three whole weeks.

'You're going to have the best time, sweetheart,' Dad said as they sped down the motorway. It was as if he couldn't wait to get rid of her either.

Alyssa fiddled with her braids. She was still getting used to her new hairstyle: Mum had had her thick curly hair braided into a gazillion tiny plaits that grazed her shoulder. It was so Alyssa could manage her hair over the summer. So she could get by without Mum.

'I'd love to spend a few days with you in Dublin, Dad,' Alyssa hinted for the millionth time. One more try couldn't hurt.

She was being extra careful to be on her best behaviour around Mum and Dad, and that had meant not badgering them with demands to stay with them over the summer. She didn't want to be a burden. Unfortunately, the hints didn't seem to have worked.

Dad sighed. 'We've been through this, sweetheart. You don't want to join my work conference. I won't have time to leave the hotel.'

Alyssa tried to hide her disappointment. She'd rather be in a dull hotel with Dad than spend the summer with a relative she had never met. Especially now that she only ever saw Dad on weekends since he'd moved out a few months ago. He and Mum both said it was temporary, but Dad showed no sign of coming home.

They drove on in silence, Alyssa's mind bubbling with unanswered questions. Earlier that week, when she'd asked Mum about Great-Auntie Jasmine and why she'd never met her, Mum had pretended she hadn't heard.

'How come I've never met Great-Auntie Jasmine before? Or any of Mum's family?' Alyssa asked now.

Dad smiled. 'Your mum can be a closed book, sweetheart.'

'She never wants to talk about them!' Alyssa said.

It was so weird. She knew all about Dad's family in Leeds, even if they only saw each other at Christmas and Easter. But Mum was so secretive, and Alyssa couldn't help wondering why.

'All I know,' said Dad, 'is that she fell out with her sister – that's your Auntie Dahlia – a long time ago. Before we met. And I've never met your grandparents because they live in Jamaica. They couldn't make it to our wedding. We're really grateful that Jasmine is able to look after you at such short notice. She has a tea shop, you know?'

Alyssa smiled weakly. It was hard to get excited about three weeks being surrounded by dusty tea leaves and an ancient great-aunt. Would she even have Wi-Fi?

Usually Alyssa and her parents went on holiday somewhere sunny over the summer break. But not this year. Alyssa remembered the crushing disappointment she'd felt when she discovered they wouldn't be going away together as a family.

It had totally ruined Alyssa's plan. She'd wanted to make sure that Mum and Dad had an incredibly fun time. So much fun, in fact, that Dad would realise what he was missing and move back home straight away.

Now, the plan had failed before it had even begun.

Mum and Dad said they were too busy with work trips for a summer holiday, but neither of them had told the other until last week. Typical. They never seemed to talk much these days.

It had been a last-minute scramble to find someone to look after Alyssa, and Great-Auntie Jasmine was the only available choice. Alyssa had found it hard to ignore the hushed telephone calls Mum made to neighbours and friends, asking them if they could look after Alyssa for a few weeks. Every time they told Mum they had other plans, like a real holiday booked with their families, Mum had sounded so disappointed.

Mum was a property lawyer, which was a job Alyssa didn't exactly understand. All she knew was that it kept Mum busy and glued to her laptop. Alyssa kept hearing Mum mutter phrases like 'big client' and 'once-in-a-lifetime opportunity'. Basically, it sounded like Mum would be in trouble at work if she didn't get this deal right. Alyssa guessed it sort of explained why Mum had pretty much taken to sleeping with her laptop.

So, Alyssa was being packed off to Great-Auntie Jasmine's for three weeks.

She couldn't help but feel a little rejected.

The car's GPS informed them that they were getting closer to Great-Auntie Jasmine's tea shop. Soon, Dad pulled the car to a stop. They had arrived.

Dad opened his arms wide. 'Come and give your old dad a hug, then!'

Alyssa hugged him awkwardly, being careful not to accidentally hit the steering wheel. His ginger beard tickled her face, and she breathed in his familiar scent, mingled with something new.

She pulled back. 'Did you change your fabric softener?'

Dad chuckled. 'Master sleuth, Alyssa! Why, yes, I did. It's called Spring Meadow or something. Is that all right with you?'

Alyssa nodded, even though it wasn't. Not at all. It was just one more way Dad had changed without her knowing. How much more would he change by the time the summer was over? If Alyssa wasn't there to help get her parents back together, would they stay apart forever?

'Alyssa, I . . .' Dad began.

She braced herself. Was Dad finally going to tell her he was moving back home?

Dad plastered on a fake grin. 'I want you to have the best time ever.'

No.

Alyssa looked out of the car window. 'The shop's all the way down there.'

'It's impossible to find a parking space, sweetheart,' Dad muttered. 'Let's see if I can find somewhere away from the high street,' he added, but then he glanced uneasily at the time. He looked stressed. Alyssa could tell what he was thinking. If he didn't hurry, he might not make his flight.

'It's all right, Dad,' she said. 'I can hop out here.'

'Are you sure? It'll only take a few minutes.'

Alyssa put on a brave face. 'It's fine. I'll be starting Year Seven in September. I can handle this.'

Dad looked relieved. 'That's my girl,' he said.

Alyssa looked out at the chaos of the high street, her heart racing. It seemed way busier than the shopping centre at home. But if she was going to secondary school next term, she'd better get used to navigating new places. Just the thought of secondary school made her tummy flip with anxiety and she pushed it out of her mind.

Alyssa gave Dad another hug and got out of the car. She wheeled her purple suitcase along, dodging shoppers and manky pigeons. Her palms were clammy against her suitcase handle. She ignored the urge to run back to Dad's car, and walked down the high street.

She scanned the rows of shops, looking for Jasmine's Teas – her great-aunt's tea shop. The high street looked like a right mishmash. Greengrocers and a couple of chain stores stood beside greasy-spoon cafes, laundrettes and corner shops that looked like they'd been around for decades. Across the road was a small park teeming with activity. It was full of kids playing football and people walking their dogs. The road was busy with traffic, but

Alyssa was surprised that the air smelled clean and fresh. She looked up and noticed brightly coloured flowers hanging from every lamp post lining the road. They seemed to perfume the air with their magical scent.

This was not what she had expected London to look like. Where were the towering statues, historic buildings and glamorous shops she'd seen on school trips? Of course, she didn't think her great-aunt lived opposite Big Ben or Buckingham Palace, but she didn't expect it to look so ... normal. As she carried on walking, her nerves eased a little. She had the vague feeling that she was returning to somewhere she'd been before. It made her feel warm and welcomed. But, as far as she knew, she'd never set foot in this part of London.

Finally, she found it. A faded hand-painted sign read *Jasmine's Teas* in swirly gold lettering. The midnight-blue shopfront framed a glass window that had a display of assorted crockery. It looked more like a charity shop than anything else.

BEEP-BEEP!

Alyssa turned to see Dad, who had pulled up on the other side of the road.

Look brave, Alyssa, she told herself.

She gave him one final wave. Then she pushed

open the creaky front door and walked in. The doorbell tinkled.

'H-hi,' Alyssa stammered. 'I'm—'

'Early!' shrieked the woman behind the till. 'My dear, I thought you were coming tomorrow!'

Great. Not even Mum's secret relative wanted her there. This trip wasn't exactly off to a great start.

Alyssa figured this must be Great-Auntie Jasmine. She wore a crimson-red kaftan thingy that flowed to her ankles, with red-framed spectacles on her nose. Her silver-streaked locs were wrapped in a matching headscarf, adding quite a few centimetres to her petite frame (with the headscarf, she and Alyssa were the same height) and accentuating her beautiful brown skin. A silver leaf-shaped brooch glinted on her chest.

'Oh, sorry,' Alyssa managed awkwardly. 'Mum and Dad had to leave for their work trips today. Dad's on his way to the airport right now. But I can call him if you want?' She reached for her phone.

Her great-aunt waved her hand. 'No need. It's a lovely surprise. Come closer, sweetness. Let me take a look at you.'

Alyssa stepped forward, and she was bundled into a rose-and-cinnamon-scented hug.

'Now, technically I am your mother's aunt, but you

can call me Auntie Jasmine. I look far too youthful to be anyone's great-aunt.'

Alyssa nodded. That was easy enough to remember. Auntie Jasmine seemed chatty and warm, and it made Alyssa feel a tiny bit less nervous.

They were disturbed by someone opening the door. It was the postman.

'Morning, Miss Jasmine!' he said brightly. He handed Alyssa a stack of white envelopes, which she passed to her great-aunt.

Auntie Jasmine took one glance at the return addresses and her face fell. She dropped them onto the counter, and looked up at Alyssa again, her face brightening.

'I'll worry about those later. For now, I'd like to welcome you to north London's premier tea emporium,' she announced. At that moment, a Jenga-like stack of boxes toppled to the ground.

Alyssa looked around. The shop seemed like it had seen better days, especially compared to the bright and shiny shops on her local high street in Milton Keynes. For a start, it seemed more like the living room of someone with a serious hoarding problem than a shop. It was impossible to tell what was for sale and what was just ... *there*.

Dozens of chests of drawers, some small and squat

and others reaching to the ceiling, lined the room. Each drawer was hand-labelled and dedicated to a particular type of tea leaf. Two small, cosy-looking armchairs and a polished mahogany coffee table took up a corner of the room in front of the till. The walls were bare, apart from an embroidered quote in a frame hanging by the till. Alyssa squinted to read it: *We are each other's harvest.*

Auntie Jasmine must be into gardening, she thought.

Although it felt chokingly warm, the smell of dried tea was fragrant and intense. A bit like flowers mixed with Christmas spices. The aroma mingled with the stuffy heat, making Alyssa's head spin. She wanted badly to get some fresh air.

'We have the largest tea selection this side of the Thames,' Auntie Jasmine said proudly. 'If we don't have it, it isn't worth brewing.'

Alyssa tugged at the neck of her white T-shirt. She was beginning to feel hot and bothered. Her skin prickled, like she had pins and needles over the surface of her entire body.

This place is going to give me heat stroke, Alyssa thought, even though Auntie Jasmine looked as cool as a cucumber in her flowing kaftan. Perhaps she would get used to it. She just had to get through the next three weeks, then she'd be home again.

They stepped through to the back (which took all of ten paces) and entered a room that seemed a world apart from the shop. This room was light, airy and made of glass. Plants of all varieties dangled from the ceiling and sprouted from giant terracotta pots. It smelled faintly like earth after a rainstorm. And it was very humid.

'This is the greenhouse!' Auntie Jasmine said, as though it was perfectly normal for a tea shop to have a greenhouse. She picked up a spray bottle and spritzed the leaves of a nearby fern. 'I believe it's time for someone's breakfast.'

'I'm okay, thanks,' Alyssa said. 'I had toast at home.'

Auntie Jasmine looked at Alyssa like she was silly. 'Not you, child,' she said with a smile. 'Pass me the plant food on the shelf.'

'So which ones are for sale?' Alyssa asked, handing her great-aunt the sticky brown bottle of plant food.

Auntie Jasmine looked horrified and cupped the petals of a nearby lily. 'We don't talk about such things in front of the plants,' she whispered. 'They're terribly sensitive.'

'Oh. My bad,' Alyssa muttered.

This woman was clearly a bit odd. Maybe there was a good reason Mum didn't talk about her family.

Mum was calm and collected most of the time. Auntie Jasmine seemed the opposite.

They pushed through the back door to reveal a huge garden. 'And this is the allotment,' Auntie Jasmine said. 'Anyone in the neighbourhood can grow vegetables here. We have cabbage, green beans, broccoli ...'

As Auntie Jasmine listed the least tasty foods known to humankind, Alyssa looked around. A morning breeze stirred through the garden; the cool air was welcomed by Alyssa's warm skin. But that didn't stop the weird prickling feeling. In fact, it was worse now they were outside.

It was shaping up to be a scorching hot summer's day. If Alyssa was at home, she'd be lounging in the garden with a stack of fantasy novels from the library by her side.

At that moment, Alyssa felt like she was being watched. She turned to see two Black girls – one who looked older than her and the other younger – staring at her with intense curiosity. They had just stepped through a door in the side wall, leading from the street straight to the allotment.

'Rosalie! Rue! Are you going to say hello to your cousin?' Auntie Jasmine said.

Cousins?

Yet another secret Mum had kept from her.

'Hi,' Rosalie and Rue said at the same time.

'I'm Alyssa,' she replied, giving a weak wave.

'I'm Rosalie, and this is Rue,' said the older one with an air of authority.

Alyssa reckoned Rosalie was thirteen, maybe fourteen. She was taller than Auntie Jasmine (which wasn't difficult) and her black hair was slicked back into a neat ballerina bun.

The younger one, Rue, was maybe nine years old. She clutched the handles of her yellow backpack and wore a shiny badge with '**She/They**' in bold letters.

The siblings looked at Alyssa as if she'd sprung up from a hole in the ground. She squirmed under their gaze.

'Hi, I'm Rue. Are you coming with us to—'

'No!' Auntie Jasmine interrupted. 'Alyssa will not be joining you at summer school. I'm afraid we're fully booked. You kids head on to morning registration now.'

Rosalie and Rue obeyed. They walked towards the back of the allotment and were soon hidden from sight by the greenery.

'My nieces stay with me every summer, even though they live down the road. They're arriving properly tomorrow night, so get ready to spend lots of time together,' Auntie Jasmine said cheerily. 'I do hope your mother comes to visit soon too.'

'She's pretty busy with work,' Alyssa mumbled.

Understatement of the year. She'd been surgically attached to her laptop for the last few months.

A flash of something shiny caught Alyssa's eye. A thick, unruly hedge lined the back of the garden. But through the bean poles and greenery of the allotment, she spotted a gap. It was a wooden door, the planks worn with age. Was that where Rosalie and Rue had gone?

A giant silver leaf was painted on the door, so faint that Alyssa almost thought she'd imagined it. It looked exactly like Auntie Jasmine's brooch. The leaf caught the sunlight and glimmered for just a second, then faded away completely.

Alyssa blinked several times, but it didn't reappear. A trick of the light.

She pointed to the wooden door. 'Auntie Jasmine, what's through there?'

'Oh, nowhere you need to worry about, my dear,' Auntie Jasmine said with a smile.

Aloe Vera
(for peaceful energy)

CHAPTER TWO

Alyssa took a seat in a worn armchair that looked older than time itself.

How on earth was she going to cope in this stuffy shop all summer? Sure, she had her fantasy novels and, if things got *really* boring, the textbooks Mum had packed so she could get a head start at her new school. But there must be some way she could keep herself entertained. After all, she was in the capital!

Maybe she could go sightseeing. Mum had begun to let Alyssa take the bus into town. Why would London be any different?

'Auntie Jasmine, do you think I could take the bus into town this week? I've got some pocket money, and—'

Auntie Jasmine shook her head. 'Don't waste your money on fancy shops in noisy central London. Why, we have all sorts of entertainment right here in the neighbourhood.'

Alyssa wasn't sure that was true. On the drive with Dad this morning, the closest thing to entertainment she had seen was a rusty swing set in the park and an old man circling the streets with a stereo fastened to his bike.

'Where? I didn't see anything,' Alyssa grumbled.

'My sweetness, I must insist that you don't bring negativity into this shop,' Auntie Jasmine said. 'I can't have the tea soaking up bad vibes.'

Alyssa sighed. 'But I've only been to London on school trips. I'd like to see more of the city while I'm here, if I can. Maybe buy some souvenirs for Mum and Dad?'

Auntie Jasmine thought for a minute. 'Well, if you insist – I'm sure we can arrange something in the next few weeks.'

It was better than 'no' but it still wasn't 'yes'. Alyssa made a mental note to ask again later.

'Rosalie and Rue are so excited to meet you properly,' Auntie Jasmine said, changing the subject.

They didn't look excited. It was like being observed under a microscope, Alyssa thought. Without Mum and Dad by her side, she felt out of place. The last thing she wanted was to meet more new people who would stare at her like she was an alien. It made her feel so awkward.

*

Auntie Jasmine said she would take Alyssa home when the shop closed later, so for the next few hours Alyssa settled in the corner with her book. The shop was like a train station. People came in and out constantly, all of them stopping by to chat. Hardly anyone bought anything, she noticed, but Auntie Jasmine had time for them all.

Later that morning, Jasmine introduced her to a young woman called Lisa. Apparently, Lisa and Auntie Jasmine managed the summer school and the shop between them. Alyssa couldn't help but wonder what the summer school was for. Mum hadn't mentioned it. Maybe it had something to do with gardening or growing stuff – Auntie Jasmine seemed really into her plants.

Lisa wore a badge that said: *Assistant Manager.* Her straight black hair was slicked back into a low bun, and her light brown skin shone with freshly applied cocoa butter. The scent of it reminded Alyssa of Mum, although Lisa looked much younger.

'Great to finally meet you, Alyssa. I'm Lisa Aydem,' she said warmly, and shook her hand.

Lisa's smart trousers and crisp blouse made the rest of the shop (and Alyssa) seem even shabbier in comparison.

'I thought Alyssa could be your assistant throughout the summer holidays,' Auntie Jasmine said. 'You know, help with those little projects you have in mind.'

Lisa nodded. 'Brilliant. This place needs all the help we can get,' she added in a low voice. 'You're the spitting image of your mother, you know.'

Alyssa smiled nervously. 'Yeah, everyone says that.' Maybe because her light brown skin was closer to Mum's complexion than Dad's, who was white with a ginger beard. 'Wait. How do you know my mum?'

'Everyone around here knows our family, darlin',' Auntie Jasmine said. 'That's what community is all about.'

'I'm an old friend of the family's,' Lisa explained. 'I went to Miss Jasmine's summer school when I was your age. Is Violet well?'

'Yep. Fine,' Alyssa said.

It wasn't quite the truth, but it wasn't *not* the truth. Because Mum never talked much these days, not since Dad had left. A conversation with Mum at the moment was like navigating a tricksy obstacle course: one wrong step and she'd shut down completely.

'Alyssa is staying with us for three whole weeks! I think Violet and her husband, Joseph, are having some marital problems,' Auntie Jasmine added in a quiet voice.

Lisa frowned. 'Oh, right. Sorry to hear that.'

Alyssa felt a prickle of anger flare up. Why was Auntie Jasmine telling strangers about Mum and Dad's situation? She made it sound like a bigger problem than it was. Dad moving out was temporary. If he was moving out for good, they would have told her.

Lisa stepped behind the till counter, glancing at the stack of envelopes left there by Auntie Jasmine before putting them in her handbag. She pressed a few buttons on the till, which opened with a bright ring.

'Any sales this morning, Miss Jasmine?' Lisa asked. 'I don't suppose someone bought something for a change?'

'Sales are overrated, my dear,' Auntie Jasmine said.

'Miss Jasmine, you know we need to actually *sell* the tea? That's how we make money.'

'We're still standing, aren't we?' Auntie Jasmine said, hand on hip. 'Besides, there's more to this place than selling tea.'

Lisa looked at Alyssa and raised her eyebrows, which made her giggle. It seemed like this was a conversation she'd had with Auntie Jasmine many times before.

'I'm going to get a coffee. That new place over the road looks nice. There's always a queue outside,' Lisa said pointedly.

Alyssa put down her book. 'Um, Lisa. Is there anything I can do to help?' She figured that she might as well make herself useful.

Lisa smiled at her. 'I like your initiative, Alyssa.'

She gave Alyssa the task of unpacking a new shipment of china tea sets for the window display. Alyssa was glad to be busy, and tried not to dwell on the fact that unpacking cardboard boxes might be the highlight of her summer.

'I wish that girl would ease up,' Auntie Jasmine said once Lisa left to get her coffee. 'This shop has stood here for nearly sixty years and it will be here for another sixty. We always manage in the end.'

Auntie Jasmine pulled up the armchair by the shop door. Alyssa had been warned by people at school that Londoners were unfriendly, but whoever said that clearly hadn't met Auntie Jasmine. She had a smile and a wave for everyone who passed by.

'I shall see you at the next community meeting, Sister Hortense!' she called after a Black woman about her age, who waved before crossing the street.

As Alyssa unpacked the delicate tea sets, something caught her eye outside the shop window.

It was an ice cream. But not just any ice cream. It was a double-cone vanilla whip with strawberry sauce and a flake. The ice cream was held in a hand, and that hand belonged to a girl about Alyssa's age. She was standing between two grown-ups who looked like they must be her parents. They also had ice creams, and they were posing for a group selfie.

The three of them looked so happy. A picture-perfect family with their picture-perfect ice cream. Alyssa felt a familiar wave of sadness. She remembered the days when she would go for ice cream with Mum and Dad. That hadn't happened in ages.

Broken families don't get ice cream together.

'Alyssa, darlin'. Are you all right?' Auntie Jasmine asked. 'You look like you've seen a ghost!'

Alyssa smiled extra wide. She couldn't stand the **thought of anyone seeing her upset, especially over** something so minor. Telling Auntie Jasmine why she was sad would make her feel silly.

'I'm fine,' she said, her lips stretched into a weird grin.

Auntie Jasmine gave her a slight smile. 'If you say so, dear.'

Alyssa watched the family cross the road to get to the park, but the feeling stayed. The more she tried to fake-smile, the worse she felt. The wave of sadness grew and grew. She felt it rising up inside her, like a pot of boiling water about to overflow.

She returned to unpacking the tea sets onto a nearby chest of drawers. A thud rang in the air, making her jump.

'Careful, Alyssa!' Auntie Jasmine said. 'Those tea sets must be handled gently.'

'I am being gentle!' she protested. When she looked down, though, there at her feet lay a teacup cracked in two. Strange – she hadn't even noticed it slip out of her hand.

'Don't move. I'll fetch a dustpan,' Auntie Jasmine said before going to the back office.

Lisa trusted you with a simple task and you blew it.

Great, now she was going to get into trouble on her first day. But before Alyssa could spend time wallowing in guilt, she stumbled back.

Suddenly she was swaying.

'Whoa!' Alyssa yelled, grabbing a nearby shelf for stability.

Was she light-headed because of the heat? Then she realised. It wasn't *her* that was swaying.

It was *the shop.*

The floorboards twisted and the ground rumbled. Metal tea caddies flew from the shelves and crashed at her feet, spilling fine tea leaves over the floor.

Alyssa ducked as a polka-dot teacup whistled by her head before exploding in mid-air. China shards scattered to all four corners of the room.

She gasped in shock. Alyssa was no scientist, but she was pretty sure objects didn't defy gravity like that. Especially not polka-dot teacups.

She stepped towards the back of the shop, unable to tear her eyes from the impossible scene. Her skin felt tingly and shivery. It was as if she had invisible lightning bolts pooling in her fingertips. Her heart pounded faster with every smash, bang and wallop.

'This can't be happening!' she muttered.

Every metal tea caddy and tiny drawer shot open, dried tea leaves bursting to the ceiling in plumes and exploding like confetti. It was literally raining tea!

Alyssa knew she had to move; it would only be a matter of time before something hit her. But she was frozen to the spot.

'Auntie Jasmine, come quick!' Alyssa yelled.

Her great-aunt bounded through from the back room. Her face was a picture of astonishment. She jumped into action.

'Get down here!' Auntie Jasmine yelled.

They crouched behind the counter, while metal tea caddies and china teapots, cups and saucers ricocheted across the room, crashing at their feet. There was no way they could make it to the front door without being hit.

'This way!' Auntie Jasmine grabbed Alyssa by the hand and led her into the greenhouse.

As Alyssa ran into the greenhouse, the sound of smashing and crashing followed. It was almost as if *she* was leaving a trail of destruction, the chaos pulling towards her like a magnet. But that couldn't be right ... could it?

Alyssa tried to catch her breath. A hot burning feeling flooded her chest and tingled down her arms, to the tips of her fingers. She was a boiling pot on the verge of overflow.

She held up her hands and got the shock of her life.

Her skin was *shimmering*. Rainbow waves radiated from her arms and hands, dissipating into the atmosphere. Could she have banged her head without realising?

Before Alyssa could find the words to tell Auntie Jasmine, a cracking sound split the air. It came from the giant terracotta pots surrounding them.

It was as if the destruction was following wherever they went. They stood in the centre of the greenhouse and watched as the pots disintegrated before their eyes. The plants popped into green dust, landing on the floor.

No, not just popped. They *exploded*. Like popcorn inside a microwave. The small shop transformed into a battlefield. Every step forward was laced with the threat of being hit with sharp shards.

Auntie Jasmine dragged Alyssa to the back door. They made it to the allotment in the nick of time.

'I think we're safe, Auntie Jasmine,' Alyssa said.

Suddenly the green water barrel beside her sprang a leak.

Then another. And another.

And Alyssa was caught in the crossfire.

'Arghhhhh!' she screamed as cold water soaked through to her skin.

Seconds later, the greenhouse shattered into a million shards of glass. As if a giant invisible fist had squished it like a paper ball. The crashing sound was deafening.

Then silence.

Alyssa looked down and saw the glass at her feet. It was like the aftermath of a hurricane or something. It was as though the greenhouse had never even existed. Every single terracotta pot was smashed. The ground was a mess of soil and tangled plants.

Her soaking wet clothes and compost-covered trainers didn't seem so important. Even if they were brand new.

Auntie Jasmine pulled Alyssa into a hug. 'Are you okay?'

No, she was very much not okay. Alyssa had thought that unloading cardboard boxes was the worst her day would get. She had never expected to have narrowly survived death-by-pottery.

She clutched her chest and felt her heart pound. 'Is it really all over, Auntie Jasmine?'

'It's all over, sweetness,' Auntie Jasmine said soothingly.

Alyssa turned to look at the wooden door at the back of the garden. If the summer school was behind that door, they would have heard the colossal smash. Where were the kids?

'I'm glad you're all right. Wish I could say the same about this place,' Auntie Jasmine said, pushing Alyssa inside before she had the chance to ask any questions.

They stepped carefully over the debris. Auntie Jasmine let out a quiet gasp.

The greenhouse and shop were unrecognisable. Every single plant and pot had been destroyed. Exposed wires hung from the ceiling and the lights flickered.

'This is unreal,' Alyssa said.

'I know, darlin'. I know.'

She felt so bad for Auntie Jasmine. This sort of damage had to be expensive to clear up. But she couldn't doubt what she saw with her own eyes.

Alyssa was going to have to say it.

'Auntie Jasmine, I know it sounds impossible,' she began. 'But everything – the tea sets and the little metal boxes – they moved on their own. No one touched them!'

'Hush,' Auntie Jasmine said. 'This ... there's a logical explanation. There's always construction work around here. Something must have gone wrong.'

Alyssa squinted. That was not what she expected her great-aunt to say. 'What construction work?'

'Oh, you know,' Auntie Jasmine replied with a tight smile. 'Renovations. Buildings being demolished. That sort of thing.'

'But you saw when everything went flying. I know you did!' Alyssa pleaded.

'We'll talk about it another time.'

Grown-ups loved that line. It meant: *Forget it ever happened because you're not getting an explanation from me.*

'Sure,' Alyssa muttered.

But she wasn't an idiot. She knew when something was being hidden from her. Although Alyssa wasn't much closer to an explanation herself, she knew this was no accident.

For some odd reason, Alyssa couldn't shake the feeling that *she'd* had something to do with the mess.

The front doorbell tinkled, disrupting the spiral of Alyssa's thoughts.

'What the heck happened?!' Lisa shrieked. She nearly dropped her coffee.

'It's not as bad as it looks,' Auntie Jasmine said matter-of-factly. 'It must be the construction work nearby.'

Lisa looked confused for a second, then she abruptly said, 'Oh. Right! Yes, the construction work . . .'

Alyssa looked at the two grown-ups with disbelief. Weren't they meant to be the sensible ones?

She crossed her arms. 'Look at the shop! How on earth did construction work—'

Auntie Jasmine raised her hand. 'That's enough,

Alyssa. I think you should wait for me at home.' She handed over her house keys. 'I need to organise a clean-up and it isn't safe here, what with the exposed wires. If you get lost, ask someone in the estate for directions. Tell them you're Jasmine's niece.'

'I can't walk back like this! I look like I had … an accident,' Alyssa said. Her shorts were embarrassingly wet.

Auntie Jasmine sighed. 'If you like, I can ask someone from the summer school to walk you home.'

And have them see her like this? No chance.

Alyssa swiped the keys. 'No, that's okay! I can handle a walk alone.' She grabbed her purple suitcase and walked out of the shop, following the directions Auntie Jasmine had given her and squelching with every step.

As Alyssa marched, she peeked through the windows of the shops along the high street. The florist, coffee shop and the takeaway looked perfectly fine. So how come Jasmine's Teas had been reduced to smithereens?

Alyssa couldn't explain why. But one thing in her mind was clear: this was the worst possible start to her summer.

Crab Apple
(for friendship)

CHAPTER THREE

Walking back to Auntie Jasmine's flat in soaking wet clothes was up there with Alyssa's most embarrassing moments ever.

Who was she kidding? It was *the* worst.

Even worse than the time she forgot her PE kit and had to do gymnastics in an old Peppa Pig T-shirt from lost property. Even worse than the time Mum and Dad had a full-blown argument in front of everyone at parents' evening.

A bunch of teenagers guffawed when she walked past, her trainers making a squelchy-fart noise with every step.

But all Alyssa could think about was what had happened in the shop. She'd seen objects hover

then spontaneously explode!

She *had*, hadn't she?

Alyssa would have known if she'd hit her head hard enough to affect her vision, surely? There was no sore spot or pain when she rubbed her scalp. Apart from the attack of the water butt, Alyssa had left the shop unharmed.

No, she'd definitely seen objects moving on their own. Judging by the look on Auntie Jasmine's face, she had seen them too. So why was her aunt pretending she hadn't? It was all so strange.

When Alyssa got to Auntie Jasmine's flat, she kicked off her compost-covered trainers and changed into dry clothes. She sank into the sofa and looked around the living room. Every surface was covered with plants and greenery of all kinds. Some were small and spiky, and others had lush green leaves the length of her forearm. Everything felt so alive.

It was the total opposite of her own house. Mum didn't like clutter, and they were both hopeless when it came to tending plants. Those little pots of basil from the supermarket never lasted longer than about three days. The greenery towering over Alyssa in Auntie Jasmine's living room brought the space to life. Plus, she had the same warm feeling she'd felt walking down the main road. She had never been here before, so why did it feel so familiar?

She checked her phone. There was a text from her friend Becky, who lived next door, as well as a selfie of her lounging in the paddling pool. Last summer, Alyssa had spent half her holiday splashing about in that pool.

Have fun in London! Seen any celebs yet? x

Alyssa sighed. In an alternate universe, she might be spending her summer weekends with Becky back home. She typed a reply:

No celebs! Just manky pigeons and loads of traffic.
Miss u x

Alyssa double-checked her notifications, but there were no missed calls from Mum or Dad.

Would they even answer the phone if she called them? Alyssa decided to check.

Dad picked up on the first ring.

'Hey, Dad, it's me. How's Dublin?'

'Hello, sweetheart! I've just boarded the plane at City Airport. Give us a wave when the jet flies over north London, won't you?' he said, chuckling.

Alyssa smiled despite the corny joke. It made her miss him even more.

'I wish I was with you,' she said.

'No, you don't!' Dad said cheerily. 'I'm going to be stuck in meetings all week. And then work will be non-stop for the rest of the summer. You're in the second-best city in the country. It's not Leeds, but I hear London has a few cool things. Enjoy it, love.'

'Dad, remember our flight to Spain last summer? Does the plane have those little caramel biscuits we loved?'

Dad muttered to someone, and Alyssa couldn't quite make it out.

'The flight attendants are badgering me to turn off my phone. Sorry, Alyssa. I'll call the second I land, all right?'

'Safe journey, Dad. Miss you,' she mumbled before hanging up.

Before she had a moment to feel sad, she rang Mum.

'Darling!' Mum said brightly. 'Is everything okay?'

'Yeah. Just calling to see how you are.'

'I can't say this conference is the most thrilling thing I've ever done. I'd much rather be on a beach somewhere than in Sheffield,' she said with a laugh.

Why did it seem like her parents were so much

more cheerful when Alyssa wasn't there? It had been weeks since she'd heard them laugh.

'How's London? I hope you're having fun?'

Fun? Yeah, if you call getting soaked by a malfunctioning water butt fun.

'I guess. Auntie Jasmine is a little odd.'

'Odd how?' Mum asked quickly.

'Oh, like she's really into her plants,' Alyssa said.

'Right. Anything more than that, sweetheart?' Mum asked, the concern clear in her voice.

Alyssa could tell Mum about the disaster at the shop. But how would she even go about describing something like that? If she told Mum there'd been a construction accident, Mum would probably get all panicky. Besides, it just sounded so weird.

'Nope,' Alyssa lied.

The call ended not long after that. Mum said she had a meeting to prepare for.

Alyssa checked the time on her phone. It was only half twelve. Auntie Jasmine wouldn't be home for hours yet.

She padded around and noticed a small balcony through the glass doors on the other side of the living room. It, too, was covered with greenery and bright petals: pot plants, flowers and herbs. Traffic sounds drifted up from the streets below. Alyssa guessed that was part of London life – she'd have to get used to the sirens.

She stepped onto the balcony. It was a riot of colours, textures and fragrances. Sunflowers and pink roses stood proudly beside the type of flowers Alyssa had only seen on school trips to the botanical gardens. She also spied tiny ripe tomatoes, green chillies and a small but perfectly formed mango tree in a heavy terracotta pot.

Alyssa pushed her thumb into the nearest mango. It had skin the colour of a tropical sunset, and the flesh yielded, releasing its perfume into the air. Ripe mango was one of her top five things to eat, up there with birthday cake and cheesy chips.

The smell brought back a memory: her and Mum eating fingers of mango standing over the kitchen sink, and Dad laughing at the mess they were making. They'd giggled as the juice dripped down their forearms, sticky and fragrant.

That was ages ago.

She pushed the thought to the back of her mind before it led to that sad feeling she knew all too well.

How was she going to distract herself for the rest of the day? She could call Becky or catch up on YouTube, but she felt too unsettled to concentrate on anything.

She had the paperbacks in her suitcase, but maybe Auntie Jasmine had something interesting too. Alyssa glanced at the living-room bookcase. The top shelf was packed with plants, their leaves dangling over the books. She parted them like a curtain and looked at the book spines. There were plenty of books on gardening, astrology and some faded novels. But there was one book that stood out from the rest. It was smaller, older and didn't have a title on the spine. Alyssa plucked it from the shelf.

It was brown and bound in leather, with curling yellow pages, about the size of an exercise book. It felt warm to the touch, as if someone had left it lying in a patch of sunshine. She opened the front cover and a small photo fell out.

The photo showed a young Black girl posing for a formal portrait. She had a mole just above her lip, like Alyssa's mum, and she was wearing a crisp white blouse. On the back of the photo, someone had written: *Euphemia Charles, aged 14*. That was only three years older than Alyssa.

'Who's Euphemia Charles?' Alyssa muttered.

Was this someone in her family? It seemed like Mum withheld family information from her like strawberry laces, a rare treat she was allowed once in a while.

She set the photo aside and looked through the book. It dawned on Alyssa that this was actually a photo album. She flicked through page after page of sepia photos, family portraits of people she'd never heard about. When she reached the colour photos, things began to get interesting.

She paused on an old school photo of two girls in matching uniforms. Alyssa recognised Mum's lively brown eyes, but not the face of the younger girl.

'It must be Auntie Dahlia, Mum's sister,' she whispered to herself.

Would she meet Auntie Dahlia this summer, or would her aunt keep her distance? Alyssa wasn't sure which option she preferred. The thought of meeting her aunt filled her with anxiety. What on earth would they talk about? But if Auntie Dahlia didn't want to meet her niece, Alyssa thought she would feel sad about that too.

The next few pages of the photo album were crowded with photos of the two sisters: smiling faces lit by the candles of a birthday cake, shared baths filled with bubbles and rubber ducks, trips to the seaside, and gleefully ripping open Christmas gifts.

The girls grew older and the hairstyles got bigger. (Alyssa giggled at the giant curly perm cascading down her mum's back – very different to the straight bob she wore now.) But halfway through the photo album the pages were blank. It was like the family had stopped taking photos after a certain point in time, sometime after the girls hit their late teens.

She remembered what Dad said about Mum and her sister on the drive here. They'd had an argument a long time ago and hadn't talked since.

Alyssa's friend Becky had younger twin brothers. She fell out with them constantly. Sometimes, if her brothers did something particularly awful (like the time they held her diary hostage in exchange for a kilo of gummy bears), Becky might give them the silent treatment for a full twenty-four hours. But never longer than that.

What had happened between Mum and her sister Dahlia for them to not talk for so many years?

Calendula
(for heart strength)

CHAPTER FOUR

The next morning, Alyssa was woken by the sound of traffic and honking horns drifting through the open bedroom window. The bright sun let her know that she'd slept late, which made sense, seeing as she'd stayed up until midnight chatting to Auntie Jasmine. Alyssa had tried asking again about what had happened at the shop, but her great-aunt continued to be evasive. Alyssa noticed that Auntie Jasmine had a knack for talking a lot without saying much at all; she didn't get a shred of useful information about the chaos at the shop or the family rift.

Alyssa stumbled into the kitchen for a glass of water.

'Auntie Jasmine?' she called. There was no answer.

A handwritten note was stuck to the fridge with a banana magnet:

Alyssa,
Gone to open the shop. See you there.
(Bring homework!)
(Don't forget to lock the front door behind you!!)
Auntie J x

Of course Mum had reminded Auntie Jasmine about her pre-secondary school homework schedule. One of the perks of finishing primary school was that there wasn't any summer holiday homework, but, even so, Mum had made sure she packed several exercise books so Alyssa 'wouldn't forget how to read and write'.

Algebra and biology couldn't have been further from Alyssa's mind, though. Finding the photo album last night had fanned the flames of her curiosity. Maybe if she could figure out what had happened between Mum and Auntie Dahlia, she could get to the bottom of it – maybe she could even help fix it.

That thought made her feel a little bit less miserable about the weeks ahead. This summer wasn't going to be as fun as a beach holiday with Mum and Dad, but perhaps it wouldn't be a complete waste of time. She might just learn something about the side of her family that Mum had worked so hard to keep secret.

Alyssa got herself a bowl of cereal and sat at the kitchen table. As she ate, she read text message updates from Mum and Dad. They both shared pictures of their boring hotel and even more boring meeting rooms. Still, the photos made her ache. She missed them so much.

She got showered and dressed. Just as she was about to leave the house, Alyssa noticed something. It was a photo on her bedside table.

She sat on the bed and inspected the photo. It was the image of Euphemia Charles from the photo album last night. 'Why didn't I notice you this morning?' she wondered.

Despite the morning sun rays drifting through the window, goosebumps prickled Alyssa's arms. She had no recollection of taking the photo out of the album and bringing it to her room. She'd spent pretty much the entire evening with Auntie Jasmine.

Maybe Auntie Jasmine had left it out for her. But why?

'Weird, weird, weird,' Alyssa said to herself.

The mental list of odd things that had happened in the last twenty-four hours was growing, and Alyssa had a feeling that Auntie Jasmine knew more than she was letting on.

Setting the photo down, Alyssa went out and made her way to the shop. She winced as she pushed open the front door to Jasmine's Teas, expecting to see loose wires hanging from the ceiling and tea debris still scattered over the floor.

But the shop looked ... fine. Not quite pristine, but exactly how it was before the mess happened. Right down to the ramshackle drawers and the stack of cardboard boxes that Auntie Jasmine meant to move.

'Hello, Alyssa,' Auntie Jasmine called from the greenhouse.

'How did you sort out the mess so quickly? It's like yesterday never happened!' Alyssa spluttered.

Auntie Jasmine stood in the doorway and put one hand on her hip. 'Is that how you greet your elders?'

'Sorry. Good morning, Auntie Jasmine.'

'That's better. Did you bring homework?'

Alyssa sighed. She'd forgotten her maths textbook. 'I forgot.'

Auntie Jasmine chuckled. 'Just between you and me, there's no place for arithmetic in summer holidays. But don't tell your mother I said that!'

'Auntie Jasmine, what about the mess? How did—'

Her great-aunt waved her hand dismissively. 'Oh, that was nothing. Lisa and I sorted it in no time. I believe she has some odd jobs for you, sweetness.'

Alyssa looked around. The same tea caddies and polka-dot teacups that she'd seen smashed at her feet were back on the shelves, as good as new. Unless Auntie Jasmine and Lisa had meticulously superglued every bit of broken pottery back together in record time, something else was going on.

Lisa gave Alyssa the task of alphabetising the tea stock and dried herbs, a job that was every bit as dull as it sounded. While Alyssa arranged canisters of basil, bay leaf and borage, she waited patiently for Auntie Jasmine to return from the allotment. She planned to start by asking about Euphemia Charles, then she would casually ask why Auntie Dahlia and Mum had stopped talking all those years ago.

However, when Alyssa had finished her alphabetising, there was still no sign of Auntie Jasmine, though she could hear Lisa in the back office. She went to the allotment through the glass conservatory (which, like the shop, was in pristine condition) and scanned the greenery.

The moment she stepped outside, Alyssa felt light-headed. Her skin prickled as if she was being tickled by invisible feathers all over her body. Her stomach churned and the rays of the midday sun felt fifty times more powerful.

What was happening?

'Whoa,' Alyssa muttered, clutching the nearest thing for support: the same water butt that had exploded all over her yesterday. 'Huh? How is this thing not covered with holes?'

'Alyssa, are you all right?' Lisa asked, coming out behind her.

'Th-thanks, Lisa,' Alyssa stuttered. 'I just feel a bit ... off-balance.'

Lisa handed her a cool glass of water. 'Sounds like sunstroke to me.'

'How can it be sunstroke? I was outside for literally two minutes!' said Alyssa. 'It sounds weird, but I got the same prickly skin feeling yesterday. Right before—'

'Just try to stay in the shade, all right?' Lisa interrupted. 'Having you around is a big help while Miss Jasmine and I are so busy. I appreciate it.'

Alyssa smiled weakly at Lisa. 'I finished sorting out the teas and herbs. What can I do next?'

Lisa beamed. 'I have just the task ...'

By the time Alyssa finished her second task of the day (sorting through the recycling – *snooze*), it was late, and Auntie Jasmine returned to lock up the shop for the night.

She chatted non-stop as they stopped at the Jamaican takeaway down the road and picked up dinner. When they got home, Alyssa sat on the sofa and replied to texts from Becky and her parents (Dublin update from Dad: still raining) while Auntie Jasmine hurried to prepare the beds for Alyssa's cousins.

Her tummy bubbled with nerves. Tonight, Rosalie and Rue were coming to stay. Like, actually live with them for the next three weeks. Even more nerve-racking, while Rosalie would be in the tiny spare room, Alyssa and Rue had to share! Goodbye, privacy.

Alyssa had only one close friend: Becky. And it might sound weird to other people, but for a long time Mum and Dad had been her best friends. Alyssa didn't like being around lots of people; small groups suited her just fine. But that meant she didn't have much experience with making new friends. She had tried, once, at an after-school club when Mum and Dad were working late, but it was so much easier to read her book while everyone else played. That felt safer.

In short, Alyssa had no idea how to act around

her new cousins.

What if we don't have anything in common? What if they don't like me? What if—

BZZZZZ!

They were here. Auntie Jasmine opened the front door and a cacophony of voices drifted down the hallway.

Rue ran into the living room and belly-flopped onto the armchair. 'Can I have an ice lolly, Auntie Jasmine? It's hotter than a camel's armpit in here!' they yelled.

Alyssa couldn't help chuckling. If a ray of sunshine was turned into a nine-year-old kid, Alyssa reckoned they would look like Rue. Their afro hair was held back with a yellow scarf and their matching dungarees brightened up the room.

Rosalie walked in. 'There's no such thing as a camel's armpit,' she said tartly. 'We've been through this, Rue.'

'Course there is, Rosalie! Every mammal has an armpit,' Rue protested.

'Don't tell me you two are arguing about camels again,' a woman said.

Alyssa got up to say hello but the words caught in her throat.

This *had* to be Mum's sister.

They looked startlingly similar. Auntie Dahlia had the same warm smile with the merest whisper of dimples. Though it had been a while since Alyssa had seen Mum smile like that.

'You must be Alyssa,' Auntie Dahlia said, with Alyssa's mum's smile.

'Hi,' she mumbled, feeling shy.

A part of Alyssa had assumed that Auntie Dahlia would be mean or bad-tempered, something that would explain why she and Mum hadn't spoken in years. But she seemed, well, nice.

Auntie Jasmine interrupted the awkward silence. 'Dinner's getting cold!' she called.

While her cousins said goodbye to their mum, Alyssa headed to the kitchen.

'Time to eat! Now!' Her cousins raced into the kitchen at Auntie Jasmine's order.

Platters of food crowded the small kitchen table: curries, rice, chicken wings covered in sticky sauce, plus coleslaw and little fried balls of dough. They had to rearrange the plates to make enough space.

Alyssa wasn't quite sure what everything was, but her tummy rumbled with anticipation.

'This looks deeeelish!' Rue said.

'I bought it all from that new Jamaican place on the high street. It's been a long day,' Auntie Jasmine said with a sigh.

Rosalie giggled. 'You never cook anything but breakfast anyway, Auntie!'

'And I'm not going to start now,' retorted Auntie Jasmine. 'I'll leave it to the experts. Dig in, folks!'

Alyssa reached for the thing that looked most familiar: the chicken wings. They were dark brown and covered in a sticky sauce. She took a huge bite, started to chew and—

Oh my gosh. My lips are on fire!

Alyssa wiped her mouth, but the tingling didn't stop. The burning sensation spread to her tongue and down her throat. She took a big gulp of juice to quell the flames, coughing at the same time. What was in that sauce? *Jet fuel?*

'Oh dear! Drink this.' Auntie Jasmine handed Alyssa a small glass of milk.

She drained the glass, and the flames in her mouth died down. Unfortunately, the milk did nothing to cool her cheeks. Her face burned with shame.

'I didn't realise how spicy it was!' Alyssa said.

'Maybe stick to lemon and herb in future, yeah?' Rosalie said with a smirk.

'You can't talk,' Rue snorted. 'Remember when I dared you to eat a spoon of Encona hot sauce and you cried afterwards?'

Alyssa giggled. She found she didn't mind the mild teasing.

'I should have warned you about the jerk chicken, Alyssa,' Auntie Jasmine said. 'Does Violet make it less spicy?'

Alyssa shook her head. 'I've never had food like this before.'

Rue looked aghast. 'You haven't had Jamaican food? No curry goat? No saltfish fritters? No—'

Auntie Jasmine held up her hand. 'Enough, Rue. We get the picture.'

Alyssa's mum was an excellent cook. Back when Mum and Dad actually liked each other, she cooked everything from Spanish paella to Malaysian noodle soups and West African jollof rice. But never the food of her own culture. Alyssa hadn't thought to question why. Now she wondered.

'A life without curry goat isn't worth living,' Rosalie said between bites. 'This is nearly as good as Mum's.'

Alyssa was only a few bites into her meal, but she couldn't help agreeing with Rosalie. This food made her feel warm and happy, right down to her toes.

Auntie Jasmine piled more spoonfuls of steaming food onto Alyssa's plate. 'Have you tried the curries? **Don't worry, they're not as spicy as the jerk chicken.**'

One tentative nibble and Alyssa was sold. The curry was the most delicious thing she'd eaten in weeks. Nicer than anything Mum or Dad had made for her in ages.

'It's incredible,' she said.

Auntie Jasmine reached across the table to pat her hand and beamed. 'I am so happy you're enjoying it.'

Alyssa nodded. 'I am.' And she meant it. The warm feeling she'd felt when she first arrived enveloped her in a happy fug. Maybe it would be fine here, after all.

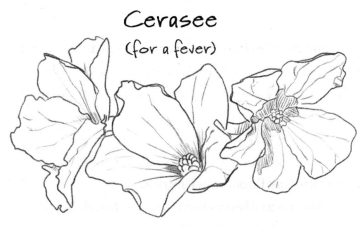

Cerasee
(for a fever)

CHAPTER FIVE

After dinner, Alyssa was finally alone with Auntie Jasmine. Rue and Rosalie unpacked their bags while she helped her great-aunt to clear the table.

'I can do the washing-up, Auntie,' Alyssa said.

Auntie Jasmine smiled and handed her the sponge. 'I won't say no, my dear! If you need me, I'll be watering my babies on the balcony.'

Once she'd finished the dishes, Alyssa headed to her bedroom to find the photo of Euphemia Charles. Now was her chance to ask Auntie Jasmine why she'd left it on her bedside table. She knocked on the door (Rue wouldn't appreciate her waltzing into their room unannounced) but her cousin wasn't there. And neither was the photo. More weirdness.

She decided that enough was enough and went to find her great-aunt on the balcony. 'Auntie Jasmine, why did you leave that photo on my bedside table? The one of Euphemia Charles?'

Auntie Jasmine set her watering can down on a small table. She looked puzzled. 'What photo? Did you just say Euphemia Charles?'

Now it was Alyssa's turn to be confused. 'You know, the small photo in the album.' She went on to explain how she'd discovered the photo album yesterday. 'You left the picture on my bedside table last night and I wanted to ask you about the girl in it.'

Auntie Jasmine was silent. This was not the reaction Alyssa had been expecting. She had been the one who put it there, hadn't she?

'I'm afraid I didn't leave it on your bedside table. In fact, I haven't seen that photo in years. Will you show me?' Auntie Jasmine said finally. 'This photo was in an old family album. I thought it was lost!'

Alyssa smiled. 'It's definitely not lost, Auntie!'

She led Auntie Jasmine to the living room and pointed to the shelf. But the brown book was nowhere to be seen. They moved every book on the shelf, but it definitely wasn't there.

'It was right here!' Alyssa said. She felt a bit silly for getting Auntie Jasmine's hopes up.

Auntie Jasmine sighed. 'Not to worry, darlin'. I thought it was too good to be true.'

'I promise I saw it. I'm not lying!' Alyssa said, her heart racing. Auntie Jasmine had to know she wasn't making things up. 'How else would I have known Euphemia's name?'

Auntie Jasmine looked puzzled. 'No one's accusing you of lying, my dear,' she said. 'It's just quite the conundrum, that's all.'

Maybe you lost it. The awful thought raced through Alyssa's head that she'd misplaced the precious photo album or damaged it somehow.

Suddenly Alyssa saw a dark blur out of the corner of her eye, followed by a thudding sound. She approached the sofa.

'I don't believe it. Did you see that, Auntie Jasmine? It was like it fell from the ceiling!'

There, on the sofa, was the photo album. And the photo of Euphemia Charles sat neatly on the top.

Alyssa looked up. There were no shelves or ledges directly above the sofa. Nothing from which the book could have dropped from such a height, unless it had been hovering in mid-air.

Her great-aunt sat on the sofa and fingered the pages of the photo album. 'Yes. This is it,' she said softly.

'Auntie Jasmine … ummm … you saw the photo album appear out of nowhere, right?' Alyssa demanded.

'I saw it too, Alyssa.' Auntie Jasmine sighed and leaned back in her chair. 'Your mother will have my guts for garters,' she muttered.

'Why? What's this got to do with Mum?'

'Because she said I was to keep you away from this "magic nonsense". The trouble is, Alyssa, that magic doesn't want to keep away from you.'

Alyssa's eyes widened. '*Magic?* Did you say *magic*?'

Auntie Jasmine nodded. 'That is exactly what I said.'

Alyssa thought about the odd things that happened since she arrived: the meltdown at the shop, the exploding water butt, the photo that wouldn't leave her alone.

She knew something strange was afoot. But … *magic*?

Magic belonged in films and fairy tales. Magic belonged in her favourite fantasy novels.

It didn't belong in her great-aunt's flat just off the North Circular.

Was this an elaborate joke? But her great-aunt didn't seem like the pranking type. Try as she might,

Alyssa couldn't think of an explanation that made more sense than magic.

'So . . . it wasn't a construction accident at the shop yesterday?' Alyssa asked tentatively.

Auntie Jasmine shook her head, her grey-tinged locs swishing over her shoulders. 'No, it wasn't. I must say, your powers took us all by surprise.'

'*My* powers? What do you mean?'

Her lips quirked into a smile. 'The mishap at the shop. That was all you.'

Guilt flooded through Alyssa. 'But . . . I didn't touch anything!'

Auntie Jasmine reached over and held her hands. 'You haven't done anything wrong. In fact, your power is a direct descendant of the woman in this photo. She's your Great-Granny Effie. I imagine that's why her photo keeps badgering you.'

Alyssa peered at the small photo. She could see the ghost of a resemblance in her jutting chin and deep brown eyes.

'She could move objects with the power of her mind,' Auntie Jasmine continued. 'That said, it's highly unusual for a young Keeper's talent to be so well developed without any training.'

'What's a Keeper?'

Auntie Jasmine removed her spectacles. 'Your

mother isn't going to like this,' she said. 'But I think you have a right to know the full story, especially if these sorts of things are going to keep happening. Magic like this is too powerful to hide for long.'

Alyssa's heart pounded. She was fed up with the grown-ups in her life not being honest with her. Finally, someone was telling her the truth.

Auntie Jasmine took a deep breath. 'Let me start from the beginning, sweetness. You, your mother and the rest of our family . . . we're descended from a line of powerful, magically inclined beings.'

'If I didn't know better, I'd say that sounds like witches,' Alyssa said sceptically. Maybe Auntie Jasmine was pranking her, after all.

Auntie Jasmine wrinkled her nose. 'I suppose you could say that. But the term "witches" makes me feel old.' She picked up the old photo. 'This is my mother, Euphemia Charles. Everyone called her Effie.' She paused. 'You know what? Let me tell you the story with a little more . . . pizzazz! Go and fetch your cousins, and then meet me on the balcony.'

Alyssa wasn't sure why her cousins needed to be involved (unless they were in on the joke too?) but she got up and walked to the tiny spare room. Rosalie was hanging up her clothes while

Rue lounged on the bed playing a noisy game on their phone.

'Um, Auntie Jasmine wanted me to get you,' Alyssa said.

They followed her to the balcony and stood around the small table. Between the plants and the garden furniture, it was a tight squeeze.

Auntie Jasmine beamed as she wrapped a shawl around her shoulders. 'It's so good to see my little ones all together,' she said. 'I've decided that Alyssa must know Our Story.'

Rue jumped into the air with excitement. 'Yes!' they cheered.

'It's about time, Auntie Jasmine,' Rosalie said with a grin.

Alyssa and Rosalie sat on the small garden chairs, while Rue bounced onto their sister's lap. Alyssa had no idea what to expect, but her cousins' excitement was contagious.

Auntie Jasmine closed her eyes and held her hands in front of her face. She took deep, long breaths. Her fingers twitched as though she was tugging on invisible strings.

A crackling sound filled the air. Like twigs being snapped. Then it stopped.

Auntie Jasmine opened one eye. 'Look at me doing

all the work when I have three descendants of Effie sitting before me! Folks, please hold hands.'

'But I'm not even a Keeper-in-Training yet,' Rue said.

'No matter. You have our magic running through your veins,' Auntie Jasmine said.

Rue slid off Rosalie's lap and stood next to their sister. The foursome held hands in a circle round the garden table.

'Now, close your eyes,' Auntie Jasmine said.

In seconds the snapping sound returned. This time it was even louder. It reminded Alyssa of microwave popcorn.

She peeked, opening one eye. There was something blocking the light, like a giant storm cloud had blocked out the sun. But it wasn't a cloud.

Dark green ivy sprouted from the balcony roof and descended downwards like a giant vine curtain towards the railing. The leaves and vines twisted together, creating a tightly woven covering that hid the city skyline.

Alyssa looked down and gasped. Their hands and arms were *glowing*. A trail of silvery light ran in an unbroken circle through their clasped hands, like electricity through cables.

The others opened their eyes just as the ivy **covering was complete. They were in a dark green** cocoon. The only light came from the glow of silver flowing through their bodies.

'It's so cool, right?' Rosalie said to Alyssa.

Alyssa's entire body fizzed with excitement and awe. 'So cool' seemed like a massive understatement.

'It's the most amazing thing I've ever seen,' she said. 'Won't people outside notice the ivy?'

Auntie Jasmine shook her head. 'People only see what they want to see. If they aren't looking for magic, they will never notice it.'

'If you think that's cool, just wait until—'

'Rue! Not yet,' Auntie Jasmine said. 'Alyssa, there's a small watering can beside your left foot. Kindly pass it to me.'

Alyssa fumbled in the dark until she felt the metal handle, and passed it to her great-aunt. The silvery glow in their arms and hands slowly faded.

Auntie Jasmine reached one hand into the watering can and produced a small palmful of silvery water. She closed her eyes, deep in focus for a few seconds, and blew.

The tiny droplets floated through the air, over to the canopy, and landed on the leaves, coating them with silver. The droplets gathered together to form a flat surface as smooth and shiny as glass. It was so bright that it illuminated their plant cocoon.

An image of a young woman appeared on the shiny surface. *Wait.* Alyssa rubbed her eyes, blinked, and rubbed her eyes again. No, her eyes weren't playing tricks on her. There *really* was a woman there. The image rippled as though she was at the bottom of a deep pool of water.

It was Euphemia Charles.

Dandelion Root
(for divination)

CHAPTER SIX

'I was younger than you when Mother decided we should leave Jamaica for England,' Auntie Jasmine said. Her voice sounded distant, as though she was in the next room. 'My father died suddenly, plunging our family into poverty. Mother did everything she could to bring in money, but being the village washerwoman wasn't enough to keep us fed. So, she took us to London in hopes of becoming a teacher, secretary or even starting her own business.'

So, this was Euphemia Charles. The image sprang to life. Through the ripples, Alyssa saw her great-grandmother writing and drawing in a book by candlelight. The ink was silver, just like the water.

The image shimmered. Now, the same woman

was packing an armful of assorted items into a battered suitcase: a leather-bound book, sheafs of paper and a small sack of glowing pebbles.

'We arrived in London with nothing, and knowing no one,' Auntie Jasmine continued, her voice almost echoey.

The image rippled again. It revealed two young girls bundled up in woollen cardigans, faces pinched by the cold. Alyssa's heart crumpled to see them looking so sad. The loneliness radiated from the image before her.

'You and Granny look very cold,' Rue whispered.

It was Auntie Jasmine and her sister, Granny Hyacinth.

'That first winter was … difficult. Mother ended up training to be a nurse. She worked hard, but times were tough. We wouldn't have survived without the small community we built for ourselves here. Our neighbours became friends, and those friends became family. Some of them were from Jamaica too. They shared their meals and their homes with us while we adjusted to a new land.

'When we moved into a small house with a tiny garden, Mother planted the bulbs and tended to them. But these weren't any old plants; this was a spell garden, and these plants had magical properties. Mother was using the knowledge that our family line was tasked with protecting many generations ago, and passed it down to us.'

The water rippled to reveal a new image: a glowing pebble being buried in a small, scrubby back garden by Great-Granny Effie while the two girls, a few years older now, looked on.

'Despite the frost and smoky city air, the plants thrived. Mother taught us how to harvest the plants and use them in spells. Spells that soothed, healed and protected.'

The image changed again: slender hands plucking leaves and buds, then grinding them into a pulp before pouring over boiling water. They were brewing tea.

'Mother used the spells to repay the kindnesses of our neighbours. The more we used our magic to help our neighbours, the more the little spell garden flourished. You see, there is nothing our magic loves more than to be used for the good of all. It soon took over every bit of space in our small home and even smaller garden.' Auntie Jasmine chuckled.

'What do you mean? How did it help the neighbours?' Alyssa asked.

'Anything from curing a nasty fever to curing an even nastier attitude from a boss or co-worker,'

Auntie Jasmine said. 'Despite what we had been led to believe, some people here weren't so welcoming to newcomers from our part of the world.'

That answer didn't make sense to Alyssa. How could a cup of tea make someone's boss be nicer to them?

'Mother had a tricky relationship with her parents. They didn't approve of her choice of husband, so she eloped with my father, Glenmore. She never spoke to her parents again after she was married. But when my grandmother died, she left Mother some money in the will. Like a peace offering. Mother used that bit of cash to rent a property on the high street. She took on fewer nursing shifts and dedicated more time to the shop.'

The image rippled to reveal a small, narrow shopfront with a glass window. The shop looked like Jasmine's Teas but the name was different. The sign read: *The Tea Emporium.*

'The shop itself was modest, but what appealed to Mother was the land that came with it. An unused patch, rich with fertile soil, and enough space for our expanding spell garden. It took some time, but we eventually moved the magical plants to their new home. They took root wonderfully.'

'Why didn't Great-Granny Effie start a shop and

spell garden in Jamaica? Why did she come all this way with you and Granny?' Alyssa asked.

Auntie Jasmine nodded patiently. 'There is a thriving spell garden in Jamaica, maintained now by your granny, my sister, Hyacinth. But what Mother needed was financial opportunity and that led her to England, along with hundreds of others in Jamaica at the time.'

Alyssa remembered Mum had mentioned something about her parents being part of the Windrush generation, though she didn't know much about it.

'I don't think it was easy for Mother to leave her homeland,' Auntie Jasmine said quietly. 'But, as a widowed mother of two, she didn't feel she had much choice.'

Alyssa saw the glowing pebbles again in the shimmering water. This time, it was two young women who covered them with soil while a much older Great-Granny Effie looked on.

As soon as the glowing pebbles were buried, the ground around them changed. A cloud of grey dust drifted upwards, magically forming hard brick-like shapes. The bricks stacked and formed a cylinder in a flurry of activity. When the dust cleared, the shape was revealed: it was a well.

All around the well, plants and branches shot through the ground, brilliantly green and sparkling with life. The biggest plant of all whooshed upwards, turning into a large tree with shiny green leaves.

This was no ordinary garden.

'That's Effie's tree. Right, Auntie Jasmine?' Rosalie asked.

'Yes. It's magically connected to the same tree in the Jamaican spell garden, back home. Hyacinth tends it. Whenever I miss her, I put my hand to the tree and feel the warmth of home.'

'So that's why Granny moved back to Jamaica,' Alyssa murmured.

She stared at the image, mesmerised by the detail.

'The pebbles were Mother's last gift to us,' Auntie Jasmine continued. 'We call them crux-pebbles. The word "crux" means "essence" and –' she gestured at the shimmering water, and the little watering can – 'that is exactly what this crux-water is: it's the very essence, the fuel, of our magic. The more we use our magic for good, the more powerful the magic gets.'

'What makes them glow?' Alyssa asked.

'I'm not sure exactly. But I do know that, as long as we have the crux-pebbles, we have the crux-water,' Auntie Jasmine said. 'They tap into an ancient energy source deep in the earth, channelling it so we can practise magic. So that we stay protected.'

'Protected from what?' Alyssa asked. But Auntie Jasmine appeared not to hear her.

Auntie Jasmine closed her eyes again. The droplets in the silver screen evaporated, and the ivy cocoon began to unwind. The green plants retracted, snapping backwards until the plant curtain receded. The dusk sky filtered through, bathing the balcony in pink-orange light. The ivy was nowhere to be seen.

Alyssa had a *bajillion* questions. But where on earth would she start?

'Can I tell you my theory, Alyssa?' Auntie Jasmine said as she set down the watering can. 'I think your magic activated yesterday because it was close to the very thing that fuels us. Our magical crux-pebbles reside in the spell garden, which is mere metres away from the shop. They're at the bottom of the well that you saw being built just now.'

That made sense. Alyssa remembered the prickly feeling all over her skin when she stepped into the allotment. It was the first time she'd ever been close to this crux, as Auntie Jasmine called it.

'Unlike the rest of us, you haven't had any

practice in controlling your powers,' Auntie Jasmine continued.

'Don't feel bad. It can take a while to control your magic,' Rosalie said.

She sounded a bit patronising, Alyssa thought.

'Tell me, darlin'. Did you see something to make you upset or angry yesterday morning?' Auntie Jasmine asked. 'Sometimes intense emotions can trigger magical disturbance.'

Alyssa remembered the perfect family taking a selfie outside the shop.

'Just a little homesick, I guess.' She didn't want to get into why seeing the family made her so upset. Especially not in front of her cousins, who might think she was a big baby.

'We haven't told Alyssa the best part,' Rue said. 'We get to spend the entire summer at Silverleaf, practising our magic!'

'Silverleaf?' Alyssa asked. 'What's that?'

'I established Silverleaf School of Plants and Potions after my mother passed away. Taking care of magical plants is a dying art, and I couldn't let mine be the last generation to know these skills. As Keepers, it is our responsibility to ensure the magic survives. Lessons take place in the spell garden, which is tucked behind the allotment,' Auntie Jasmine said.

'Does that mean everyone who goes to the summer school is a . . . magical being, too?' Alyssa asked. She was hesitant to call herself a magical being because, as far as she was concerned, she was incredibly normal.

Auntie Jasmine shook her head. 'Not like us. But the beauty of plant magic is that anyone can harness it, if they are willing to open their mind and work hard. As magical beings, the plant magic comes to us more naturally.'

'But we still have to work hard, too,' Rosalie chipped in. 'Harnessing magic isn't easy, even for us.'

'That is correct, Rosalie. The children help tend the garden and in return they are trained in how to use the magical plants. At Silverleaf, they learn how to channel botanical magic,' Auntie Jasmine said.

'Why just kids?' Alyssa asked. 'Aren't grown-ups allowed?'

'Oh, we have a few grown-ups. There's me, Lisa and my ex-partner Debbie who runs the secondary spell garden at her home, which isn't far from here. But we are a rare bunch: some of my best students are now disbelieving grown-ups. After a while, the spell garden simply fades from memory. As children grow up, many become far too focused on things like logic and common sense to believe in magic. And if you don't believe it, you can't see it.'

Sounds just like Mum. She thought Alyssa's fantasy novels would rot her brain and grumbled if Alyssa ever suggested watching a movie about magic.

'Wait. Does that mean Mum has magic too?' Alyssa asked.

Auntie Jasmine nodded. 'We all do in this family.'

'But if Mum's magical, why would she hide it?'

And why would she keep it from me?

It was hard for Alyssa to imagine her sensible mum, who could barely keep a house plant alive, as a magical being channelling plant magic like Auntie Jasmine. But the truth of her magical heritage was clear.

And the thought was unsettling.

Auntie Jasmine wrapped her shawl tighter around her shoulders and said, 'I cannot explain your mother's actions.'

'Mum said that she hasn't spoken to Auntie Violet since before I was born,' Rosalie added.

'My dad said they fell out. But he wouldn't tell me why,' Alyssa said.

'Do not ask me to account for the actions of those girls. One spell misfired and before we knew it—' Auntie Jasmine broke off. Alyssa thought she looked sad.

'What happened?' Rue asked. The three kids stared at their great-aunt.

'I've said enough. Alyssa has had plenty of family bombshells for one day, hmm?' Auntie Jasmine said.

'You mentioned that a spell misfired. Is that what happened to me at the shop yesterday?' Alyssa asked. She remembered the trail of destruction she had left.

'Don't worry, sweetness. That won't happen again,' Auntie Jasmine said, as if reading her mind.

'How do you know?' Alyssa asked. 'What happens if it does? It must have taken ages for you to clear that up!'

'A time-reversal spell hides a multitude of sins,' Auntie Jasmine said with a smile.

'We can do time-reversal spells?' Rosalie gasped.

'*I* can do time-reversal spells,' Auntie Jasmine said firmly. 'And only in exceptional circumstances. It uses a great deal of crux-water and only works with inanimate objects.'

'Are you going to do a time-reversal spell every time Alyssa makes a mistake?' Rosalie asked.

Alyssa felt like a silly child. Just when she'd been starting to like her cousin.

'That's out of the question,' Auntie Jasmine said. 'I'm afraid there is only one solution I can see: Alyssa, you must come to Silverleaf and learn to control your powers. However, your mother must not find out. I promised I would keep you away from magic. But yesterday proved that's just not possible – you and the magic have too powerful a connection, my dear.'

It was getting late. The dusky sunset had faded to blue, and the city skyline twinkled in the distance. A breeze ushered in fresh, cool air. Alyssa wasn't sure she liked the idea of keeping secrets from Mum. But hadn't Mum done the same thing to her? Maybe it was all right for Alyssa to have a secret of her own.

She looked down at her hands and flexed her fingers. The thought of having this hidden power made her feel more nervous than that time she had to give a talk in assembly.

Yet ... she had to admit, it was also kind of exciting. Alyssa had always wanted an adventure, like the ones she read about in books. The stories that transported her from her suburban bedroom into fantasy realms and magical kingdoms. To think only yesterday she'd thought that the most exciting thing to happen this summer would be alphabetising tea leaves.

From tomorrow, Alyssa would be swapping chores in the tea shop for lessons at Silverleaf School of Plants and Potions. For the first time since she'd arrived, her summer was beginning to perk up.

Dog Blood Bush
(for healing)

CHAPTER SEVEN

Auntie Jasmine had sent all three children to bed an hour ago, but Alyssa was far from sleepy. Her mind fizzed with the new information she'd gathered that evening. It was all she could think about.

Just a few hours earlier, Alyssa had felt strange about sleeping in the same room as Rue, who was practically a stranger. But now they shared this secret. Their bedroom had space for twin beds and not much else. The window was open and the curtain swayed with the cool night breeze. The faint noise of sirens drifted up from the street below. It seemed to Alyssa like London never slept.

'I don't know how I'd cope if Mum and Dad

decided I couldn't be a Keeper,' Rue said. 'Rosalie would lose it. She studies non-stop.'

'What sort of studying?' Alyssa asked.

'Mainly memorising. How else are you going to remember the plants and their magical properties?' Rue said. 'They're the basis of our spells.'

This surprised Alyssa. After all, she didn't know anything about magical plants and she'd still managed to make a giant mess in the tea shop.

'I have a lot to catch up on,' she muttered. She was used to being top of the class at school and didn't like the idea of being left behind.

'So your mum never mentioned magic to you once? Not in your whole life?' Rue asked.

'Never! She's not even mentioned you guys.'

'Wow. We knew about you, but only because Auntie Jasmine talked about you and your mum. Mum always clams up when we ask her anything,' Rue said. 'Why do you think they don't talk any more?'

'I know as much as you,' Alyssa said. It was a complete mystery. She shifted on the bed to face Rue. 'What do you think Auntie Jasmine meant by a spell misfiring?'

'Mum will be at my grounding ceremony tomorrow. We could ask her then,' Rue said.

'What's a grounding ceremony?' Alyssa asked.

The door creaked open and light from the hallway filled the bedroom. Rosalie stood at the door. Unlike with Rue, who was open and friendly, Alyssa still wasn't sure what to make of Rosalie.

'It's when your seedling is planted to measure your magical growth,' said Rosalie. 'It's a symbol of acceptance into our community and marks the start of becoming a Keeper-in-Training.' She sounded like she was quoting a textbook word for word.

'They usually happen when you're ten, but mine is a year early. Must be cos I'm so talented. And after the ceremony everyone gets this sick tattoo! Show her, Rosalie,' said Rue.

Rosalie smiled. 'It's only visible to those who have magical training or share our lineage.' She rolled up her T-shirt sleeve to reveal a leaf design that shimmered and glowed on her shoulder. It was just like Auntie Jasmine's brooch.

'I hope you know what you're getting yourself into, Alyssa,' Rosalie continued. 'Magic is a serious business, you know.'

Alyssa bristled at Rosalie's tone. Why did she have to sound like such a know-it-all? 'I'm sure I can handle it,' she said, although she wasn't entirely sure she believed that herself.

'Ignore her,' Rue whispered when her sister left the

room. 'Rosalie is thirteen going on one hundred and thirty. She forgets that magic is meant to be fun! The rest of Silverleaf are friendly. They'll be so excited to meet you.'

'How many kids are at Silverleaf?' Alyssa asked, feeling a familiar dread in the pit of her stomach at the thought of so many new faces.

'Only about a dozen. We're a pretty tight bunch,' Rue said. They must have noticed the sour look creeping onto Alyssa's face. 'What's the matter? Aren't you excited?'

No, Alyssa was the opposite of excited. The idea of making new friends made her want to curl up like an armadillo. She was so awkward in front of strangers. It was bad enough with Rue and Rosalie, and they were family. Besides, what was the point of putting in all that effort with new people if she would be leaving in three weeks?

What if they thought she was too quiet, or too annoying, or . . . whatever. It was much easier to keep to herself.

'So, Rue,' Alyssa said, swiftly changing the subject. 'What are you wearing for your grounding ceremony tomorrow?'

As Rue breathlessly talked through their outfit, Alyssa felt her tummy bubble with anxiety.

Maybe Rosalie had a point. Did Alyssa know what she was getting herself into?

Alyssa stood in front of the wardrobe. What was the appropriate outfit for one's first day at a magic school?

She had no clue what sort of magical shenanigans would take place at Silverleaf. It was in a garden, so she figured it was best to wear something she didn't mind getting muddy. Finally, Alyssa settled on a *Black Panther* comic-book T-shirt, a pair of faded grey leggings and old sandals.

Auntie Jasmine was practically giddy. She woke them at the crack of dawn with a special breakfast: buttery scrambled eggs, toast and sweet golden-brown slivers that her cousins called fried plantain. Alyssa had never eaten plantain before, not that she would tell her cousins that.

In just two days Alyssa had eaten more Jamaican food than she'd ever had in her whole life. She wasn't complaining, but she did think it odd that it was yet another thing Mum had kept hidden from her. Why had Mum rejected everything about her family so completely? They all seemed really nice. And the food was amazing!

As Auntie Jasmine piled breakfast onto their

plates, she gazed at them lovingly. 'It's so good to see you kids together,' she said.

'Hurry up, slow coaches!' Rue yelled half an hour later, as they left the flat. They were dressed in the green dress with a matching scrunchie and white trainers with green laces that they'd picked out last night. They had a shiny new badge pinned to their dress: it was a striped rainbow in yellow, white, purple and black with the letters '*ENBY*' over the top.

'What does your badge mean, Rue?' Alyssa asked. 'Is it to do with Silverleaf?'

Rue's face lit up. 'I'm glad you asked! It's my nonbinary badge. It shows people that I'm not completely a boy or a girl, even though I was assigned female at birth.'

Alyssa smiled. 'Enby, like NB. Cool! I'll remember that. And it's a cute badge.'

'Thanks!' Rue said. 'I have *loads*.'

Rue jogged ahead while Rosalie and Alyssa walked down the stairwell.

'I remember my grounding ceremony,' Rosalie said wistfully. 'My seedling shot up twenty-three centimetres on the first day. It's a Silverleaf record! And it means I'm on track to become Keeper Supreme once Auntie Jasmine steps down.'

'Oh. Cool,' Alyssa said. Words like 'seedling' and

'grounding ceremony' didn't mean much to her yet. It sounded like a whole other language. 'What's a Keeper Supreme?'

'It's the most powerful a Keeper can become! A Keeper Supreme is in charge of maintaining the spell garden and conducting the protective spells that keep the neighbourhood safe. It's a very important role,' Rosalie said, her eyes sparkling.

Auntie Jasmine had said the same thing last night, but Alyssa didn't know what she'd meant.

'Safe from what?' she asked. The neighbourhood seemed so normal. What could possibly threaten it?

'Our magic protects the community from anyone who tries to harm it. If the spell garden wasn't here, our corner of London wouldn't feel quite so friendly and welcoming. Mum says that all over London, people are being forced to leave their homes because greedy companies want more money for their land. Our protection spells prevent things like that from happening.'

'How?' Alyssa asked.

Rosalie smiled. 'Only Auntie Jasmine knows exactly how the protection spells work. All I know is that her shop hasn't had a rent increase in three decades. And have you also noticed how the weather is always perfect?'

Alyssa's eyes widened with shock. 'You mean it's this sunny every single day?'

'Not every day,' Rue said. 'We need rain, but the protection spells mean it only rains at night.'

'That's unbelievably cool,' Alyssa said. A whole summer of perfect weather was the stuff of dreams.

Alyssa, Rosalie and Rue walked through the estate courtyard while Auntie Jasmine lagged behind. She got stuck into conversation with every neighbour they passed.

The tower block was nothing like Alyssa's street at home. In her quiet neighbourhood, all the two-storey houses had identical hedge-lined front gardens and spacious drives. Aside from Becky's family, they didn't really know their neighbours.

At first glance, the block of flats seemed harsh and grey against the dazzling blue cloudless sky. But then Alyssa looked closer. The ground-floor flats *did* have front gardens with little dark red fences. And those gardens were filled with deckchairs, potted plants and gnomes. Kids played hopscotch and drew colourful chalk designs on the pavement while the sound of a dozen different radio stations drifted from the windows. Rosalie was right: it *had* felt friendly and welcoming from the moment Alyssa had arrived.

'Should we wait for Auntie Jasmine?' Alyssa asked once they left the estate and reached the zebra crossing.

Rosalie shook her head. 'I think Rue will combust if we don't get to the spell garden soon. They've been excited about this for months.'

As they walked down the high street together, the waft of perfumed air hit Alyssa's nostrils. She looked up and saw the hanging baskets of flowers on the lamp posts that she'd spotted on her first day.

'What sort of flowers are those?' she asked. 'They smell amazing!'

Rosalie smiled and winked. 'They're some of our magical plants. They're enchanted to soak up the air pollution from the traffic by the main road – you won't find a nicer smelling street in all of London.'

'That's so clever,' Alyssa said in awe. What other magical tricks did her family have up their sleeves?

They arrived at Jasmine's Teas. Alyssa pushed open the front door and was greeted by the potpourri smell. Despite the fact she'd only been here for two days, it already felt familiar.

'Morning, gang! Excited about the ceremony, Rue?' Lisa asked. She was standing behind the counter, at the till.

'Excited? I barely slept!' Rue squealed.

'I heard you'll be joining us for the day, Alyssa,' Lisa said, squeezing her shoulder.

Rue tugged on her wrist. 'Come on!'

Alyssa took Rue's hand and allowed herself to be dragged through the greenhouse, followed by Rosalie. Rue really was very excited. They all jogged through the allotment, careful not to step on the greenery. At least Alyssa and Rosalie were. Rue tore across the soil, a flash of green over brown.

Auntie Jasmine had arrived at the allotment now, and she stopped to chat to an older man, too absorbed with tending to his plants to notice the children skipping past his plot.

'Good morning, Mr Begum. How are the onions?' Auntie Jasmine asked.

'Let's keep going,' Rue whispered. 'Mr Begum owns the hardware shop opposite. He and Auntie Jasmine can chat about onions for *hours*.'

The trio reached the back of the allotment. They pushed the tangly hedge aside to reveal the wooden door.

'So what's the password?' Alyssa asked.

'What do you mean?' Rosalie asked.

Alyssa blushed. It had been out of her mouth before she'd realised and now she was embarrassed.

'Uh, isn't there a magical password? Or – or a

spell you have to say?' she stammered. 'Something to unlock the door and protect it from intruders. I always read about them in books.'

Rue and Rosalie looked at each other, then burst into giggles.

'Auntie Jasmine has that covered,' Rosalie said. 'Intruders won't even see the wooden door. Only those inducted into the spell garden can see it. You're able to see it for the same reason you saw my tattoo last night. Because you're family.'

'Magic is in our blood,' Rue said proudly. 'Now let's go!'

They pushed open the wooden door and stepped inside.

Dandelion
(for the appetite)

CHAPTER EIGHT

Alyssa walked into a huge garden enclosed by high brick walls. The blue sky and tall buildings surrounding the garden were visible through a haze, as if there was a film covering the entire garden. She looked around. All she saw were lush green plants and trees.

The traffic noise from the main road disappeared when the wooden door shut behind them. A hush hung over the grounds.

'Where's the magic school?' Alyssa asked. She had been expecting a building of some sort, but it was just a . . . garden.

Rosalie giggled. 'This *is* the magic school! Silverleaf is right here.'

A gravelled path with bushes and greenery on both sides began at the wooden door and led to a low-fenced central enclosure with long benches laid in a circle. In the middle of the benches was a giant bronze dish standing on wooden legs. Alyssa reckoned it was wider than her outstretched arms. There were no desks, whiteboard or stationery that she could see, but there was a large round wooden table outside the enclosure. It was unlike any school she'd ever been to.

She realised that Rue and Rosalie were already skipping down the path, rushing eagerly towards their friends. They had already abandoned her.

Alyssa walked slowly to delay having to talk to new people. As she went, she took in the scent of the warm, slightly damp air. But there was something else in the air here. An energy so charged that it seemed to coat her skin like a satin scarf. She'd felt it at the tea shop yesterday, the moment she'd stepped into the allotment. There was only one thing it could be.

'*Magic*,' Alyssa whispered. She reached out to stroke a nearby leaf that was so lushly green it looked artificial. The leaf moved out of reach.

Alyssa gasped. Had it ... Did that plant just *move* by itself? It seemed weird to think it, but she had the distinct feeling that it hadn't liked being touched.

'Some of the plants are grumpy first thing in the morning,' said Auntie Jasmine, coming up behind Alyssa and making her jump.

'Sorry,' she said. 'Are there any I should avoid?'

'Oh, just the ones with poisonous fangs,' replied Auntie Jasmine.

Alyssa gave a nervous laugh, then noticed her great-aunt's straight face. Before Alyssa could ask where exactly the fanged plants lived so she could steer clear of that part of the spell garden, Auntie Jasmine had turned away.

'Morning, buttercups!' she yelled over the laughter and chatting. 'Prepare for registration in a few minutes.'

All around Alyssa, kids her age and older chatted to one another, while younger ones climbed trees and played ball games. Just the thought of having to introduce herself to one of them made her want to leave Silverleaf forever. Talking to new people was so nerve-racking that Alyssa generally did her best to avoid it.

But if she left, Alyssa would never discover how to control her powers. And she couldn't risk trashing the shop again. Plus, she'd never discover why Mum didn't talk about her family.

Alyssa took her phone out of her pocket. She

could check her messages to avoid making eye contact with anyone. But her screen wouldn't even switch on.

'Phones don't work in the spell garden,' a voice said. Alyssa looked up to see a boy a little older than her. He was skinny with dark brown skin and friendly eyes.

'They don't?' said Alyssa.

The boy shook his head. 'Nope. I found out on my first day too. Must be something to do with that,' he said, pointing to the translucent haze between the spell garden and the sky.

'You kids spend enough time on those infernal devices as it is,' Auntie Jasmine said. 'The spell garden is a phone-free zone.'

Alyssa slipped her phone back into her pocket. 'Sorry, Auntie Jasmine.'

Auntie Jasmine winked at her, then made her way into the central enclosure.

The boy smiled. 'I'm Leon, by the way.'

'Nice to meet you. I'm Alyssa,' she said, fiddling with her braids. She hoped she wasn't blushing too hard.

'Oh, I know who you are. You're Miss Jasmine's niece, right?'

Alyssa was surprised. 'How did you know?'

'Miss Jasmine said her niece was coming and she wasn't meant to know about Silverleaf or the spell garden,' Leon said. He paused. 'But you obviously do now!'

She smiled shyly. 'Yep! It happened last night,' she said. 'I found out everything.'

Leon raised one eyebrow. 'Bit of a bombshell, huh?'

Alyssa laughed. Leon was easy to talk to. 'You're telling me. How long have you known about this place?'

Leon settled cross-legged on the grass and Alyssa did the same. The ground felt warm under her hands. 'About two months. I met Miss Jasmine when our takeaway opened. She said she needed help running her garden, and I thought, *It beats mopping the floor.*'

He explained that Auntie Jasmine had invited a select bunch of local kids to Silverleaf. She'd given them a tour, explaining the spell garden's magical purpose and its place in the community.

'If we want to join, we can,' Leon said. 'Like any other summer school.'

'Do your parents know ... about the spells and stuff?'

Leon shook his head. 'They wouldn't believe me if I told them. They think we're out here learning about tadpoles and growing our own watercress.'

'So, I guess you're not born magical?' Alyssa asked. It still felt silly saying it out loud.

Leon shook his head. 'That's just your family. The rest of us have to use the magical plants to create spells and hope we catch up. I heard about what you did to the shop on Monday,' he said, smirking.

Alyssa's cheeks flushed. Before she could answer, a melodic sound rang through the spell garden. The laughter and chatter died down. The younger kids jumped down from the trees and everyone made their way to the enclosure in the centre of the spell garden.

'C'mon,' Leon said, jumping up, and they walked to join everyone else.

As she and Leon approached the enclosure, Alyssa yelped and grabbed Leon's arm. What was that she'd seen out of the corner of her eye?

Colourful creatures flashed through the undergrowth, moving too fast for Alyssa to see what they were. Her heart beat faster. She had expected to see a few pigeons and insects, but no one mentioned anything about the spell garden being home to *wild animals*.

It took her a few seconds to realise that no one else had moved. The rest of the group was looking at her with concern. Including Leon.

All except for Rue, who was trying their best to hold in laughter. They lasted about three seconds before exploding into hysterical giggles.

'You are too funny!' Rue said once they'd caught their breath.

Alyssa folded her arms. 'I don't see what's so funny.'

'They're just plants, silly!' Rue said. 'This isn't your average garden. The plants wake up in the morning, just like us. They like to wait until the spell garden is a bit busier before putting on a show. It's their way of saying hello, I guess.'

The once green garden was now a multicoloured explosion. Giant petals unfurled, reaching towards the sky. The green bushes sprouted tiny purple berries, making a popping sound as they appeared. Another shrub, which Alyssa had mistaken for a pile of twigs, shot up from the ground with a sprinkle of yellow confetti-like petals.

The sight was so mesmerising that Alyssa's embarrassment eased. She was too in awe of her surroundings to care about feeling silly. It was as though the plants were welcoming her to their magical community.

She heard a deep yawning sound and felt a rumble beneath her feet. She followed the sound to a large tree at the edge of the garden. Its roots shifted just underneath the ground.

'That's Effie's tree,' Rosalie said. 'It's the oldest plant in the spell garden.'

They were interrupted by a young boy with red hair running towards them. 'Look at what Simran found!' he said breathlessly.

Simran followed behind him. Alyssa could see that the girl was struggling to keep a smile off her face. Once she reached the rest of the group, she unfurled a scrap of fabric in her hands. It was hiding a small glass jar filled with blue petals. It didn't look that special to Alyssa.

'Oh my gosh!' Rue said.

Rosalie did a double-take. 'Is that what I think it is?'

Simran nodded so hard her fringe bounced. 'The parrot petals bloomed early this moon cycle. Ollie covered for me while I pinched a few before Lisa or Miss Jasmine noticed,' she whispered.

'Um, what's a parrot petal, Rue?' Alyssa whispered. She didn't want anyone else to hear how clueless she was.

Rue's face lit up. 'Everyone, this is Alyssa, our cousin. She's trying parrot petal for the first time!' she said loudly.

'Shhh!' Ollie said. 'You know they're contraband for Keepers-in-Training.'

'I can't believe you don't know about parrot petals, Alyssa,' Simran said in a low voice. She wrapped the small jar back in the fabric and tucked it into her rucksack.

'Yeah,' Ollie said, flicking his red hair out of his eyes. 'Didn't your magic smash up the tea shop?'

'And the greenhouse! I heard it was smashed to smithereens,' Simran said.

Alyssa's face flushed. 'It was totally an accident!'

Simran and Ollie looked impressed. 'Whoaaa,' they said at the same time.

'Get this, guys,' Rue said. 'Her mum didn't tell her about magic at all. She only found out yesterday!'

'You mean, you made that massive mess in the shop without even trying? I need to concentrate super-hard just to do a basic tea spell,' Simran said. 'I guess that's the perk of having magic in your blood.'

'Yes, Alyssa has a slight advantage,' Auntie Jasmine said as she approached the huddle. 'Remember, though: non-magical beings can harness magic just as powerfully as magical beings. But it won't get any easier if you spend lesson time chatting instead of learning. Please go ahead with registration, then get started on your tea spells without me. I need to give Alyssa a tour of the spell garden.'

Alyssa was relieved. Everyone had been welcoming so far, but she couldn't shake the feeling of being an outsider. They all knew so much more about the spell garden than she did. They all belonged here.

Enchanter's
Nightshade
(for enchantment)

CHAPTER NINE

Auntie Jasmine walked Alyssa to the very edge of the garden. They climbed a small hill covered with grass and wildflowers, following a narrow stream flowing with silvery water. When Alyssa looked up, she could see the taller buildings surrounding the shop, and Auntie Jasmine's block of flats in the distance. The spell garden was a bubble of green surrounded by concrete and brick. It was so surreal.

In fact, it was so surreal that it made her feel dizzy. Alyssa staggered slightly, holding on to Auntie Jasmine's arm for support.

'What's the matter, child?' Auntie Jasmine asked, concerned.

'Just feel a bit weird all of a sudden,' Alyssa said.

It reminded her of how she'd felt before the incident at the shop.

'Of course! Being so close to the crux well is activating your magic. I forgot to give you this earlier,' Auntie Jasmine said. She reached into the pocket of her kaftan and pulled out a cloth-wrapped rectangle. 'Eat these.'

Alyssa unwrapped the cloth and nibbled at the round biscuits inside. 'Are they magical too?'

'No, just plain old ginger snaps. The ginger will settle you. Non-magical plants can be powerful too, you know!'

Alyssa munched her way through the stack of biscuits. Sure enough, her dizziness calmed and she felt normal again.

'Will I get this feeling every time I'm in the spell garden?' she asked.

'It depends on how long it takes you to acclimatise to the magic, sweetness. Your body feels the magic but your mind hasn't fully accepted it, so you are not yet in alignment. There is a way to speed up that process, though ...' Auntie Jasmine trailed off, thinking. Then she turned and waved her arm over the lush green before them. 'Every plant you see here has a special purpose, whether it's a tiny blade of grass or Effie's tree itself.'

Alyssa nodded.

'We channel our magic into two types of spells,' Auntie Jasmine continued. 'The most used are the tea spells. We brew different magical plants into special teas that soothe and heal.'

'What's the second type of spell?' Alyssa asked.

'Protection spells. Only an advanced Keeper like myself can cast those. We have one over the spell garden right now. Look!'

Auntie Jasmine gestured upwards, and Alyssa's eyes followed to the brick wall surrounding the spell garden. Just above the brick wall was a misty haze, like warm air shimmering from a radiator. That was what Alyssa had noticed when she'd first entered the garden.

'I see it!' she said.

'There's also a protection spell over the entire neighbourhood,' Auntie Jasmine told her.

'Protecting it from what?'

'Well, for one thing, the spells help to stabilise the weather disruption caused by climate change,' Auntie Jasmine said. 'And they protect the community from anyone who would seek to cause harm or disruption. When I first moved here, hardly anyone wanted to live in this neighbourhood. It wasn't seen as fancy or nice. But now? There are people who would pay a pretty penny to own a piece of the neighbourhood that we worked so hard to build. Like those blasted developers who would sell their own granny to get their hands on this land.'

'Why here?' Alyssa asked. She liked the neighbourhood so far, but it seemed very normal to her.

'The short answer is money,' Auntie Jasmine said. 'Over the years, the value of this area has shot up – just like everything else in this city. Our landlord could make a lot of money if they booted us out and rented to a fancier shop owner. Luckily, our spells won't let it get that far.'

'But what happened at the shop when I first arrived ... that didn't involve tea or protecting anyone. It was spontaneous!' Alyssa said, confused.

'Don't you worry, sugarplum,' Auntie Jasmine said. 'We'll soon have you trained up and in control of your powers. The spell garden is a closely guarded secret, and I'd like to keep it that way.'

They reached a well that was built of grey weathered stone. Alyssa recognised it straight away. It had been part of Auntie Jasmine's story on the balcony last night. Even if she hadn't recognised it, Alyssa would have understood its importance: the closer she got to the well, the more her skin prickled and tingled.

'This is the crux well,' Auntie Jasmine said. 'Without this old thing, there'd be no spell garden.'

Alyssa peered down the well. She caught a glimpse of crux-water at the very bottom, glinting silver.

'Wow. It's so deep,' she said. Her words echoed around the stone walls.

Auntie Jasmine turned and Alyssa did the same. From where they stood, the entire spell garden rolled out from beneath their feet. Alyssa saw the enclosure with benches where the other kids did their lessons, like a clearing in the forest. It was surrounded by greenery, leaves and bushes that swayed despite the still air.

'A pipe in the well allows the crux-water to roll downhill and nourish every single plant in this garden,' Auntie Jasmine said. 'It was my own invention.'

'Why can't you use normal water in the garden?'

'We do for the vegetable patches. But the magical plants need magical water. For the same reason that plants thrive on the stuff that wouldn't sustain us as humans. Can you imagine having a bowl of sunlight for dinner?'

'Oh.' Alyssa wanted to take back her silly question. 'Where does it come from?'

'Right at the bottom of that well is a small mound of crux-pebbles, twelve in total. They connect to a power source deep within the earth, drawing up the crux-water and enabling it to flow. The more our magic is used for the good of the community, the more we have crux-water in abundance.'

'A power source, like electricity?' Alyssa asked.

'Not quite,' Auntie Jasmine said. 'The truth is, I don't know what exactly the source is. My theory is that my mother was drawn to this neighbourhood for a reason. I think this earth is above a ley line.'

Now this was something familiar to Alyssa. 'I've read about those in books!'

Auntie Jasmine clapped her hands. 'Wonderful! So you know that ley lines are underground lines criss-crossing the earth that carry powerful supernatural energy.'

Alyssa nodded happily. Finally, there was something in this spell garden that she knew about.

'Well, I reckon that two or more ley lines intersect in this very spell garden. And that when they combine with the crux-pebbles, we get our crux-water.'

They made their way back down the hill, Alyssa being careful not to trample the bright blue wildflowers. She still didn't know where the fanged plants were. Until she did, she was treating every plant, no matter how small, with caution.

Auntie Jasmine steered them towards another

part of the garden where it seemed like every possible type of plant was smooshed together.

'The spell garden looks chaotic but it's actually divided into several distinct zones. There, we have what I call our backbone plants. Every single spell requires at least one of these,' Auntie Jasmine said.

She reached down and tugged gently at a bush with tiny fronds. Auntie Jasmine crushed the leaves in her palm, releasing a scent exactly like banana milkshake. It was so sweet and delicious that Alyssa's mouth began to water.

'Banana fern. Brew a tea with a few of these leaves and the drinker will fall head over heels with the first person they see,' Auntie Jasmine said.

'Wow, really? How many leaves?' Alyssa asked, thinking of Mum and Dad. Could a magical tea get them back together?

Auntie Jasmine chuckled. 'Thinking of casting a love spell, are we? Forcing people to do things against their will is the costliest magic there is. Besides, our magic should only be used for the good of the community. It becomes very costly when it's used for selfish reasons, because the crux-pebbles are sensitive to wrong intentions. It means that the crux-water doesn't flow as freely.'

No magical tea spell, Alyssa thought, disappointed.

A buzzing sound nipped past Alyssa's ear. She saw a flash of gold and swatted at it.

'The flicker-bees don't sting!' Auntie Jasmine said. 'So there's no need to be rude.'

'Rude to *bees*?'

'Flicker-bees are nearly as important as the crux-water to the health of the spell garden,' Auntie Jasmine said.

She whistled and held out her palm. Several flicker-bees settled in the crook of her hands, vibrating gently.

'Come close. Flicker-bees are very friendly.'

Alyssa peered into Auntie Jasmine's hands and saw that the flicker-bees were the size of her thumb. They were paper-thin and shone like gold tinsel in the sunlight. As well as the sound of their vibrating wings, Alyssa heard something else. A quiet squeaking sound like a gerbil.

'Are they ... talking?' Alyssa asked, eyes wide with awe.

Auntie Jasmine nodded. 'Oh, they're most intelligent. And they produce fabulous honey, which we save for special occasions.' She lifted her palms, releasing flicker-bees into the sky. 'Magical or not, all bees are to be treasured. We humans can't survive without them, you know.'

It seemed as though the spell garden was full of weird and wonderful surprises. Alyssa had seriously underestimated her great-aunt. When Alyssa had first arrived, Auntie Jasmine had seemed like a slightly odd old woman with a hoarding problem. But now Alyssa could see how wise and knowledgeable she was about this amazing magical world.

Next, they reached a part of the garden that was shaded by the branches of Effie's tree. It looked like a grand oak tree that had stood there for centuries, its trunk thick and ropey.

'Press your ear against the trunk and tell me what you hear,' Auntie Jasmine said.

Alyssa did as she was told. At first, she heard nothing but the sound of her heartbeat. Then something else.

'It sounds like . . . the sea?' she said hesitantly.

Auntie Jasmine grinned. 'Precisely! This tree is twinned with another in the Jamaica spell garden, the one that your Granny Hyacinth tends. On a good day, you can hear the cicadas and crickets. It was the first tree Mother planted in the spell garden.'

'What's the Jamaican spell garden like?' Alyssa asked.

'Oh, I haven't been to visit. This spell garden

keeps me too busy for things like holidays,' Auntie Jasmine said cheerily.

'What about those plants?' Alyssa pointed to a neat patch that looked like the allotment behind the tea shop. This one had rows of dark green leaves and trees growing clusters of banana-like fruit.

'That's my little vegetable patch. Mother taught us how to grow her favourite foods from back home. Do you know how much they charge for plantain and callaloo on the high street these days? Daylight robbery,' she muttered.

They walked around the edge of the spell garden while Auntie Jasmine plucked leaves and berries, naming their scents and properties. Alyssa dawdled, hoping to spend more time alone with Auntie Jasmine and less time looking like a friendless loser among the other kids.

'Do you feel at home here, Alyssa?' Auntie Jasmine asked.

Alyssa shrugged. 'I mean ... not yet. I miss Mum and Dad. But I'm sure that will change soon,' she added, not wanting to disappoint Auntie Jasmine.

'It'll take time,' Auntie Jasmine said gently.

Talking about Mum and Dad made her stomach churn with longing. She quickly changed the subject, in case getting upset caused another 'mishap', as Auntie Jasmine had called it.

'Why aren't the plants labelled?' Alyssa asked.

'Ah! That would be cheating. Keepers should recognise a plant from sight alone,' Auntie Jasmine said. 'You'll learn in time.'

Alyssa gulped. She hoped she wouldn't let Auntie Jasmine down.

Fogfruit
(for weakness)

CHAPTER TEN

'Let's go down to meet the others,' said Auntie Jasmine. 'But watch out for the bunny shrubs, dear. They like to feed on the crux-water dew that gathers in this part of the spell garden.'

Alyssa looked down. 'I can't see any – OH!'

To her shock, the grass was moving. Little round shrubs the size of hedgehogs shuffled silently across the ground.

'Do they bite?' Alyssa asked, hopping out of the way.

Auntie Jasmine crouched down. 'Not this one, darlin'.'

She plucked a pinch of fur from the bunny shrub and held it up to the sunlight. It looked like fluff from a dandelion.

'Brewing a tea with these leaves gives you courage. But, whatever you do, never chew the leaves. Not unless you want long front teeth and a furry nose,' Auntie Jasmine said.

Alyssa nodded, trying hard to commit that fact to memory. She imagined turning up to her first day of secondary school with a furry nose, and couldn't stop a smile.

They reached the enclosure. Rue, Simran, Ollie and a few others were standing around the large wooden table that she'd seen earlier. Glass jars full of ingredients, bronze spoons and even a set of scales covered the table. It seemed to Alyssa that blending a tea spell wasn't much different from baking a cake.

'Now this is what I like to see!' Auntie Jasmine said, rubbing her hands together. 'It looks like we have some exciting tea magic at hand. What are you working on, Simran?'

Simran brushed her black fringe out of her eyes. 'It's a tea blend for my neighbour's cat. Smudge is always getting stuck in trees. I'm hoping this blend will get him to stay on the ground, if I can sprinkle it into his food.'

'Fascinating,' Auntie Jasmine said.

'You should add some potato flower for its grounding properties,' Rosalie said.

Auntie Jasmine beamed. 'Fabulous idea, Rosalie.'

They moved around the table to Ollie, who was scribbling a spell on a notepad.

'Ollie. Can you tell me the three basic plant types that are the backbone of every spell?' Auntie Jasmine asked.

'Plants that heal, plants that protect and . . . plants that ward off evil,' he said.

'Evil?' Alyssa asked.

'Yeah, like Ollie's toxic farts!' Rue whispered. The other kids burst out laughing.

'Oi!' Ollie shouted. His red hair and freckles seemed even more apparent when he blushed.

'Rue! That is not the behaviour of someone about to have their grounding ceremony,' Auntie Jasmine chided. 'Tell us the number-one rule of the spell garden.'

Rue stood up. 'All spells must benefit the community. They must not be used for personal gain.'

'That's right. Spells may be conducted only if they benefit people other than yourself,' Auntie Jasmine said seriously. 'The reason this spell garden thrives is because everything we do is for the good of the community. Even if they don't know it,' she added with a chuckle.

'I can't wait to make a tea spell,' Alyssa said. 'Once I know more about the plants.'

Auntie Jasmine grinned. 'Spoken like a true Charles woman! Perhaps once you're an official Keeper-in-Training, you can join in. For now you'll have to observe.'

Alyssa smiled and nodded, trying to hide her disappointment. She wanted so badly to tinker with the magical plants like the other Silverleaf students. But there was no chance of her becoming an actual Keeper-in-Training. Not if Mum had anything to do with it.

'Fabulous,' Auntie Jasmine said. She turned to the other kids. 'We're going to have a mini spell challenge! I would like you all to come up with a three-plant blend to cure homesickness.' She gave Alyssa a sideways glance. 'That's one we haven't tried in a while.'

The kids cleared their spaces, eager to get started.

'Auntie Jasmine, can I join in?' Rue asked.

'As you will officially be a Keeper-in-Training in a few hours, yes, you may,' Auntie Jasmine said.

'How long do we have, Miss Jasmine?' Leon asked.

'Ten minutes. Starting ... now!' Auntie Jasmine clapped her hands and produced a pocket watch from her kaftan, which ticked quietly.

The kids got to work while Alyssa looked on. They **passed around glass jars full of brightly coloured** powders, dried petals and leaves. She noticed that every student seemed to have a different approach. Rosalie measured each substance carefully using tiny copper spoons, while Rue tipped powders into their measuring bowl using eyesight alone (and rather clumsily, Alyssa thought).

Ollie knocked over a bottle of sparkling midnight-blue powder and sneezed, spraying the powder into the measuring bowl of his neighbours.

'Ugh, Ollie! You've contaminated my spell!' Simran said.

'My bad,' he said sheepishly.

'Accidents happen,' Auntie Jasmine said gently. 'You have enough time to start over.'

Alyssa tiptoed around the table while everyone worked. They were concentrating so hard that all was quiet apart from the tinkle of metal and glass. She was mesmerised by the shimmering powders and jarred concoctions – nothing like the dusty non-magical tea leaves Auntie Jasmine sold in the shop. She could feel the magic radiating from them.

Suddenly a shrill alarm pierced the air.

'Time's up!' Auntie Jasmine said, stopping the pocket-watch alarm. 'Please line up your measuring bowls in front of me for inspection.'

The kids did as they were told. Soon there were

several copper bowls filled with assorted powders at the top of the table. Auntie Jasmine lifted each one and inspected them individually.

'Well, this one has far too much cackle root,' she muttered. 'And I don't know what possessed one of you to add viper weed.'

Finally, Auntie Jasmine selected three bowls and separated them from the rest. 'These are the three bowls that I think are worth testing. Who made them?' she asked.

Rosalie, Simran and Leon put up their hands.

'Now for the real test. Does it cure homesickness?' Auntie Jasmine asked. 'Alyssa, would you care to be our guinea pig?'

'Me? I – um …' Alyssa said. She couldn't exactly say no with all those people staring at her. She sighed. 'I'd be happy to, I guess.'

'Fabulous!' Auntie Jasmine said. 'Rosalie, Leon and Simran. Please can you draw crux-water from the tap?'

They went to the giant bronze dish that was in the centre of the enclosure. Rosalie, Leon and Simran took turns drawing water from the metal spout at the dish's edge. Silvery liquid dribbled into miniature copper teapots produced from a hidden shelf beside the tap.

'Is that a crux-water tap?' Alyssa asked Rue.

Rue nodded without taking her eyes off her sister. 'Yep. Saves us a trip to the well every time we do spell work.'

'Come, children.' Auntie Jasmine beckoned them to follow her to the giant bronze dish, and sat down on the nearest bench.

Alyssa watched as Rosalie, Leon, then Simran each poured their tea blend into a teapot and gave it a stir.

Simran glanced up and caught Alyssa gazing at the faint steam coming from her teapot's spout. She smiled and said, 'The teapots are magic – they heat the crux-water as we stir the tea.'

Auntie Jasmine motioned to Alyssa. 'You stand here. At the front.'

Alyssa's tummy twisted with nerves. What had she got herself into? Not only was she standing up in front of the entire spell garden, she would have to try a completely new and untested magical tea. She hoped the nervousness wouldn't show on her face.

'Um, Auntie Jasmine,' she whispered. 'Are the magical teas definitely safe?'

'Of course, darlin',' Auntie Jasmine said. 'Besides, you're only going to have a sip. Any effects, ill or otherwise, will last just a few minutes or so.'

That was only slightly reassuring. She hoped that Rosalie, Leon and Simran knew what they were doing.

'The teas have brewed, Auntie Jasmine,' Rosalie said. 'Shall we pour?'

'Yes, please!' Auntie Jasmine said excitedly. 'Testing new teas never gets old.'

Alyssa was presented with three very small cups of hot tea. The liquid in each cup glittered in the sunlight, but the smell from each cup was very different.

'Go on,' Auntie Jasmine said. 'Tell us what you think.'

Alyssa took a deep breath, then she gingerly sipped the first cup. The warm liquid slid down her throat like molten honey. To her surprise, it was actually quite nice.

'This one is sweet. Kind of reminds me of cough syrup mixed with peppermint,' Alyssa said.

'But how does it make you feel?' Auntie Jasmine asked. 'Did it cure your homesickness?'

Alyssa closed her eyes. The faint cough-syrup taste reminded her of sick days spent at home with Mum when she was little. They'd watch daytime TV under a duvet on the sofa. If anything, the memory made her more homesick than ever.

She shook her head sadly. 'Sorry.'

Leon looked at the floor, disappointed. That must have been his spell.

'Better luck next time, Leon,' Auntie Jasmine said. 'I would advise using a touch more daisy-petal extract next time for a cheerful boost.'

Next was Simran's tea. Alyssa took a gentle sip and spluttered. It was the strangest sensation – the tea vibrated gently as it passed through her lips and down her throat. Before she could stop herself, Alyssa found herself laughing and couldn't stop.

'What's so funny?' someone murmured.

'Simran, how much tickle root did you use?' Auntie Jasmine asked.

'Just a pinch! I thought laughter would be the best cure,' she replied.

'Understood. But be more careful next time,' said Auntie Jasmine.

Alyssa was still giggling uncontrollably. She laughed so much it made her tummy hurt and she clutched her sides. Luckily, it was infectious. Soon everyone was laughing too, and the sound of their joy rang through the air.

Then, as quickly as Alyssa's giggles started, they stopped. Alyssa didn't want to disappoint Simran, but the homesickness was still there when she thought about Mum and Dad. When everyone had calmed down, it was time to try the next tea.

Rosalie stared as Alyssa took a sip. The taste was subtler than the others, sort of like watered-down fruit squash. Alyssa thought about Mum and Dad, and for a few seconds she felt the familiar pang of homesickness. Then something changed: a warmth spread from her throat to the tip of her toes. She felt lighter and free, like she could float on air.

'Well?' Rosalie asked.

Alyssa thought about Mum and Dad. There was no pain at all. Just excitement that she would soon see them again.

'I think it worked!' she said.

'Yes!' Rosalie cheered.

'Well done, Rosalie. Can you share your tea blend?' Auntie Jasmine asked.

'I used a blend of sunflower petal, midnight-rose extract and the tiniest pinch of wing weeds,' she said proudly.

'Wing weeds?' Alyssa asked.

'It's a weird-looking moss that grows on the highest branches of the spell garden. Very tricky to get hold of,' Rue said.

'So that's high up in the air – just like sunflower

petals, because they are the tallest flower. Is that right?' Alyssa asked.

Rue nodded. 'Seems like you're getting it! Wing weeds lift the spirits.'

Alyssa felt relieved. This weird magical world was starting to make sense.

Lisa appeared in the enclosure. 'Sorry, I had tons of paperwork. I hope I haven't missed Rue's big moment?'

'Not at all!' Auntie Jasmine said brightly. 'In fact, we have a slight change of plan.' She laid her hand on Alyssa's shoulder. 'How would you like to become a Keeper-in-Training today as well?'

'I'd love it!' Alyssa said. She would feel like she really belonged.

'I had the idea last night. I thought you might need more time to understand the spell garden, then I saw how you watched the other students. You were mesmerised! And I can sense that you feel a strong connection with the spell garden,' Auntie Jasmine said. 'I can't deny what is flowing through your veins. No one can. And I cannot deny you the opportunity to learn about this important part of yourself.'

'It was the weirdest thing. It felt familiar and brand new at the same time,' Alyssa said.

Auntie Jasmine smiled. 'I'm so pleased to hear that. Planting your seedling and becoming part of our community officially should ease the magic sickness too.'

Alyssa felt giddy with anticipation. 'Thank you, Auntie Jasmine!'

'Don't thank me yet,' she said, giving her a wink. 'Now, if you'll excuse me, I have an extra place at the seedling plot to prepare. We can only have grounding ceremonies once per moon cycle so I must get a move on.'

Everyone gathered at a corner of the spell garden where thin, green stalks sprouted from the ground. Most of them were small – the height of daffodils in spring before the yellow flowers bloomed. A few were much taller and a couple were almost the same height as Alyssa. Mini wooden sticks planted in the ground beside each seedling had a name written on each.

Auntie Jasmine beckoned Alyssa and Rue to the front of the crowd. The other Silverleaf pupils stood behind them in a semicircle.

Alyssa felt her heart race. What if she made a fool of herself in front of all these people?

'Thank you, everyone, for attending the first grounding ceremony of the summer,' Auntie

Jasmine said to the small crowd. 'As you know, the grounding ceremony is when a Keeper-in-Training's seedling is planted to measure their magical growth. It signifies the beginning of their magical education – my apologies for starting a little later than usual this summer. I have been somewhat distracted recently.'

Alyssa's cheeks coloured. Was she the distraction?

'Once their seedling reaches maturity and bears fruit, they are considered fully fledged Keepers,' Auntie Jasmine continued. She gestured to the row of seedlings behind her. 'There's nothing you, I, nor any other member of this magic school can do to hurry this growth along. No amount of crux-water or compost will influence their growth. It's purely a measure of one's magical skill, and that comes through hard work, and a little luck.'

Alyssa looked closer at the seedling labels. The tallest one belonged to Lisa, which made sense. She was a Keeper's Apprentice and would soon be ready to look after her own spell garden. It was the size of a small tree, and small plum-like fruits in various shades of green sprouted from it. Alyssa wasn't surprised to see that the second-tallest belonged to Rosalie. It towered several centimetres over the **other seedlings.**

'Auntie Jasmine, where's your seedling?' Alyssa asked.

'My seedling is now a tree, somewhere in the spell garden. It was planted more moon cycles ago than I care to count.' Auntie Jasmine chuckled. 'Rue, would you please pick your seed?'

Alyssa was relieved that her cousin was going first. She followed her actions carefully.

Auntie Jasmine held a beige sack open and Rue reached her hand in. She pulled out a roundish bean-like seed that was dusty with soil. It was only when Alyssa looked closely that she realised the seed was pulsing and changing colour, shifting from deep purple to sky blue.

'I've got a good feeling about this one,' Rue said.

They bent down and picked up a bronze trowel, digging a small hole in the patch. Once they'd buried the seed and covered it with the damp soil, Auntie Jasmine handed them a small watering can. Rue trickled crux-water over the seed, liquid silver seeping into the ground.

Then they waited. Apart from the shuffling bushes and rustling leaves, the spell garden was silent.

'It's coming!' Auntie Jasmine whispered.

Alyssa squinted. It was very small, but yes. A tiny green shoot was poking its way through the soil.

'Come on,' Rue whispered.

Suddenly the seedling went from being barely visible to a real plant. It happened in a matter of milliseconds – the seedling thrust into the air! Alyssa couldn't believe her eyes. The seedling was now the length of her forearm and a light greenish colour.

'This'll never get old,' Alyssa whispered to herself. Seeing magic unfold before her eyes made her feel giddy, like anything was possible. But . . . would the same thing really happen for her?

'Fabulous work, Rue!' Auntie Jasmine said, and the rest of the magic school burst into applause.

'Yes!' Rue cheered. 'It's a big one, right?'

Rosalie hugged her sibling. 'Well done, Rue. It's not quite as big as mine,' she teased.

'Yeah, well, I'm the youngest-ever Keeper-in-Training. Top that!' Rue said.

'We're not finished yet!' Auntie Jasmine said, quietening the crowd. 'Alyssa, won't you choose your seed?'

Don't mess this up. Don't mess this up. Don't mess this up, Alyssa repeated in her head.

If her seedling refused to sprout for whatever reason, Alyssa knew she would be devastated. Two days ago she hadn't even wanted to be here, and now this felt more important than ever. She couldn't bear the thought of being back in the dull tea shop knowing that magic, actual magic, lay beyond the allotment. It would make the boredom ten times more crushing.

She did the same as her cousin, reaching into the sack for a seed. Just like Rue's, the seed pulsated in her palm. Almost like it had a heartbeat.

Alyssa dug a hole, placed the shimmering seed in the ground, covered it with soil, then doused it with crux-water.

'Have I done it right?' she asked Auntie Jasmine. Her great-aunt nodded.

Then they all waited.

Her heart pounded in her chest. Why was nothing happening? Imagine if she was the first person in Silverleaf history to have a seedling that just … didn't?

Just then a sound like paper being ripped interrupted Alyssa's spiralling thoughts. It was coming from the ground, from the place where she had planted her seed.

The seedling, as tiny as a single watercress, peeped through the soil. Alyssa felt her cheeks colour. She didn't want to catch anyone's eye. This was just her luck. Her seedling was the size of a fingernail.

'Don't feel bad,' Rue said quietly. 'You're new to all this.'

'Wait,' Auntie Jasmine said. 'This seedling hasn't finished growing.'

In an instant, the green shoot burst up several more centimetres. Now it was the same height as Rue's.

Everyone clapped and cheered.

Alyssa couldn't believe her eyes. She had a real seedling of her own. Here was proof of her magical heritage right before her eyes. It was proof that she belonged.

Foxglove
(for breaking enchantments)

CHAPTER ELEVEN

The grounding ceremony wasn't over yet. After they planted their seedlings, it was time for Alyssa and Rue to receive their markings.

Lisa drew the tattoo, a leaf pattern, using a feathered pen filled with crux-water. It tickled their skin while Alyssa and Rue struggled to hide their giggles.

Once they had their tattoos, she and Rue were officially Keepers-in-Training. More importantly for the other Silverleaf pupils, that meant everyone could finally eat.

Alyssa hadn't realised that the grounding ceremony would end with a party. She followed the others as they made their way to the corner of the spell garden nearest to the entrance, and she was surprised to see that the area had filled up with grown-ups.

'Do all these people know about the ... you-know-what?' Alyssa asked Leon. 'We're literally surrounded by magical plants. I can feel the magic in the air!'

Leon smiled. 'It's wild, right?' He giggled as a bunny shrub snuffled at his feet. 'But what can I say? They just don't see it. Grown-ups are way too logical for all that. They think they're here for a party to kick off the first week of Miss Jasmine's summer school.' He paused to wave at two older people. 'I'm just going to say hi to Mum and Dad – see you in a bit!'

All the grown-ups had brought food and drink, which was laid out on a long wooden table. Heaped dishes of steaming jollof rice, crispy samosas and wontons, flaky sausage rolls and salads jostled for room on the table.

Alyssa was suddenly starving. She piled her plate high, but made sure to save room for dessert. There was a slice of lemon drizzle cake with her name on it.

She hung back from the party and wandered around the spell garden with her plate of food. At last, she found a nice spot under Effie's tree. Even though everyone had been friendly, the morning had taken its toll. There was so much to process, from Auntie Jasmine's tour of the spell garden to her surprise initiation as a Keeper-in-Training. She wanted a little bit of quiet time to herself.

Perhaps tomorrow she would get started on her first magical tea blend, though she had no idea what spell she would work on first.

What she'd thought would be a dull few weeks in a stuffy shop now had the promise of something extraordinary. She was part of a magical community. She had an untapped power flowing through her veins.

And she had a big secret to hide from Mum and Dad.

'Come down! Mum's here!' Rue arrived, interrupting her thoughts. 'I'm gonna ask her about Auntie Violet ... I mean, I've asked before, but I think she'll have to give me a real answer with you here.'

Alyssa followed her cousin to the party. What would Auntie Dahlia have to say about falling out with Alyssa's mum years ago?

They found Auntie Dahlia and Rosalie chatting on the lawn.

'Mum, Alyssa and I were wondering something,' Rue said.

Auntie Dahlia turned to them and smiled. 'Yes, sweetpea?'

'Well, it – it was more Rue than m-me,' Alyssa stammered.

'When was the last time you talked to Auntie Violet?' Rue asked.

Auntie Dahlia's smile faltered. 'It's been . . . a while.'

'Why?' said Rosalie.

A cloudy look settled on Auntie Dahlia's face. 'That's all in the past,' she said. 'Besides, it's not my place to talk about it. That is something for Alyssa to discuss with her mum.'

'But . . .' Rue began.

Auntie Dahlia looked like she wanted to say something else, but then she seemed to make a decision, gave a nod and said very firmly, 'I'll see you later, kids.'

With that, she walked back to the party. It was clear the conversation was over.

'I told you, Rosalie!' Rue whispered. 'Mum's hiding something.'

'Just like my mum,' Alyssa said.

She wanted so badly to know this big secret. It felt as though Mum had been one great big enigma lately. Suddenly understanding a bit more about her mum's past seemed like it might help Alyssa understand her better. And if she could do that, then, just maybe, she could work out how to get her parents back together again.

'Don't worry, Alyssa,' Rue said. 'We'll figure it out before the summer is over.'

Alyssa heard a whistle from the other side of the spell garden. It was Simran, Ollie and Leon, beckoning them over. She and Rue walked through bushes and shrubs until they reached a small clearing hidden by greenery. The chatter and laughter of the party seemed to disappear behind them.

Barely able to contain her excitement, Simran unscrewed the small jar of parrot petals. It released an odour that reminded Alyssa of menthol.

'You guys know the drill,' Simran said.

'I don't!' Alyssa and Leon said at the same time. The others giggled.

'Parrot petals bloom for three days each moon cycle,' Rosalie said, coming up behind them. 'They have transformative qualities if you scrunch the petal and inhale the fragrance.'

'All right, Miss Textbook,' Rue said. 'Basically, give the petals a sniff and weird things happen to you.'

'That's why they're contraband,' Ollie said with glee. 'Anyway, they're not particularly helpful for the community, which means they just drain the crux-water.'

'If they're contraband, then why are *you* here?' Leon asked Rosalie.

Alyssa had wondered the same thing. She clearly wasn't the only one who had picked up on Rosalie's goody-two-shoes vibe.

Rosalie crossed her arms. 'Someone's got to supervise you lot. Remember what happened last summer, Rue? It took days for Ade's thumb to reappear.'

Rue shrugged. 'Yeah, but it did come back. So what's the problem?'

'How do you know how you'll change?' Leon asked.

Ollie grinned. 'You don't. That's the fun of it!'

Simran shook the jar of petals. 'Take one and pass it round.'

Alyssa had already tried magic once today, but there was something exciting about doing it unsupervised. It made her a bit nervous but in a good way.

They stood in a circle, each of them holding a bright blue parrot petal. Alyssa watched Rosalie carefully: she scrunched the petal in her hands and wafted the glittery dust into her face.

Alyssa followed Rosalie's lead. The dust tickled

her nose and made her cough a little. She didn't feel any different, though.

'How long until – *WHOA!*' Leon yelped. Suddenly he was several centimetres taller. His jeans barely covered his knees.

Rue burst out laughing. 'You're like a giant!' they said in an impossibly squeaky voice.

'You sound like there's a mouse in your throat,' Ollie said to Rue, giggling. 'Did it work for me? I don't feel any different.'

Ollie's freckles had turned traffic-light red!

Rosalie nodded. 'You need a mirror – *OH!*' Her voice had changed too. Unlike Rue, it sounded like a megaphone: so loud and echoey it could be heard across the entire spell garden.

'Shush, Rosalie!' said Simran's slightly muffled voice. Everyone turned towards her.

Her voice was muffled because a curtain of dark hair covered her face, growing down to her knees.

'Whoa, Simran. Your fringe is epic!' Rue said.

Alyssa touched her scalp and looked down her body. Everything seemed unchanged.

Just my luck. The magic didn't work on me.

She was about to ask the others if she'd changed. But she couldn't. Because her voice had disappeared.

Oh NO!

Alyssa tried to talk but it was no use. No sound, not so much as a squeak, came from her mouth, even as she tried her hardest to yell. She grabbed Rue's arm to get their attention.

'Alyssa! What is it?' Rue asked.

Alyssa waved her hands in front of her mouth and shook her head, miming that she couldn't talk.

'You can't talk? That's a new one,' Ollie said.

I want my voice back! Alyssa tried to say.

Rosalie put one hand on her shoulder. 'Don't worry, it's temporary,' she said in a whisper that echoed round the clearing.

'You sure about that?' Leon asked, panic in his voice. 'I'm still getting taller.'

Rue chuckled. 'Don't be silly,' they said in a normal voice. Then they looked up. 'Oh!'

Alyssa looked up too. Leon was towering way above them now – at least twice his usual height. It looked like he was on stilts.

'Is that ... meant to happen?' Simran asked. Her fringe was shrinking back to normal.

Alyssa glanced at the rest of the kids. Ollie's freckles had returned to their usual colour. She tried talking and was relieved to find sounds coming out of her throat.

'I can talk!' she gasped finally.

'I'm still growing!' Leon whimpered. His knees loomed above them. He crouched to avoid hitting his head on a nearby tree branch.

'Rosalie, what's going on?' Rue asked. 'The transformations never usually last longer than a minute or two.'

'I ... I don't know!' Rosalie said. She looked worried, and that made Alyssa worry too. What if Leon never went back to his normal size?

'Leooooooooon!' A voice echoed across the garden. It was instantly recognisable. 'Get down from that tree this instant before you break your neck!'

Rosalie's eyes filled with fear. 'Auntie Jasmine! If she catches us, we'll be banned for the rest of the summer!'

'You need to get down, Leon!' Simran called.

Everyone moved out of the way, dodging Leon's gangly limbs as he bent to the floor. He sat down and his legs stretched across the clearing, as long and straight as a ladder.

Anxiety bubbled in Alyssa's tummy. What would they do if they couldn't fix Leon? Even worse, what if Auntie Jasmine found out she'd broken the rules on her first day as a Keeper-in-Training?

All of a sudden, Leon's feet shot forward another few centimetres.

'He's still growing!' Rue gasped.

'How many parrot petals did you inhale?' Rosalie asked.

'What do you mean, inhale? I thought we were meant to chew!' Leon said.

Rosalie's eyes widened in shock. 'You *ate* one?'

'Oh no!' Rue exclaimed. 'Rosalie, we can fix this, right?'

Alyssa turned to Ollie. 'What's so bad about eating parrot petal?' she whispered.

He uttered one word. 'Permanent.'

'Okay, let me think!' Rosalie said. 'We need something that will reverse the spell before it sets in for good.'

'WHAT?' Leon yelled.

'Keep it down!' Rosalie said. 'I need to think.' She bolted into action and roamed the clearing. She bent down to pluck different plants, sniffing the leaves.

'You got any bright ideas, Alyssa? I heard you've got some power in those fingers,' Leon said.

Alyssa shook her head. She had no clue what to do.

You have all this power but no idea how to use it, she said to herself.

Rosalie came back and dumped an armful of greenery onto the ground. She sat cross-legged beside Leon and began tearing the green stems and white petals into tiny pieces. Whatever she was doing, it looked nothing like a spell.

'Our equipment is on the other side of the spell garden,' she explained. 'So we have to make do.'

'You found nurse blossoms!' Ollie said.

'Yep,' Rosalie said. 'And there should be just enough crux-water in the stems to power the spell.'

She piled the sticky mess of torn flowers into a heap and held her palms over them. 'Come on ...' she muttered.

'It's not working! Why isn't it working?' Leon said.

'Doesn't it need to be brewed like tea?' Alyssa asked.

'Do you see a kettle anywhere?' Rosalie snapped. 'It will work – just give it time.'

'Hey, guys! Where are you? You're missing out on cake.' The voice pierced the clearing. It was Lisa. It sounded like she was headed in their direction.

'She's coming!' Simran whispered.

'Rosalie, you need help!' Rue said.

'No! I've got this!' she said.

Alyssa felt a familiar tingling in her fingers. Suddenly she knew what to do.

She thrust her palms over Rosalie's. Immediately a silver-white light shot out from their hands and **ignited the nurse blossoms into a short burst of** flame. It **went out as swiftly as it had sparked into** life, and left behind a white dust.

'Leon, rub this on your legs!' Rosalie whispered. 'Quick!'

'Guys! You're being very quiet …' Lisa said. She was getting closer.

'Nothing's happening!' Leon whimpered. If anything, his legs had grown longer. His feet disappeared into a bush on the other side of the clearing.

'I know! You need to *eat* it!' Rosalie said. 'You ate the parrot petal, so now you need to eat the antidote.'

Leon grimaced. He took a fingerful of dust and swallowed. As soon as he did, he clutched his stomach.

They heard the rustle of grass and a strange clicking sound.

'Lisa's coming!' Rue whispered as Leon's lanky limbs retracted in jerky movements.

'Does it hurt?' Ollie asked.

Leon shook his head. 'No, but it feels really weird.'

'There you are!' Lisa said, bursting into the clearing. At that exact moment Leon was back to his usual not-so-tall self.

'And that's why you never, ever harvest viper weed on a full moon,' Rosalie said loudly.

Alyssa nodded. 'Thanks for that, Rosalie.'

Lisa narrowed her eyes at them. 'What are you up to? Why are you lying down, Leon?'

'I tripped!' Leon said.

'I'm giving Alyssa a weed lesson. We wouldn't want her to harvest the wrong plants,' Rosalie said brightly.

Alyssa was impressed at how smoothly and easily her cousin lied. She grinned at Rosalie, who winked back. Maybe she wasn't such a goody two-shoes, after all ...

'How considerate of you!' Lisa smiled, though her eyes were still slightly narrowed. However, if she suspected they'd been up to no good, she didn't say anything. 'Miss Jasmine wanted me to tell you that it's time for cake.'

Everyone followed Lisa back to the party, although Alyssa and Rosalie hung back to help Leon. He was a little wobbly but otherwise fine.

The three of them looked at each other before bursting into quiet giggles.

'I thought we were done for,' Rosalie said.

Leon dusted a stray twig off his shorts. '*You* thought you were done for? That was the scariest thing that's ever happened to me!'

'Yeah, it was super-scary,' Alyssa agreed. But she had to admit that it had also been kind of fun.

'You two make a good team, you know that?' Leon said.

'Thanks,' Alyssa said, smiling.

She'd only spent one day at Silverleaf, and she was realising there was so much she didn't know. She couldn't wait to get started with her training.

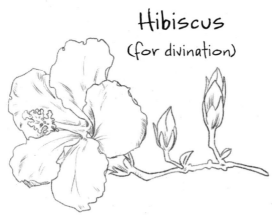

Hibiscus
(for divination)

CHAPTER TWELVE

Alyssa spent the rest of that week listening extra carefully during her Silverleaf sessions. She took detailed notes and devoted her evenings to memorising the names of plants. Before she could start work on a particular tea, she had to get to grips with the basics, Auntie Jasmine insisted.

Auntie Jasmine also gave Alyssa special sessions where she learned to control her powers. This involved lining up rows of pine cones while Alyssa focused all her concentration on knocking them over. Auntie Jasmine reasoned that if Alyssa could summon her surge of magical energy at will, she could better control it. So far, Alyssa had managed to knock over one pine cone. It was so frustrating!

Where was her magic when she wanted it to appear? Auntie Jasmine, however, was optimistic that she'd improve.

It was hard work, but Alyssa was committed to getting as good at spell work as possible in the short time she had. After all, if she could get her head around magic, maybe she could do something to help fix her broken family. At the very least, she could cure nervous butterflies on the first day of school next term. *That* was a tea that could benefit lots of people, including Alyssa, so it was within the rules. At least, that's what she hoped.

On Friday evening after Silverleaf sessions had ended for the day, Auntie Jasmine announced that tonight was the monthly local community meeting. And her nieces were going with her, whether they liked it or not.

'Mastering magic is important, but so is being of service to the community,' Auntie Jasmine said.

Alyssa had been looking forward to going home and calling her parents. She had been here since Monday and hadn't spoken to them on the phone in four whole days.

'I'm not even part of this community,' Alyssa grumbled.

Auntie Jasmine looked at her sideways. 'Don't

be absurd. Of course you are! You're a Keeper-in-Training, darlin', which means you are an essential part of this community.'

*

When they arrived at the meeting, Alyssa's heart sank. It was in a ramshackle hall where the windows were fastened shut and she knew that her legs would end up stuck to the plastic seat. Despite the hot evening, the hall was packed with people of all ages.

Rosalie and Rue said they were going to the playground and somehow managed to quietly back out of the hall. Alyssa had no such luck. Auntie Jasmine held her arm and insisted on introducing her to everyone, including the corner-shop owner Mr Rasheed, Margaret, who ran the laundrette, and Mr Jackson, who sold her compost for the allotment.

At last, when it was time for the meeting to start, everyone sat in a circle. Auntie Jasmine chaired the meeting while a woman she introduced as Debbie took notes. Debbie was around Auntie Jasmine's age but her denim dungarees and bright-striped T-shirt made her seem much younger.

The elderly Caribbean man sitting next to Alyssa nudged her. 'You wan' some?' he whispered, a brown paper bag in his hand. It smelled like strawberries.

Alyssa nodded, reached in and took a small

handful of cool, ripe fruit. She bit into one and her eyes lit up.

'Best strawberries you ever had?' he asked, a twinkle in his eye.

'Yeah!' she said. They really were. 'Thank you.'

'From your auntie's allotment,' he whispered.

Alyssa chewed thoughtfully. The strawberries were delicious. She wondered if the magic of the spell garden somehow seeped into the allotment. Could they be *magic* strawberries?

'Now to the next point on the agenda,' Debbie said. 'Has anyone else received letters from Forsythe Developers?'

A few people nodded.

'Our takeaway has only been on the high street for two months,' one woman said. 'Already the landlords want to hike up the rent! And they want to change the name of the neighbourhood to Midtown City. What's wrong with Holloway?'

Auntie Jasmine and Debbie looked at each other.

'You can't be serious, Gloria. We haven't had a rent increase in these parts for decades,' Auntie Jasmine said.

'Mark my words, there are changes coming to this neighbourhood, and I don't like it,' said the man beside Alyssa. His voice boomed through the cramped hall. 'I've lived and worked here for over forty years, but it's only now that the council has a problem with my fruit stall.'

'What do you mean, Mr Brown?' Auntie Jasmine asked. She sounded concerned.

'I mean that I've been ordered to pack up and leave! Unless I spend my life savings on some ridiculous permit. *Forty-four years* I've served this community, selling fruit six days a week, rain or shine,' he said. His voice cracked with emotion.

'This is most alarming. Surely there must be something we can do?' Debbie said.

Murmurs of worry rippled through the hall. Alyssa realised it was about more than just buying Mr Brown's delicious strawberries. Everyone seemed upset at the idea of losing him.

But hadn't Auntie Jasmine said that the spell garden protected the community? They didn't have anything to worry about, then ... did they? She took the commotion as an excuse to slip outside and get some fresh air. The hall building was on the edge of a small park. Apart from a few groups of people having evening picnics, Alyssa couldn't see anyone else – and she couldn't see a playground. Where were her cousins?

'Hey!' a voice behind her said loudly.

Alyssa turned. It was Leon.

'Oh, hey. You got pulled into this too?' she asked.

'Yeah, Mum and Dad take these community meetings seriously. They haven't missed one since they opened the takeaway.'

'Did you sneak out like Rue and Rosalie?' Alyssa asked.

Leon shook his head. 'I didn't set foot inside in the first place. Once you're there, it's impossible to leave!'

'*Now* you tell me,' Alyssa said, rolling her eyes and grinning at Leon.

'There you are, Alyssa!' yelled Rue, waving from the swings that were practically hidden behind a cluster of trees.

Alyssa and Leon walked round the trees, towards the small playground. Rosalie was sitting on a swing next to Rue, hunched over an exercise book.

Rue waved at Alyssa, but Rosalie barely looked up from her book.

'Where were you?' Rue asked.

'You abandoned me!' Alyssa said. 'It was so hot and stuffy in there.'

She spotted another group of kids hanging out by the roundabout. They looked about the same age as the Silverleaf kids, but, judging by the stony glare one of the girls gave her, Alyssa guessed the two groups weren't exactly the best of friends.

'Do you know those guys?' she whispered to her cousins.

'You could say that,' Rosalie muttered, putting away her book. 'They go to the *other* summer school, Hemlock. It's in the spell garden that Auntie Debbie runs; it's about a mile from here. Debbie loves to experiment with growing plant hybrids, but Auntie Jasmine prefers to keep the original plants as they are in her spell garden, so she said Debbie could start a second garden.'

'You mean there's another crux well?' Alyssa asked.

'No, but there's a magical underground pipe that connects our garden to theirs,' Rosalie said. 'Their spell garden would be nothing without ours.'

'Wait, you said *Auntie Debbie*. You mean that blonde woman in the meeting is our aunt too?' Alyssa asked.

'No, silly!' Rue chuckled. 'She and Auntie Jasmine were together for years. So she's like an auntie to me and Rosalie.'

Suddenly a football flew into their group and slammed against the nearest swing.

'Watch it!' Rue yelled. They threw the football back to the other kids with equal force.

'They're just salty because they have the second-best garden,' Rosalie said loud enough for the other group to hear.

The blond boy who'd kicked the football approached them. 'Your spell garden might be bigger but you should see the plant hybrids we're creating. They make your plants look like puny weeds.'

Rosalie smirked. 'If you say so, Kieran.'

Even if Alyssa didn't know much about this other spell garden, she could tell one thing for certain: Rosalie and Kieran had history. The air simmered with angry words unsaid.

'You don't even know how many awesome spells Rosalie has!' Rue yelled. 'Just you wait and see.'

'Ooh, I'm scared. *Not*. Rosalie and spelling aren't the best combination, am I right?' Kieran said smugly. His friends burst into mean giggles.

'Oi, shut up!' Rue yelled.

'Leave it,' Rosalie said. She got up from the swing, picked up her rucksack and left the playground.

'Should we go after her?' Alyssa asked. What had Kieran meant? And why had Rosalie allowed him to wind her up like that? She usually seemed unbothered by what other people thought of her.

Rue shook their head. 'She just needs some space.'

'Finally!' Leon said as the grown-ups filed out of the

community hall. 'The meeting's over. I need to get my parents. Otherwise Dad will stay and chat for hours.'

Alyssa's tummy rumbled, reminding her that she was ready to eat. Mr Brown's strawberries were delicious but they weren't dinner.

'Let's go and find Auntie Jasmine,' Alyssa said. As they walked towards the community hall, she turned to Rue.

'What did Kieran mean about Rosalie's spelling?'

'Kieran and Rosalie went to the same primary school. They did *not* get on,' Rue said. 'Kieran and his mates were awful to Rosalie when they found out she's dyslexic. All it means is that it takes her a little longer to read, but they made her life hell. She even wanted to move school.'

'That sounds tough,' Alyssa said. She thought she might understand why Rosalie pushed herself so hard during Silverleaf lessons.

They found Auntie Jasmine deep in conversation with Mr Brown. She gave him one final embrace as they approached. 'I'm so, so sorry. If only we'd—'

'If only what? It is not your fault,' Mr Brown said.

She nodded, but the sad expression didn't leave her face. If Auntie Jasmine believed Mr Brown, then why did she look so upset?

It couldn't be her fault, could it?

Ground Ivy
(for coughs)

CHAPTER THIRTEEN

There were no Silverleaf lessons on Saturdays, so Lisa roped Rosalie, Rue and Alyssa into sorting out the tea shop. She insisted it needed a good decluttering, even though Auntie Jasmine disagreed. She'd been in a funk since the community meeting yesterday evening, and didn't seem quite her cheerful self.

Even Rosalie grumbled about having to spend the day helping at the shop. 'I could be practising my taxonomy,' she muttered.

Although Alyssa would have much rather been outside, she didn't mind a day off from the spell garden. Auntie Jasmine was still making her practise controlling her magic, and she was rubbish at it. Try as she might, Alyssa just couldn't summon that tingling feeling in her hands again.

Rue slumped against the shop wall. 'How can one tiny shop contain so many boxes?' they huffed.

The cousins had been sorting through old stock all morning. Lisa wanted to make way for new stock, but Auntie Jasmine refused to throw anything away. When she thought Lisa wasn't looking, she'd stuff a box of tea into the pocket of her burnt-orange kaftan.

Alyssa took a closer look at the tea blends lining the shelf. Among the tea varieties she recognised, like English breakfast and chamomile, there were small tins with beautiful handwritten labels, including *A Good Night's Sleep*, *Butterflies Be Gone* and *Stress Away*.

'Auntie Jasmine, does the butterfly tea blend really get rid of nerves?' Alyssa asked.

'Why, yes. It's a very special tea blend I invented to ease nervous butterflies in the tummy,' Auntie Jasmine said.

Alyssa's eyes lit up. That was just the thing she needed for starting Year Seven!

'It really works!' Rosalie yelled from the greenhouse at the back, where she was misting the plants. 'I used it on my first day of secondary school.'

'Just a shame no one buys it,' Lisa muttered.

Auntie Jasmine sighed. 'You know as well as I that my special blends are *not* to be exchanged for money. They are given to those who need them. It's for the good of the spell garden.'

So these *are the magical teas*, Alyssa realised. Suddenly the dull tins seemed a lot more interesting.

'The space is looking neater already. I can see the wall for once!' Lisa said.

Privately Alyssa agreed, though she would never say so to Auntie Jasmine. The shop looked better when every surface wasn't covered with old boxes. It no longer looked like someone's cluttered living room.

Auntie Jasmine grumbled in the worn armchair. 'It's fine. If you like boring and generic,' she huffed.

'Just watch! We'll attract the sort of customers who actually buy stuff,' Lisa said.

'Oooh, a tea shop!' A young couple stopped outside and poked their heads through the door.

'Do you sell matcha lattes?' one of them asked.

Auntie Jasmine groaned. 'This is a fancy latte-free zone.'

Lisa put on a bright smile. 'I'm afraid we don't do coffee, but can I interest you in—'

'No worries. We'll try the coffee place across the road,' they said before leaving.

'Yet another reason we should have a coffee machine,' Lisa mumbled.

Someone tapped on the glass window. Alyssa saw a Black woman about the same age as Auntie Jasmine. Her great-aunt rose from her chair and gestured for the woman to come inside.

'Sister Hortense! I was so sad to hear about Princess,' Auntie Jasmine said, clasping both hands around hers.

The woman took a seat in the opposite armchair and dabbed at her eyes with a handkerchief. 'Thank you, Jasmine. I miss her ever so much.'

'I'm glad you stopped by. When I heard that your cat had passed, I whipped up a special tea blend,' Auntie Jasmine said. She reached for the top shelf and pulled down the tin labelled *Grief Relief*. 'It contains sage, marjoram and just a dash of hawthorn leaf. Plus a few secret ingredients.'

Sister Hortense peered at the tin. 'Do I drink it or season my chicken with it?'

'Just add hot water, let it steep for a few minutes and drink. I guarantee you'll feel like a new woman,' Auntie Jasmine said. 'In fact, I will brew you a cup right now.'

Alyssa watched with interest.

Auntie Jasmine flicked on a small white kettle

behind the counter and busied herself making a special cup of tea for her friend. She served it in a normal-looking mug. There was no silvery glow or weirdness of any sort.

'Princess was such a special cat,' Sister Hortense said, her voice quivering slightly. 'True, she was the laziest creature that ever walked God's green earth, but I would give anything to have her back.'

Auntie Jasmine rubbed Sister Hortense's shoulder as she sipped the hot tea.

'I know, my friend. You gave Princess the best possible life. We will all miss her.'

Sister Hortense patted Auntie Jasmine's hand. 'Thank you. You know, Jasmine, I feel better already.'

Auntie Jasmine turned to Alyssa. 'Darlin', let me introduce you to a good friend of mine. This is Sister Hortense.'

'You're telling me this is Violet's pickney?' Sister Hortense exclaimed. 'I never thought I'd see the day!'

Auntie Jasmine laughed. 'That's her all right, Hortense! Alyssa is staying for the summer.' She bent down and whispered something to Sister Hortense.

'Oh, I am sorry to hear that,' Sister Hortense replied loudly. 'Divorce?'

Alyssa froze. Who said anything about divorce?

Auntie Jasmine nodded. 'It seems that way.'

Sister Hortense peered over her spectacles. 'It's good to meet you, little one. Mind you tell Violet that I say hello.'

Alyssa nodded and tried to be polite, but the D-word was ringing through her mind.

'I hope she still remembers me all these years later,' Sister Hortense continued. 'Though I still recall the fire like it was yesterday. Terrible business.'

Alyssa snapped back to reality. She remembered Auntie Jasmine's words from earlier that week.

One spell misfired ...

Did she mean that it had caused a literal fire? It would explain why Mum never had candles in the house. Alyssa remembered the scented candle she and Dad had bought Mum for Mother's Day a few years ago. Mum had seemed to like it but she never used it once. In fact, Alyssa couldn't recall seeing it ever again.

'The fire? What fire?' Alyssa asked.

Out of the corner of her eye, Alyssa saw Auntie Jasmine shake her head.

Sister Hortense caught her breath. 'Nothing for you to worry about, child. I should be getting on.'

She thanked Auntie Jasmine and left in far better spirits than when she'd arrived. That didn't surprise Alyssa – she'd seen how powerful a few leaves could be.

Auntie Jasmine had said that using magic for selfish reasons, like a love spell, was against the rules. But now that divorce was being mentioned... Surely for an emergency like this it would be okay? Besides, Auntie Jasmine would never have to know.

'I don't see why Sister Hortense couldn't pay for that tea. Do you think I could walk into that new coffee shop over the road and expect a free latte?' Lisa said, stamping on cardboard boxes to flatten them.

'For the last time, Lisa, we are not like the other shops,' Auntie Jasmine said tartly.

That's for sure, Alyssa thought. However, she couldn't understand why Auntie Jasmine didn't want to smarten the place up. The new coffee shop might not be as interesting or as cosy as Jasmine's Teas, but it had one important edge: paying customers.

At that moment, a minivan parked outside the shop. Alyssa wouldn't have thought anything of it, if it wasn't for the expression on Auntie Jasmine's face.

'I don't believe it. It's not enough to harass me with endless letters – now they're turning up to my door!'

'Who is, Auntie Jasmine?' Alyssa asked. The minivan looked perfectly normal to her. It was off-white and had a grey logo on the side with **FD** in big, bold capitals.

'It's Forsythe Developers,' Auntie Jasmine said, not taking her eye off the van. 'And they are not welcome.'

She marched outside, closely followed by Lisa. Alyssa watched through the window as her great-aunt knocked on the minivan door.

Rue and Rosalie came in from unpacking boxes in the greenhouse to see what the fuss was about.

'Whoa, Auntie Jasmine looks super-annoyed,' Rue said.

They watched as Auntie Jasmine told the people in the minivan to keep it moving, while Lisa looked on, a little embarrassed.

'Forsythe Developers. Why have I heard that name before?' Alyssa asked.

'Because Auntie Jasmine can't stand them. They keep offering her money to leave the allotment and the shop, and they won't take no for an answer,' Rosalie said.

Before Alyssa could ask why being offered money was a bad thing, Auntie Jasmine and Lisa came back into the shop.

'You could at least have a meeting with them, Miss Jasmine,' Lisa said.

'Absolutely not. Those parasites won't be happy until they own every brick in this neighbourhood. No one wanted a shop in here when my mother opened this place. And now? You should see the offers I receive from these big, big companies, trying to get me to leave before my lease is up for renewal,' Auntie Jasmine said. 'Not a week goes by that I don't hear from Forsythe Developers. This neighbourhood is shedding scraps of its soul by the day.'

Having lots of money didn't seem so terrible to Alyssa. 'Why don't you accept the money and move, Auntie Jasmine?' she asked. 'You could get a bigger shop.'

Auntie Jasmine looked horrified. 'And uproot the allotment? There are tomato patches in that garden older than you! Mark my words: this community would not last one week without this place. Moving is out of the question.'

'If we carry on this way, Miss Jasmine, we might not have any choice,' Lisa said as she picked up a heap of cardboard boxes.

Auntie Jasmine pointed to the embroidered quote behind the till and read it aloud. '*We are each other's harvest.* When we help one another, we all reap the rewards. That is something we must never forget.'

Alyssa felt a stab of empathy for Lisa. Auntie Jasmine didn't want anything to change, even as the rest of the world moved on.

'Lisa, let me help,' Alyssa said. She picked up the

remaining flattened boxes and trailed behind her to the recycling bin by the allotment.

'Cheers, Alyssa!' Lisa said when they were outside.

'I don't understand why Auntie Jasmine doesn't want the shop to make money,' Alyssa said.

'I'm trying to turn this shop into something special before it gets left behind. The neighbourhood is changing so quickly. But Miss Jasmine doesn't like change.'

'I get that,' Alyssa replied quietly. It seemed like everything at home was changing and she didn't like it one bit, so she could understand Auntie Jasmine being upset.

'Sometimes change is good!' Lisa muttered to herself.

Alyssa wanted to ask Lisa more – Lisa seemed almost as annoyed as Auntie Jasmine – but they were interrupted.

'Hey, Alyssa. We're going to get lunch now,' Rosalie called from the greenhouse.

'How about you three get some ice cream while you're out?' Lisa handed Rosalie a ten-pound note. That would cover more than just ice cream.

They didn't need to be told twice. 'Thanks, Lisa!' Alyssa, Rosalie and Rue yelled as they ran out into the street.

'Come on,' Rue said. 'Let's take the long way to the shop.'

While they walked, Alyssa told them about Sister Hortense mentioning the fire. 'Has your mum ever talked about a fire from her childhood?'

'Nope,' Rue said.

'I don't understand why Mum would keep that from us,' Rosalie said.

'Unless it was related to why she and my mum don't talk any more,' Alyssa said.

They passed all sorts of shops on the high street, including a new supermarket with electric sliding doors and a security guard. Alyssa hadn't noticed that a few days earlier.

'I bet this place sells ice cream,' she said, pausing outside.

Rosalie shook her head. 'Mr Rasheed's shop sells ice poles for twenty pence. That leaves us plenty of change for chicken and chips.'

'Plus, Mr Rasheed's is the only one that sells my favourite flavour. Purple!' Rue said.

They passed the chicken shop where they bought steaming hot cardboard boxes packed with wings and fries. Alyssa couldn't wait to dig in. They walked out of the shop with a carrier bag of food.

Rosalie paused outside a shiny building and looked up.

'That's so weird. This is definitely Mr Rasheed's shop, but it looks completely different,' she said. 'Where's he gone?'

Alyssa peered through the window. Whatever this shiny new store was, it wasn't a corner shop.

Gorse
(for romance)

CHAPTER FOURTEEN

This new shop had floor-to-ceiling glass windows and an electronic sliding door. The sign above the door said *WÜF* in giant polished iron letters. It looked like the sort of place that sold paper-thin laptops rather than anything edible. It didn't feel part of the community like the other places on the high street.

'I was here just last weekend,' Rue said. 'Mr Rasheed would've told me if he was moving away. He said we were his favourite customers.'

'Maybe he had to move really quickly,' Rosalie said. 'I hope he's okay.'

Alyssa noticed the board beside the door: *Opening Offer! 20% off Artisan Ice Cream.*

'Look, there's a fridge inside. It must be an ice-cream parlour,' Alyssa said.

They were hit with a delicious cool breeze once they stepped inside. The air-conditioning felt heavenly against Alyssa's clammy skin. The smell of fresh paint lingered in the air.

'The shop looks totally different. It's so light and spacious,' Rosalie said.

Rue rushed to the counter. 'Sweet! They have loads of flavours. Wonder if they have purple ...'

Rosalie took in the polished parquet flooring, the smooth white surfaces and minimalist shelving. 'Just one scoop, Rue. Something tells me it'll cost more than an ice pole.'

Alyssa and Rue pressed their fingers against the glass. The counter was topped with towering glass jars of posh biscuits. They gazed at the dazzling array of ice creams and sorbets swirled into metal tubs glittered with frost.

Alyssa read out the labels, hoping they'd have her favourite: cookies 'n' cream.

'*Liver and Onion. Sardine Surprise. Rabbit Ripple,*' she said aloud. Strange. Then she looked at the biscuit jars. 'Homemade dog cookies?'

Rue pretended to gag. 'What sort of ice-cream shop is this?'

'An expensive one. For only the most refined of canines,' said a voice that was as chilly as the air.

Alyssa looked up. A man in a pristine white apron had appeared behind the counter. He brandished a silver ice-cream scoop in a way that made it look like a weapon.

'You mean, this is ice cream for *dogs*?' Alyssa asked. Wow. They really did have everything in London.

'Ohhh,' Rue said. 'That explains the disgusting flavours.'

The man looked at them with horror. 'Are those ... fingerprints?!' His voice reminded Alyssa of a wasp buzzing, all nasally and crisp.

He hustled them away from the glass counter and cleaned the surface with a white cloth he produced from inside his apron.

'Excuse me, do you know where Mr Rasheed's gone?' Rue asked. 'His shop used to be here and they sold purple ice poles.'

The man frowned. 'This shop is mine now, and I can assure you ... this establishment shall not ever sell an iced pole.'

He turned round and noticed Rosalie hovering by the door. 'Hey, you! What's that in your pocket?' he demanded. 'Empty it, now!'

Rosalie's eyes widened in shock. 'There's nothing in my pockets! Why would I want one of your smelly dog biscuits?' The slight tremor in her voice betrayed her fear.

'Look. I don't have all day, young lady. Empty your pocket and then leave my shop.'

Since Alyssa had arrived, everyone in the neighbourhood had been so welcoming and friendly. Why was this guy being so rude? They'd only come in to look around. How dare he accuse Rosalie of stealing?

'Let's go,' Rosalie said, opening the door.

'What's your problem?' Alyssa yelled at the man. She was so loud she even surprised herself.

It wasn't like Alyssa to raise her voice, especially to a grown-up. But she couldn't stand the way this horrible man talked to them. Mum had taught her to be prepared for moments like this. Moments when someone would treat her unfairly based on how she looked. But Alyssa had never experienced it for herself. Until now.

The shop owner's face was puce with rage. A vein throbbed in his temple. He stepped towards Alyssa. 'What did you say to me?'

The swirling emotions of fear and rage bubbled inside her. Despite the frigid air-conditioning, she felt a familiar warmth in her fingertips. She knew what was about to happen, but she just couldn't control it.

It all happened in a millisecond.

THUMP.

THUMP.

SPLAT.

The sounds came from behind the counter. Splodges of brown and beige ice cream exploded against the glass with so much force that it nearly shattered. Alyssa knew this was her fault and tried hard to rein in the chaos. She did her best to focus on something happy, something to calm her down, but she couldn't shift how small this rude man had made her feel.

'Not the new fridge!' the man yelled. 'What's happening? You kids need to leave, now! Don't make me call the police.'

That was the final straw. Alyssa could no longer hold back.

The fridge began to rumble and shake. The ice cream melted in a matter of seconds. Now it was like thick milky soup but hotter than lava and exploding in spurts. The white walls were covered in smelly beige stains. Huge splodges of Sardine Surprise splattered the owner square in the face as he struggled to contain the mess with his apron.

Rue covered her nose. 'Can anyone else smell that?'

But Alyssa wasn't listening. She was too overwhelmed by the anger that was unspooling all around her. The metal shelving units lining the wall buckled like matchsticks and boxes of dog biscuits collapsed to the floor with a massive crash.

The biscuits scattered everywhere. Suddenly there was a yelping sound followed by the sound of paws slipping against the polished wooden floor as a spaniel puppy with floppy ears bounded in from the back of the shop. It rushed towards the spilled biscuits and ate its fill.

'No, Colin!' the snooty shop owner shouted. 'You can't eat those biscuits! Gluten gives you the runs!'

He ducked the sprays of ice cream coming from the counter to drag Colin away from the biscuits. The puppy snarled and snapped in the man's arms.

'Guys, we need to move. Now!' Rosalie said urgently.

Alyssa knew she was right. They could be in serious trouble. They had to leave.

Thankfully, the shop owner was too distracted with the destruction around him to notice the girls **rushing out of the door.**

'Good luck with Colin's diarrhoea!' Rue yelled before the door shut behind them.

Once they were clear of the shop, Rosalie yanked the other two into a nearby alleyway. She turned to Alyssa and grabbed her hands.

Rainbow waves were radiating from Alyssa's fingers. The magic was unmistakable.

'*What do you think you're playing at?*' exclaimed Rosalie.

Alyssa hid her hands behind her back. 'It was an accident!'

'I saw you!' Rosalie yelled. 'You used magic in front of a normie. Do you have any idea how irresponsible—'

'And cool!' Rue interrupted. 'Alyssa did us all a favour. That grumpy dude was seconds away from losing his rag.'

'But using the magic in that way drains the crux well! Auntie Jasmine would be so disappointed. She's stressed enough as it is, since that community meeting about the developers,' Rosalie said. 'Let's hope Auntie Jasmine doesn't find out about this.'

'It really was an accident. I think it happened because he made me so . . . angry,' Alyssa said. Even though her heart was pounding, she felt in awe of her own power.

'Alyssa, you have got to learn to control yourself,' Rosalie said.

'I'm trying! I've been practising with Auntie Jasmine, but we're not making much progress.'

'Give it up, Rosalie,' Rue said. 'No one got hurt – it just made a big mess. And it was the least that uptight jerk deserved.'

Alyssa managed a weak smile at Rue.

The hint of a smirk crossed Rosalie's lips. 'He was a piece of work, wasn't he?'

The three of them looked at each other before bursting into laughter. They crossed the road and walked to the small park. However, as they ate their slightly cold chicken and chips, the enormity of what had just happened dawned on Alyssa.

'It was as bad as the mess I made in Jasmine's Teas,' she said. 'Maybe I should have stopped at smashing the shelving units?'

'You think?!' Rosalie said. 'Our magic is supposed to be used for the good of the wider community. That's, like, the first rule!'

'That overpriced shop wasn't exactly for the good of the community. Didn't you say it took over a place that had been there for years?' Alyssa said.

'She has a point,' Rue said. 'Alyssa did us a favour.'

Alyssa turned to Rosalie. 'I don't know how I did it. You won't tell Auntie Jasmine, will you?'

'Course not. I'm no snitch,' Rosalie said.

'I can't wait to see what you do next!' said Rue, grinning. 'Wish I'd filmed it!'

'It's really unusual to harness magic without spell work. No plants, potions or incantations,' Rosalie said thoughtfully. 'Let's be scientific about this and retrace your steps. What happened both times just before your magical mess?'

Alyssa concentrated. So much had happened in the last six days. The first morning at the shop felt like weeks ago.

'The first time it happened, I'd seen a family posing for a selfie with ice cream outside the shop,' Alyssa said.

Rosalie quirked one eyebrow. 'Okay. And just now?'

'It happened after that guy accused you of stealing. He looked at us like we were something on the bottom of his shoe.'

'So now we're getting somewhere. The second time your magic went haywire was because someone made you upset and angry. But that doesn't explain the first time. Why would seeing some random family upset you?'

Alyssa felt her face flush. Rosalie was right, of

course. Why would seeing some random family have been so upsetting? Her cousin wanted a logical explanation, but Alyssa had none.

'If you don't tell us the truth, then we won't get anywhere,' Rosalie said.

'Auntie Jasmine always said that magic and emotion are closely connected,' Rue added.

Alyssa took a deep breath and let the truth out. 'Because I haven't had ice cream with Mum and Dad since last summer. All they do these days is argue.'

Her cousins were quiet for a moment.

They probably think I'm ridiculous, Alyssa thought.

Rosalie and Rue looked at each other and then Rosalie finally spoke. 'When Mum and Dad split up, it took some getting used to. But now they're mates,' she said.

'It's hard, though,' said Rue, 'especially if you're an only child. At least I have Rosalie.'

'Thanks,' Alyssa said quietly.

Her cousins finished their food, but Alyssa found she had lost her appetite. Talking about Mum and Dad breaking up made it feel more real.

Even though Auntie Jasmine had warned against casting love spells, all Alyssa could think was this:

If I can just figure out the right tea spell, I'll never have to get used to Mum and Dad being separated. It would be for the greater good if they stayed together ... wouldn't it?

Ironwood
(for positive
energy)

CHAPTER FIFTEEN

Sundays in the spell garden were for maintenance. While Jasmine's Teas was closed, everyone mucked in to take care of the plants. Literally. Equipment had to be checked for rust, plants pruned and flower beds weeded. The lucky ones got the fun jobs, like harvesting flicker-bee honey straight from the hive.

The unlucky ones got up close and personal with the compost heap.

Alyssa and Rosalie were given the job of weeding the soil where the plants for the persuasion spells were grown. Alyssa would have preferred a task that got her up close and personal with one of the plants she needed for her love spell – *where was the banana fern Auntie Jasmine mentioned, anyway?* – but it was better than turning the compost.

She pulled on a pair of thick chain-metal gloves that reminded her of a knight's armour.

'Are these really necessary?' she asked.

Rosalie nodded solemnly. 'Oh, yes. It's called viper weed for a reason. Look out for the spiky red orbs and tug from the root.'

Alyssa looked at the viper weed in front of them. So these were the fanged plants. Crimson spheres sprouted from the stem. They were the size of a ping-pong ball and covered in tiny tooth-like spikes. She carefully avoided the orbs, grasped the stem at the base and pulled hard. It came out far easier than she'd expected.

'What happens if this is used in a spell?' Alyssa asked, holding up a viper weed. It had a scent that reminded her of the sourest rhubarb. The smell alone made her mouth pucker.

Rosalie shrugged. 'Depends on the spell and the Keeper casting it. It could give you a case of perma-tickles or kill you instantly.'

Alyssa dropped the viper weed.

'That's why Keepers-in-Training don't use certain plants in our spell work, especially if they're freshly harvested,' Rosalie said. 'They can be unpredictable.'

As they were weeding, Alyssa caught a whiff of something she recognised. 'Do you smell that? It's like banana milkshake.'

'You must have accidentally cut a banana fern,' Rosalie said without looking up. She was absorbed with uprooting a particularly stubborn viper weed.

The banana fern! Fancy seeing that here, thought Alyssa, as she noticed the spiky-leaved bush among the viper weed. *Okay, so what did Auntie Jasmine say about how to use it?*

'Brew a tea with a few of these leaves and the drinker will fall head over heels with the first person they see.'

Now was her chance.

Alyssa bent down by the plant, clearing away the leaves to find the biggest ones. She tugged at the plant and broke off a small handful of leaves. Rosalie sniffed the air. The banana scent was impossible to miss.

'What's that in your hand?' Rosalie asked.

'It's ... um ...' Alyssa hated the idea of lying to Rosalie, but she couldn't tell her what she planned to do. She knew that sort of spell was off limits to Keepers-in-Training. 'It's banana fern,' she admitted. 'I just ... liked the smell.'

Rosalie continued looking at Alyssa suspiciously,

so reluctantly she dropped the leaves to the ground. She'd have to try again another time.

*

Something felt different at dinner that evening. Auntie Jasmine wasn't as chatty and she barely spent any time watering her 'plant babies' on the balcony. Alyssa and her cousins did the dishes and cleared up the kitchen while she had an early night.

'Is Auntie Jasmine all right? She said she was fine, but I'm not sure I believe her,' Alyssa said to Rue, handing them clean plates to dry. They had a washing-up assembly line going. 'She seemed weird.'

'I'm not sure,' Rue said. 'Maybe we should bring her tea in bed?'

'Good idea,' Alyssa said.

Rue opened the tea cupboard. It was crammed with boxes, canisters and jars stuffed with dried tea leaves. 'Where do we start? We need something calming.'

Alyssa rooted through the heaving cupboard. 'Rooibos . . . hibiscus . . . lemon balm . . . I don't know what any of them are good for.'

'There's a simple formula we use for tea blends,' Rosalie said. 'You guys will learn it in a few weeks, I reckon.'

Rue rolled their eyes. 'Of course, Rosalie never resists a chance to show off.'

Rosalie crossed her arms. 'Any better ideas, Rue?'

'I'd love to hear the formula,' Alyssa said.

Rosalie jogged to the next room and returned with a leather-bound exercise book filled with sheaves of paper. She flicked through her notes until she found the right page. 'Here we go! I have a basic magic tea formula right here.'

Alyssa read the list out loud over her shoulder:

One of leaf
Two of fruit
Three of flower
Four of root

'That's not very helpful,' she added. 'Sounds like half of it is missing.'

'Yeah. I was hoping for a proper spell,' Rue said.

'We just need to choose the plants based on what we want to achieve,' said Rosalie.

'Huh?' Rue asked.

'Okay, say we want to brew a tea to make Auntie Jasmine feel energised. We use plants with energising properties: leaf, fruit, flower and root, like the rhyme says.'

'But we can't make magic tea outside the spell garden, right?' Alyssa asked.

'It's forbidden for Keepers-in-Training to use magic outside Silverleaf, but there are plenty of non-magical plants with healing properties,' Rosalie said.

Together they flicked through Rosalie's notes in search of plants with healing properties. Eventually they settled on what they needed.

'So we have cerassee for the leaf, orange for the fruit, chamomile for the flower and valerian for the root,' Rosalie said.

'Eww, not cerassee!' Rue groaned.

'What's that?' Alyssa asked.

'It's an old Jamaican remedy. Mum always makes it for us when we're sick,' Rue said. 'I'd rather go to school than drink that.'

'It tastes gross but it works,' Rosalie said.

Alyssa listened carefully. If this formula worked for Auntie Jasmine, she could use the same formula to blend her tea for Mum and Dad.

While Rosalie brewed Auntie Jasmine's tea in a small teapot, Alyssa and Rue flicked through her exercise book, which she'd filled with notes and lots of sketches.

Alyssa admired the neat ink drawings of nurse

blossom, cackle root, cat's claw and other weird and wonderful magical plants.

'I didn't realise you liked to draw, Rosalie,' she said.

Rosalie looked up from her tea preparation. 'Oh,' she said shyly. 'I find it easier to remember things visually rather than writing them down. My dyslexia means I think in pictures rather than words.'

Alyssa smiled. 'They're really cool. I wish I could draw like that.'

'Thanks,' Rosalie said quietly. 'If only my teachers at school thought the same. They think I'm not paying attention when I'm drawing in class. Anyway ... it's ... whatever.'

She took the tea tray to Auntie Jasmine's room like she was in a hurry. Then she shut herself in her room.

Had Rosalie looked a little sad talking about her dyslexia? Alyssa couldn't imagine her intelligent, bold cousin struggling with anything, let alone schoolwork.

Alyssa and Rue played on their phones, looking up every now and again to show each other something on their screens. The flat was so much quieter with Auntie Jasmine in bed. It didn't feel right. If she was up, she'd tell them to put their phones away. She'd say something like—

'Don't tell me you kids are glued to those infernal devices!'

Alyssa and Rue dropped their phones. 'Auntie Jasmine!' they said in unison.

Auntie Jasmine stood in the kitchen doorway in her red silk dressing gown and yawned.

'Are you feeling better?' Rue asked.

'Getting there,' she said, taking a seat at the kitchen table.

Rosalie burst into the room. 'I thought I heard you! Did the tea work?'

'Why, yes,' Auntie Jasmine said. 'Thank you all. I have more energy and I even feel less anxious about those developers. What did you put in it?'

Alyssa watched Auntie Jasmine carefully while her cousins described their healing tea recipe. Auntie Jasmine didn't have her usual glow, but she definitely looked better than she had earlier.

The tea had really worked. And it didn't even have any magical ingredients! Alyssa couldn't help imagining what a real magical tea could do for Mum and Dad. It could fix *everything*.

'Now, while I've got the energy, I need to water the balcony garden. Do I have any volunteers?' Auntie Jasmine asked.

'I'll help!' Alyssa said cheerfully.

The next chance she had, she was going to focus on the love tea spell for Mum and Dad. Starting with the ingredients she needed from the spell garden.

Honeysuckle
(for abundance)

CHAPTER SIXTEEN

When Rosalie wasn't looking, Alyssa pinched the exercise book and stayed up late reading it in bed. Using her phone, she devised a shortlist of different plants (some magical, some ordinary) that she could brew in her magical tea for Mum and Dad.

After painstakingly reading the notes, turning the pages quietly so as not to disturb Rue's snores, Alyssa wrote down the plants that had healing and loving properties in her exercise book. Although some sounded familiar, she hadn't yet learned about most of them at Silverleaf yet. Her first recipe was going to include the following:

Banana fern leaf (One part)

Passionfruit (Two parts)
Rose petal (Three parts)
Mandrake root (Four parts)

She was excited to begin experimenting. The thought of blending the different tea elements reminded Alyssa of when she and Mum used to bake muffins on Saturday mornings. Every weekend they would challenge themselves to come up with a brand-new flavour: strawberry and cardamom; lemon and coconut; even mango and chilli.

They hadn't invented any cakes since Mum and Dad started arguing. In fact, now she thought about it, the last time they'd baked together was before Christmas. That meant Mum and Dad had been arguing solidly for almost nine months. Her lip trembled. Then she steadied herself. If the plan worked, things would be back to normal in no time.

She went to sleep smiling.

*

The next morning, Alyssa, Rosalie and Rue arrived at Jasmine's Teas and greeted their great-aunt. She had left home to open the shop before they woke up.

'Good morning, Auntie Jasmine!' Alyssa trilled. 'Isn't it a beautiful day?'

But Auntie Jasmine didn't seem happy at all. 'Morning, my dears,' she muttered. The dark circles were visible under her eyes. It looked like the tea's healing powers had worn off.

'Are you okay, Auntie?' Rosalie asked.

Auntie Jasmine smiled weakly. 'I think I caught a chill in the night. Why is it so cold in August?'

'Cold?' Rue said. 'Auntie, it was boiling last night. We slept with the windows open.'

Auntie Jasmine yawned in response. She couldn't have been more different to the cheerful, energetic woman Alyssa had met just a week ago.

'Morning, all!' Lisa said as she entered through the front door. 'Sorry I'm late, the queue for the coffee shop was a mile long. Another new place opened and they're giving away free iced lattes to celebrate their opening. Genius marketing strategy.'

'What new place?' Auntie Jasmine asked.

'The one between the barber shop and the Ethiopian restaurant. Get this – it's fully machine-operated. You select your flavour on the touchscreen and it dispenses into a little cup!' Lisa said excitedly.

'But that's where Margaret's laundrette used to be!' Auntie Jasmine gasped. 'She didn't say she was closing. I only saw her at the community meeting on Friday.'

'I think it happened pretty quickly,' Lisa said. 'It's like they popped up overnight. I think we should do it here. All we'd need is—'

'I don't believe this. The last thing this high street needs is more bloomin' lattes!' Auntie Jasmine interrupted.

Lisa rolled her eyes. She looked pretty frustrated. 'Forget it,' she mumbled.

'Was Margaret a friend of yours, Auntie Jasmine?' Alyssa asked.

'Everyone in this neighbourhood is a friend, sweetness. Margaret's laundrette has been here longer than this place,' Auntie Jasmine said. She coughed a few times, and Alyssa thought she looked washed out.

'I think you kids should get to registration, don't you?' Lisa said, changing the subject.

'Lisa, would you mind handling registration today? I didn't sleep at all well,' Auntie Jasmine said, letting out another big yawn.

'Sure,' Lisa said, and everyone except Auntie Jasmine hustled out of the shop, through the allotment and into Silverleaf.

'Can I work on my new spell idea, Lisa?' Rosalie asked.

'You know the rules,' Lisa said. 'Mondays are for

taxonomy. However, if you complete your lesson in the morning, you can practise whatever you like in the afternoon!'

Alyssa smiled to herself. It sounded like she'd have the entire afternoon free to experiment – if she kept her tea spell secret.

*

After a morning of struggling to memorise the myriad categories of magical plants in the spell garden, in the afternoon Alyssa managed to break away from the rest of the group, who were busy on their personal projects. She claimed the bright sunlight was giving her a headache and she needed a glass of water. Luckily, Lisa believed her fib without any further explanation.

Alyssa stood in front of the store cupboard, which was more like a shed lined with shelves of jars and canisters. Some of the jars glowed jewel-bright colours and some radiated warmth. Others vibrated gently on the shelf, as though the magic inside was bursting to get out. Some were filled with powders in luminous rainbow colours and others contained what looked like greyish soil. All of them held wondrous possibilities.

Alyssa's heart beat faster and her fingers tingled with anticipation.

She leaned forward to study the labels. She only needed one plant. Passionfruit and rose petal could be found easily on the high street, and she knew where the banana fern grew. But the mandrake root? That was a plant she had never come across. Hopefully it was in one of these jars.

'Pretty awesome collection, right?'

The voice made Alyssa jump. She turned to see Lisa.

'Oh! Yeah, really cool,' Alyssa said.

Lisa stepped into the shed. 'Some of these jars are older than me. I should suggest an inventory audit to Miss Jasmine. If an ingredient is too old and stale, the magical properties become unpredictable. Are you looking for something in particular?' she asked.

'Erm, I was looking for something to help with a headache,' Alyssa said. 'Then I got distracted by all the jars. It's a lot to take in.'

Lisa smiled. 'Of course. I practically grew up in this spell garden. I forget how weird it must be for you. Violet still doesn't know you're here dabbling in spell work?'

Alyssa shook her head. 'She's so busy with work these days. I'm sure she wouldn't notice if I grew a third arm, let alone learned about magic.'

'Maybe Violet had the right idea.' Lisa sighed.

'Leaving magic behind for a real job. At least she's made something of herself,' she said quietly. 'Anyway! I find that a mug of feverfew tea sorts out a headache nicely. You can find that yourself, can't you? Remember that top-shelf ingredients are off limits until your seedling reaches the next level.'

'Of course,' Alyssa said brightly.

When Lisa left the shed, Alyssa turned her attention to the top shelf. She noticed a jar of dried banana fern, but she wanted to use fresh for her spell. It would be more potent, and her parents needed all the help they could get.

At the very end of the shelf was a tall thin jar labelled *Root of Mandrake*. Inside, it held what looked like a shrivelled brown carrot with two legs.

'Typical,' she muttered to herself as she stretched out her arm. The jar was out of reach.

Alyssa looked up again at the shelf. The dust clouding the outside of the jar indicated that the ingredient hadn't been used for a while. Auntie Jasmine seemed so distracted . . . Surely she wouldn't notice if a touch of mandrake root had gone, would she?

But there was another problem. How would Alyssa reach the top shelf? There were no chairs or ladders in the shed, and the other students would notice if she dragged one of the wooden stools inside.

Then it hit her. Alyssa might not have a stool, but she did have the power to move objects with her mind. The only problem was, those objects usually ended up getting smashed. The mess in Jasmine's Teas and the snooty dog ice-cream parlour still lingered in her mind.

'Alyssa, you have no choice. You can do this,' she whispered to herself.

Her powers appeared to awaken at times of heightened emotion. As Rosalie had said, magic and emotions were linked. She needed to think of something that would make her angry or sad.

Alyssa didn't have to search long. The day that Dad moved out stuck out in her mind. It was a memory she often skirted around because of the pain it caused: one day, Dad went to work and simply didn't come back. He called Alyssa and told her he and Mum were 'having a break' and it 'would all be sorted soon'.

When Alyssa had asked Mum what had happened, she'd said exactly the same. Word for word. It had made Alyssa feel like, behind the comforting words, something was being concealed from her.

She felt the familiar swell of pain and anger rising in her. The air around her fingers shimmered as she held onto the memory. Now, she turned her focus to the glass jar, trying to get it to inch forward into her open hands. It took all of Alyssa's concentration to hold both thoughts in her mind at once.

A scraping sound interrupted Alyssa's concentration. The jar was moving! She tugged on the sadness and hurt in her memory, forcing herself to relive it. The jar kept moving, slowly, until suddenly it launched off the shelf and dropped straight into Alyssa's hands.

'Ooof!' Alyssa grunted. She hadn't expected it to be so heavy.

There was no time to celebrate her mini victory. Carefully but quickly, she twisted open the old jar. It released a fug of stale air that smelled faintly of apples. Alyssa snapped one of the shrivelled legs off the mandrake root, wrapped it in a paper towel and put it in the bottom of her rucksack. She hoped it would be enough.

As Alyssa was about to leave the store cupboard, she paused. What should she do with the jar? Lisa and Auntie Jasmine would notice if she left it on the floor – and Lisa knew that Alyssa had been in there last.

She could try and levitate it back onto the shelf, but that required more precision and power than Alyssa felt she was capable of. She would have to do it the old-fashioned way. Alyssa began to rearrange the bottom shelf, moving dusty jars out of the way, until there was space for the mandrake jar. She pushed it to the back of the shelf and concealed it with the other smaller jars.

With any luck, Lisa wouldn't do that inventory audit any time soon.

*

Gathering the mandrake root had been easier than expected, so Alyssa spent the rest of the afternoon dabbling with other ingredients for her tea spell alongside her friends. Getting hold of the bits and pieces would be a doddle. She might even have a successful tea recipe by the end of the week!

Rosalie was working on a tea blend that could boost concentration (so students would focus more on their homework and less on their phones – *typical Rosalie*, Alyssa thought) while Leon had an idea for a tea spell that made boiled broccoli taste like pepperoni pizza. Lisa argued that it was hardly for the wellbeing of the community, but Leon claimed that anything that got kids to eat more greens could only be a good thing.

'Thanks for the help, Alyssa. What are you working on?' Rue asked. They had just finished gathering the ingredients for a tea spell that would cool down the drinker – perfect for pets struggling in the heat.

'Umm …' Alyssa faltered. She had to think fast.

'I reckon it's a love spell,' Rosalie teased. 'She seemed very interested in the banana fern yesterday.'

'Yes! But … it's not what you think,' Alyssa began. 'It's to help with the love of … of … chores. Mum's always saying my room is a mess. I thought this tea would help me love housework and make her life easier.'

'Housework? *Borrring!*' Rue exclaimed. 'Don't let my mum hear about that. My bedroom at home is organised chaos – just how I like it.'

'Does anyone know where I can find some bunny shrub?' Alyssa asked, changing the subject. She'd have to be extra careful when preparing the tea spell in front of everyone else. Especially Rosalie.

The afternoon passed in a blur (time flew when you were conducting secret spell work). That evening, Alyssa and her cousins helped Lisa to lock up the spell garden. They walked through the allotment and into Jasmine's Teas through the back door. There, they found Auntie Jasmine sitting on an armchair holding a letter.

'Auntie Jasmine, I nailed today's taxonomy lesson!'

Rue said brightly. 'I finally know the difference between . . .'

Rue trailed off as they realised Auntie Jasmine wasn't listening.

'Everything okay, Auntie?' Rosalie asked.

'I-I'm afraid it is not,' Auntie Jasmine said quietly.

'What's going on?' Lisa asked.

'It's the landlord. They're asking for three months' rent in advance,' Auntie Jasmine said. 'Or we will be evicted: the tea shop, the allotment and the spell garden.'

'They can't do that!' Rosalie gasped. 'That's, like, a violation of your human rights. Or something.'

'Sadly, this is them being reasonable. At least they're giving us the option to stay,' Lisa said. 'Forsythe Developers have offered the landlords around here a ton of cash to clear out their tenants so they can purchase the units.'

'Oh, yes, very generous,' Auntie Jasmine said sarcastically. 'They want to boot out the people who made this neighbourhood special and give it a shiny new rebrand. Midtown City is a terrible name. So bland and boring!'

'So all we have to do is raise three months' rent in advance and we get to stay?' Alyssa asked.

Auntie Jasmine sighed. 'You make it sound easy,

sweetness. The trouble is that the shop makes just enough to get by. Earning triple the profits by the eighteenth of the month is a tall order.'

The eighteenth? Alyssa was due to go home on the twentieth. That didn't leave much time at all.

Rue gasped. 'That's only eleven days away! This is so unfair.'

'What puzzles me is why this is happening in the first place. What is happening to our protection spells?' Auntie Jasmine said. 'In the last couple of weeks, the power seems to be fading. I can't work out why.'

'Maybe we've used too much magic recently?' Lisa said. 'Alyssa's arrival shook things up a bit. That time-reversal spell was costly, and hardly for the good of the community. I'm sure it will be under control again in no time.'

Had Alyssa's arrival really disrupted the community so much that it was affecting their magic? The thought made Alyssa feel very guilty.

Auntie Jasmine shook her head. 'I don't think that's it, Lisa. We've been doing more spell work than ever for the good of the community, yet the crux-water is still low. I can't understand it.'

'What can we do about it?' Alyssa asked. She hated the idea that this might be her fault.

'First, I need to persuade the landlord to give us more time. This deadline is beyond unreasonable,' Auntie Jasmine said. 'Secondly, I'll check the crux-water levels tomorrow and work out exactly how much we're losing. Whatever the reason, we may have to expect some changes around here.'

'What sorts of changes?' Rue asked.

Auntie Jasmine looked out of the shop window mournfully. 'I wish I knew, sweetness. I wish I knew.'

Alyssa's heart sank. She hated seeing Auntie Jasmine like this. Looking at her cousins and their worried expressions, she could tell they felt the same. But this sounded like grown-up stuff. What could a bunch of kids do to help?

Mahogany
(for strength)

CHAPTER SEVENTEEN

On the way to the spell garden the next morning, the mood was sombre. Alyssa, Rosalie and Rue walked together while Auntie Jasmine decided to sleep in. She said she'd call Lisa and ask her to check on the crux-water levels. Alyssa could tell that she was obviously deeply worried about the crux-water, but seemed too ill to check on things herself.

'This is so weird,' Rue muttered as they crossed the estate courtyard. 'Auntie Jasmine never has a lie-in. She must be *very* ill.'

'I hope she'll feel better soon. I've never known there to be a crux-water shortage,' Rosalie said. 'The letter from the landlord must have really upset her.

Mum couldn't believe it when I told her. Can you imagine life without the spell garden?'

Rue shook their head. And, even though Alyssa had only been a Keeper-in-Training for a week, she felt a twinge in her tummy at the thought of losing this special place. Not only had she discovered she had magical powers and was learning to use them, she'd made friends, got to know her cousins. Plus, staying at Silverleaf, making her magic love tea, might be her only chance to get Mum and Dad back together again. She hoped everything would work out – *it had to.*

Tuesdays at the spell garden were for seed-sowing, and there was always a race to get the shiniest trowel set. The threesome pushed through the wooden door of Silverleaf and heard murmuring voices. More than usual.

It didn't take them long to figure out the source of the voices. Alyssa followed her cousins to the central enclosure, where they saw a bunch of other kids sitting in their spot.

'What are you doing here?' Rosalie shrieked.

The kids turned round. Alyssa recognised them as the ones she'd seen in the playground during the community meeting. They were from Hemlock, the rival school. Silverleaf pupils were sitting on one side of the enclosure and Hemlock pupils on the other.

Lisa and Debbie entered the enclosure together.

'Ah, I see you guys have met,' Lisa said.

'What's going on?' Simran asked.

'Miss Jasmine asked me to check the crux-water levels this morning as she isn't feeling very well,' Lisa began. 'She's resting until she's feeling better.'

Rosalie looked downcast. 'I knew it was strange for Auntie Jasmine to sleep late,' she muttered.

'Do you think she's going to be okay?' Ollie asked.

Debbie nodded. 'Of course, petals. And while Lisa minds the shop, I will look after both magic schools. Which means we will share a space until Jasmine's health is restored.'

There was uproar among the kids.

'*Share?* With *them*?' Rue spluttered.

The blond boy Alyssa had seen at the playground stood up. 'Believe me, we're not happy about this either,' he said.

'As if things could get worse,' Rosalie muttered.

'Oh, you'll manage,' Lisa said, chuckling. 'In my day, there was only one spell garden and we all shared just fine. You already share the same crux-pebbles; now you will share the same space too.'

Alyssa raised her hand. 'Will the crux-water shortage affect our spell work?' she asked, thinking about her tea spell.

To her surprise, her question was met with much muttering among both the Silverleaf and Hemlock kids. Alyssa sat on her hands; she'd forgotten that they didn't know about the crux-water being low.

'Well, I'm glad one of you is focused enough to care about your lessons,' Lisa said pointedly. She hushed the whispers and continued. 'Now, everyone, I can see that a few of you are worried, but there's no reason to be alarmed. Jasmine and I are investigating it and for now we just need to be careful about how much we use. The short answer to Alyssa's question is no: your type of spell work uses up very little magic. But I'm afraid anything larger than a basic tea spell will have to wait.'

Alyssa nodded, reassured.

Seed-sowing lessons were postponed, as this used unnecessary crux-water. Instead, Lisa told them to get on with their personal projects. For Alyssa, this was the perfect time to begin mastering her tea blend. While her friends thought she was working on her housework tea blend, she would work on the love tea spell.

Lisa walked over to their little group. 'Guys, I need volunteers to prepare the lunch. We have double the mouths to feed. Leon and Alyssa, you haven't been to our kitchen yet, I don't think ...'

Leon and Alyssa exchanged glances. They couldn't exactly say no, could they? They got up and followed Lisa to the kitchen.

*

The kitchen was tucked away from the main enclosure. From the outside it looked very basic: just a countertop, a huge sink and lots of small cupboards.

Lisa gave Leon and Alyssa a brief tour and handed them two aprons. Tuesdays were Jamaican chickpea curry and steamed basmati rice.

'But where's the oven? The stove?' Alyssa asked. It looked like a toy kitchen. 'And I'm not usually allowed to use a massive knife like that at home,' she said, pointing to the bronze knives in a wooden block on the counter.

'Oh, you've never cooked in an enchanted kitchen, have you?' Lisa said. 'You're in for a treat. All you need to do is put the prepared ingredients in the pot, think about what you want to make and the kitchen will do the rest. The knives are charmed so they'll only cut food, not you,' she said with a chuckle.

Alyssa's eyes widened. 'No way!'

'Wow!' Leon said. 'If only Mum and Dad could see this.'

Lisa nodded. 'However, you have to *really* imagine

the meal in your mind: the smell, the flavour and the appearance.'

'How much crux-water does this use?' Leon asked. 'Seems like loads!'

'Actually, it replenishes the crux-water, because feeding hungry kids counts as doing something good for the community. Besides, you're doing the chopping and the food prep – the magic simply speeds up the process,' Lisa said.

Alyssa nodded. It made sense to her.

'And don't forget to put food waste in the compost bin,' Lisa added. 'Have fun!'

Leon turned to Alyssa. 'Apart from chickpeas, do you know what goes into a chickpea curry?'

Alyssa laughed. 'Your parents literally own a Jamaican takeaway! I thought you'd be the expert.'

Leon shrugged. 'I stay out of the kitchen – our head chef is too grumpy.'

Together they rooted through the cupboards and pulled out the ingredients they assumed they'd need: onions, garlic, powdered spices, jars of chickpeas and a small sack of rice.

They found knives and chopping boards, which were made from the same bronze metal as the magical tools in the spell garden. As Alyssa measured spices and Leon washed the rice, they settled into an easy rhythm. Tipping canisters of brightly coloured powders into a bronze bowl felt like magic to Alyssa, anyway.

It reminded her of cooking a special meal every year with Dad for Mum's birthday – Mum's favourite meal in the world was anything she didn't have to cook herself, she'd always tell them. It was a tradition they'd had for as long as Alyssa could remember.

As she diced the onion using the trick Dad taught her (to keep the cut side down so the smell doesn't make you cry), the warmth of that special memory suffused her whole body. Cooking with Dad was always fun. They'd pretend to be the hosts of their own cooking show – and Mum loved whatever they prepared.

Even more reason why I need to get this magical tea blend right, Alyssa thought. She wanted Mum and Dad back together more than anything.

'Alyssa, can you help me fill the pot with water? It's heavier than I thought,' Leon said.

'Sure!' Alyssa said cheerfully. She put down her knife and helped Leon lift the heavy bronze pot into the giant sink.

As the pot filled with cold water from the tap (the normal kind, not silvery crux-water), Alyssa saw

Leon's eyes go wide at something behind her. He lifted his arm and pointed.

'How did you do that?!' he gasped.

Alyssa turned to see the knife chopping the onion. All by itself!

'Wow, Lisa wasn't kidding,' Leon said.

They watched, transfixed, as the knife neatly yet swiftly diced onion after onion into small cubes. The only sound in the kitchen was the dull, rhythmic thump of the knife blade hitting the wooden chopping board.

While the knife did the prep work, Alyssa and Leon didn't have much to do. They passed the time exchanging their favourite jokes. Several corny jokes later (Leon's gags were even cheesier than Dad's), the vegetables were prepped and the uncooked rice was in the pot.

'So, I guess we put the lid on and wait until it's cooked,' Leon said, after he chucked in the last jar of chickpeas.

'Oh, and we have to visualise, just like Lisa said!' Alyssa added. 'There's just one problem: I've never had Jamaican chickpea curry before. How can I visualise what I can't taste?'

'What do you mean you haven't—? You know what, never mind,' Leon said. 'I'll visualise the curry while you handle the rice. You've had rice before, right?'

'Of course!' Alyssa said. 'Mum's is the best.'

They put the lids on their pots and closed their eyes. Alyssa imagined the biggest pot of fluffy white rice. She imagined its warm, steamy scent and delicate flavour. She imagined it so vividly that she could taste it in her mouth.

The pot lid grew hot under hand. She opened her eyes. 'Leon, I think the rice is cooked already!'

They lifted the lids and the aroma of basmati rice mingled with the rich scents of the chickpea curry. The rice was warm and fluffy and the chickpea curry simmered gently.

Leon chuckled. 'Now this is the sort of magic Mum and Dad would love to know about! They wouldn't have to put up with their moody cook any more.'

'We did it!' Alyssa said. 'And in perfect time,' she added, looking at her watch. 'I'll ring the lunch bell.'

The long wooden bench and table outside the kitchen filled up with hungry Hemlock and Silverleaf kids in a matter of minutes. It was a tight squeeze, made even more awkward by the tension between the two groups, but they managed.

Leon and Alyssa handed out plates of curry and rice, passing them down the bench. Alyssa's heart thumped. What if they didn't like their food? Thankfully, it was eaten with no complaints, to her relief. A few people even went back for seconds.

'I wonder if Auntie Jasmine is feeling better,' Rosalie muttered between mouthfuls of rice.

'I bet she's thinking about how to smooth things over with the landlord,' Alyssa said. 'You never know – she might have sorted it by the time we get home.'

'I really hope so,' Rosalie said. 'If it doesn't get sorted ... well, I don't even want to think about that.'

'Yes, Jasmine told me the whole story last night,' Debbie said. She was sitting further down the bench. 'It would be an almighty shame if the spell garden had to close because of corporate greed.'

A silence fell over the table. Both Hemlock and Silverleaf kids stopped eating and chatting.

'Why would the spell garden close?' Ollie asked worriedly.

'What'll happen to the plants?' Simran added.

'And what about our lessons?' a girl from Hemlock called Eniola asked.

'Fiddlesticks,' Debbie muttered. 'Don't worry, children,' she said in a louder voice. 'No one is closing our spell gardens.'

Kieran narrowed his eyes. It was clear that he,

as well as the rest of the kids, didn't believe her. Nonetheless, everyone continued to eat their lunch.

After they'd helped Lisa and Debbie to clear up (the enchanted dishwasher made this much easier), Alyssa and Leon made their way to the enclosure. Finally, Alyssa could crack on with her magical tea blend. She had the mandrake root in her rucksack; what she needed next was the banana fern.

But, as they arrived, they were met with an unlikely sight: both Hemlock and Silverleaf were sitting *together*. About twenty or so kids sat in a circle while Rosalie talked.

'And they said that we had to come up with the money by the eighteenth, or we lose the land,' Rosalie said. 'It's the eighth today, so we have ten days.'

'Unbelievable,' Kieran muttered. 'Please tell me you at least have a plan?'

'Hey! We only found out, like, twelve hours ago,' Rue snapped.

'That's a no, then,' Eniola said drily.

Rosalie crossed her arms. 'Do you have any bright ideas? Raising three months' worth of rent in less than two weeks isn't easy, you know.'

'When my school needed a new climbing frame, we did loads of things to raise money,' Ollie piped up. 'Selling lemonade, a bake sale, dog walking ...'

'That's not a bad idea,' Rosalie said. 'We can all do something to raise money. Plus, Auntie Jasmine is so loved around here. I bet the community will be happy to contribute!'

'Lemonade and cupcakes won't raise anywhere near enough,' Kieran scoffed. 'We need to think bigger! I say we throw a massive club night and sell tickets. My big bro is a DJ and he does it all the time. He's *minted*.'

'Oh, yeah? Using which venue, genius?' Rue said.

'Guys, quit arguing!' Leon shouted. 'Whatever we decide to do, it's only gonna work if we put aside our differences and work as a team. We can all agree that we want to save the spell garden, right?'

Everyone nodded.

'So let's try to act like we don't hate each other. At least for the next week,' he said. 'The fact is, these are great ideas and we don't have to choose just one. How about we split into teams?'

'Yes!' Eniola jumped up. 'And the team who raises the most money wins?'

Leon looked confused. 'Wins what?'

'The title of superior spell garden, of course,' Kieran said smugly.

Rosalie's eyes widened. 'You're on! May the best team win,' she said, getting up to shake Eniola's hand.

'That ... isn't what I meant,' Leon muttered.

Ivy
(for good luck)

CHAPTER EIGHTEEN

Auntie Jasmine was still under the weather when Alyssa, Rosalie and Rue got home, but she seemed to perk up when she heard their fundraising plans. She said it was an excellent idea and gave it her blessing, even if it meant putting spell garden lessons on hold for a week or so.

Alyssa was torn. She wanted to help her friends figure out how to save the spell garden. She really wanted Auntie Jasmine to be back to her usual bubbly self.

But she also had a deadline of her own. If she didn't have her magical tea blend before she returned to Milton Keynes, there was no chance of getting her parents back together. She only had twelve days now until Dad picked her up.

After two days of intense fundraising planning where they made leaflets and stuck posters around the area, on Friday morning the Silverleaf kids prepared for their first job: walking the neighbours' dogs. If each of the kids found at least three dogs to walk, they were set to raise hundreds of pounds in one morning alone!

'Good luck today, children!' Auntie Jasmine said quietly before she left for the spell garden. She looked weaker than usual.

'Auntie, are you sure you shouldn't stay home and rest?' Rosalie asked, concerned.

Auntie Jasmine shook her head and coughed. 'I can't afford to rely on your fundraising alone, my dears. I need to get to the bottom of this crux-water shortage. I'm going to see if there's anything I can do to strengthen our protection spells. We've been doing more spells for the community than ever – our crux-water should be thriving. It's very puzzling.'

There it was. Alyssa's familiar feeling of guilt. The crux-water shortage had started so soon after she arrived. Perhaps it really was down to her.

'Is there anything we can do to help?' Alyssa asked.

Auntie Jasmine smiled. 'This is something I can

handle. I won't be able to relax until I know why our protection spells are fading, and how to fix it,' she said.

As soon as they finished breakfast, Alyssa, Rosalie and Rue went to pick up their dogs from around the estate. Most of the neighbours seemed thrilled to have someone take this job off their hands, and the fact that it was helping Auntie Jasmine's shop was a bonus. Between the three of them they had six dogs, including three hyperactive cocker spaniels, two stout French bulldogs and an ancient wheezing terrier. With nothing but blue skies overhead, the conditions looked perfect.

'This is the easiest job ever. Why didn't we think of it sooner?' Rue said as they walked to the local park, pulled along by the excitable cocker spaniels. 'We could have been rolling in it!'

'Save that enthusiasm for when it's time to pick up the dog mess,' Rosalie said, laughing. 'Did you remember your tea blend, Rue?'

'Yep,' Rue said, patting their back pocket. 'I'll use it if the dogs get overheated. Hopefully it'll help them cool down.'

As her cousins chatted, Alyssa wondered what the Hemlock kids had planned. They hadn't seen their rivals since Tuesday at the spell garden.

The Silverleaf kids had agreed to meet in a designated spot at the local park – the same one that was next to the community hall. But when they got there, the park looked different.

Leon, Ollie, Simran and a few other Silverleaf kids, all with dogs, hovered around the gate, which was locked.

'What's all this?' Rue asked.

'It's locked! The sign says the park is now "Pay to Play", whatever that means,' Leon said.

Alyssa peered at the official-looking sign nailed to the gate. 'It says this is a fee-paying park. We need to tap a contactless card to get in. Is this a London thing?'

'You have got to be kidding!' Rosalie said, reading the sign for herself. 'It's being run by Forsythe Developers. That's the same company trying to kick us out of the shop.'

'Looks like they don't want us in the park either,' Alyssa muttered crossly.

'It's fifty pence an hour. I'll pay it this once,' Rosalie said. She reached into her rucksack for her purse and tapped a card. 'Mum and Dad gave it to me for emergencies. I reckon this counts.'

When they all got into the park, Alyssa, Rosalie and Rue sat under a shaded tree with their dogs and counted how many pets the Silverleaf kids had. Rosalie produced a clipboard from her rucksack. (*What teenager carries around a clipboard?* Alyssa wondered.)

'Er, who brought the rat?!' Rosalie shrieked.

'Um, Mr Jackson insisted on giving me his ferret Toby to walk,' Ollie called. He held on tightly to the leash of a grey ferret that was rolling around on the grass. 'He paid me double!'

'Just keep it well away from me! It looks like we have nineteen dogs – and one ferret,' Rosalie added, then she called out to rest of the Silverleaf kids, 'I've laid out water bowls by the gate because it's a hot day. Keep an eye on your dogs for the next ninety minutes, okay? And don't forget to pick up after them!'

Lisa waved from the railings as she walked back from the coffee shop. 'Good luck!' she yelled.

Everyone headed for the designated dog enclosure. The second that the dogs were let off their leashes, they immediately bounded off in one hundred different directions. Alyssa was assigned the three cocker spaniels, and kept a close eye on them as they rooted around the hedges and played with the other pups. One hour flew by.

'I could get used to this,' Leon said as they lounged

on the picnic table by the little doggy park. 'It's easy money!'

'Imagine if we did this every day?' said Alyssa. 'We'd have the rent money in no time.'

'Uh-oh.' Rue held out their hand. 'I think it's starting to rain!'

'Seriously? There wasn't a cloud in the sky when we arrived,' Leon said.

Rue pointed to an angry-looking storm cloud hovering on the horizon. 'Whoa. It looks like it's gonna pelt it down any minute.'

Alyssa realised that she hadn't experienced any bad weather since she arrived in Holloway. She remembered what Rosalie had said about how it only ever rained at night, thanks to the crux-water protection spells. What did it mean that the nastiest storm cloud she'd ever seen was now moments away?

It must *be related to the crux-water shortage*, she thought, with a lurch in her stomach.

Within seconds, the storm cloud blotted out the sun, turning the sky into steel. Thick bullets of water pelted to the ground at rapid speed.

Rosalie sprang into action. 'Everyone, grab your dogs and meet under the big tree!'

The rain didn't seem to bother the dogs in the least. In fact, some of them, like Alyssa's cocker spaniels, positively loved it. They splashed in puddles and rolled in the mud as if it was their job. By the time Alyssa had rounded up the pups and attached them to their leashes, she was soaked to the skin and nearly as muddy as the three dogs.

Everyone huddled under the tree waiting for the rainstorm to pass. The dogs, their leashes tied to the park's nearby metal fence, frolicked in the rain and drank thirstily from the dog bowls Rosalie had laid out earlier.

'I'm so c-c-c-old,' Simran said, shivering.

'We can warm up later,' Rosalie said gently. 'We need to return the dogs first.'

After what seemed like an age, the beating rain slowed to a drizzle.

Rosalie's phone buzzed. 'Great! I'm already getting worried text messages from the owners. We said they'd have the dogs back by noon. Let's get moving.'

'Um, guys? We have a problem,' Ollie said, pointing to the heap of dogs. They were totally still.

'Oh my gosh, they're dead!' Rue screeched.

Rosalie rolled her eyes. 'Calm down, Rue – they're obviously not dead. I can see them breathing from here.'

Rosalie was right, of course. The dogs weren't dead. However, they did seem to be in an unusually deep sleep. They approached the dogs and shook them, but it was no use. Some snored and others twitched their legs as they chased postmen in their dreams. Even Toby the ferret was dozing.

'They did run around for quite a long time. Maybe they're tired?' Ollie suggested.

'I'm not sure about that. My gran had the most annoying beagle called Jack, and he never slept like this,' Leon said.

'Do you think it's related to magic?' Alyssa asked. 'Maybe Rue's tea spell was too strong.'

Rue shook their head and brought a small metal flask out of their back pocket. 'Impossible. It's all in here! I didn't even get the chance to use it.'

'It might not be Rue's tea blend, but something magical seems likely,' Rosalie muttered. 'First things first, though, we need to get these dogs back to their owners. Asleep or awake,' she said decisively.

Rue crossed their arms. 'How are we supposed to do that? Carry them?!'

'Have you got a better idea?' Rosalie replied.

There was silence. No one did.

Countless sweaty walks later, all the dogs had been returned to their owners. The kids took turns minding the sleeping dogs in the park while the others hauled their charges back to their owners like sacks of potatoes.

Simran had the bright idea of commandeering a few wheelbarrows from the allotment, which made the job a little bit easier. But the hardest part was explaining to each of their customers why their dogs had returned filthy and fast asleep.

'I've never known Alvin, Simon and Theodore to sleep like *this*,' said a gobsmacked neighbour when Alyssa and Leon wheeled three snoozing, mud-splattered cocker spaniels to their door.

'Well, they had a really good time at the park,' Alyssa said.

Leon chuckled awkwardly. 'Yeah! You should have seen 'em go!'

The neighbour tutted and reluctantly handed over a crisp banknote. 'I understand you're doing this to save the old tea shop?'

Leon and Alyssa nodded.

'Sir, we are cold, wet and exhausted. We wouldn't be doing this if we didn't have a good reason,' Alyssa said.

'That shop is an institution in this neighbourhood. It would be a tragedy if it was lost,' the neighbour said kindly as he handed over another banknote.

Leon and Alyssa dropped the wheelbarrow back to the allotment and handed their cash over to

Rosalie. She asked Lisa to keep it in the shop's safe for now.

'So ... any ideas for our next fundraiser? I don't want to see another dog leash, like, ever,' Alyssa said. 'That was so tiring.'

Rue wrinkled their nose. 'Same. I never want to go near another dog, or ferret, for as long as I live.'

'Let's sleep on it,' Rosalie said thoughtfully. 'I haven't seen any sign of Hemlock's fundraising activities, and we brought in a lot of cash today. We might even have a head start!'

As they turned a corner, though, they spotted a group of kids handing out bright yellow flyers to passers-by.

Hemlock kids.

Rosalie sighed. 'I spoke too soon.'

'Now we know what Hemlock got up to,' Alyssa said, pointing to the group.

Kieran approached them, casting his eyes over their muddy clothes.

'Looks like you guys got caught in the rain,' he said, smirking. 'Can't have been easy carting those sleeping dogs around the neighbourhood.'

Rue crossed their arms. 'A little rain didn't stop us raising loads of cash,' she said.

'Wait, how did you know about the sleeping dogs?'

Rosalie asked.

Kieran shrugged. 'Good luck with the rest of your fundraising,' he said with a smile. 'If you'll excuse me, we have more flyers to hand out.'

'We'll leave you to it,' Rue said. 'Because you're going to need all the help you can get.'

'I bet they used magic on us!' Rosalie muttered angrily. 'I don't know why I didn't see it sooner! A few sips of valerian-infused crux-water could knock out an elephant! They could have slipped it into the water bowls while we were distracted.'

'Typical Hemlock behaviour,' Rue muttered. 'Plus, a selfish waste of crux-water.'

'It doesn't make sense. We're all working towards the same thing,' Alyssa said. 'Why would they sabotage us?'

Rue gave Alyssa a funny look. 'We talked about this: whoever raises the most money gets to call themselves the best magic school! We'll never live it down if we lose to Hemlock.'

As they waited at the traffic lights, a bright yellow flyer caught Alyssa's eyes.

'They're having a bake sale tomorrow afternoon at the community hall,' she said, scanning the flyer.

Rue sighed. 'That's such a good idea. Why didn't we do that?'

'Who says we can't?' Rosalie asked. 'If they are gonna use magic to mess with our plans, why shouldn't we have a bit of fun with theirs?'

Passionflower
(for peace and calm)

CHAPTER NINETEEN

The cousins got home and immediately formulated a plan. To get their own back on Hemlock, all they needed to do was out-bake and out-sell them at their own fundraiser. The problem? By now it was late afternoon, and even if they spent all night baking, they wouldn't be able to make more than a few dozen cakes in Auntie Jasmine's tiny kitchen.

Luckily, they had a perfect solution: the spell-garden kitchen. They resolved to sneak in that night and use a touch of magic – they might even be able to make enough cakes to supply the entire neighbourhood! There was no way Hemlock could compete. Even better, as it was for the good of the community, it would help the crux-water shortage.

'Oi! Wake up!'

Alyssa's slumber was rudely interrupted by someone whispering in her ear.

'It's time.' It was Rosalie, nudging her awake. Alyssa was immediately alert.

'Are you sure I can't come?' Rue grumbled.

'Sorry, Rue, but we need you to stay here. Remember to text us if Auntie Jasmine wakes up, all right?' Rosalie said. 'She'll have a fit if she catches us sneaking out this late.'

Having shaken off her sleepiness, Alyssa threw on some clothes, stuffed her phone into her pocket and laced her shoes in record time. Together, she and Rosalie slipped out of the front door, then dashed down the flights of stairs and across the courtyard. They walked in silence until they reached the high street.

Alyssa checked her phone. It was nearly one o'clock in the morning, but the high street seemed busy: bars and pubs that were empty during the day were now filled with jostling people. The takeaways glowed invitingly and seemed busier than ever. Even the barber shop was open.

But there were also a few empty shops that Alyssa could have sworn hadn't been there earlier in the week. The occasional dark window punctuated the otherwise lively street.

'Friday nights around here are always busy, especially on a hot night like this,' Rosalie told her.

'I love it. Where I live, no one makes a peep after ten o'clock,' Alyssa said.

They paused at the traffic lights and waited for the green man to appear.

'Is there usually so much traffic at this time of night?' Alyssa asked. Rosalie didn't reply.

Alyssa turned to see her cousin looking at an empty shop window.

'Mum's going to be gutted,' Rosalie said. 'This place used to be her favourite fabric shop. It's run by a pair of old Ghanaian ladies. I swear she only shopped here a few weeks ago.'

They peered at the white poster with bold black print pasted inside the glass:

MIDTOWN CITY ART GALLERY
OPENING 18 AUGUST
VISITS BY APPOINTMENT ONLY

'Midtown City sounds so silly,' Alyssa said. 'What's wrong with Holloway?'

'The developers want to make this area sound posh and expensive. New name, new buildings, new shops. To make room for the new people,' Rosalie muttered. 'Come on. We need to keep moving.'

They reached Jasmine's Teas but Rosalie marched straight past. 'I know a shortcut to the spell garden,' she said. 'The door to the allotment will be locked at this time.'

She walked past the row of shops and ducked under the barriers of a supermarket car park at the end. Alyssa followed her lead, keeping her back to the shop wall until they reached the other side of the car park.

Hidden by a tangly shrub was a corner of the wall where the bricks had crumbled. It left a narrow space for a person to creep through.

'I discovered this secret entrance last summer,' Rosalie said.

Alyssa raised an eyebrow in surprise. Rosalie was the last person she would have expected to know about a secret entrance. The more she got to know her cousin, the more she liked her.

From there, it was a matter of stepping through the dark allotment and making their way to the spell garden. The wooden door creaked open for them without any fuss.

Alyssa didn't know what to expect from the spell garden at night. But it certainly wasn't what she saw before her.

The entire garden was awash with a silver-blue glow. It wasn't coming from the night sky or light bulbs. It was coming from *inside* the plants. Every leaf, stalk and stem glowed in the dark, illuminating the garden.

'It's the crux-water,' Rosalie said quietly. 'It's in every plant and it glows in the dark, so there's no need for night-lights. Pretty smart, eh?'

'It's incredible,' Alyssa whispered.

She could tell the garden was sleeping. As she stepped gingerly onto the gravel path, she could feel a deep and steady pulsing beneath her feet. The brightly coloured petals and shuffling bunny shrubs had retired for the night, leaving the sleepy glow in its place.

'It's amazing. Thanks for bringing me here,' Alyssa said.

'It's nice to hang out here with no one else around,' Rosalie said. 'Not a word of this to Auntie Jasmine, yeah? We're not allowed in the spell garden unattended, especially not this late at night.'

They headed to the spell-garden kitchen, but soon realised that it was too dark to bake – the illumination of the night sky and softly glowing plants wasn't enough to help them see what they were doing. However, Rosalie had the bright idea of filling large glass jars with glowing crux-water from the tap in the enclosure. The jars lined the kitchen counter and acted as makeshift night-lights, filling the kitchen with a spooky glow.

'This will have to do,' Rosalie said, sighing a little.

'It's so cool!' Alyssa chirped, rooting through the cupboard for baking ingredients. 'We have tons of flour, sugar, eggs and oil. Loads of spices too. What else are we going to flavour it with, though?'

Rosalie smiled. 'Whatever we can dig up in the garden. We have berries, nuts and plenty of fruit.'

'The possibilities are endless,' Alyssa said, her mind racing through potential delicious cake flavours. 'How about a lemon and raspberry cake? And a carrot cake? A cinnamon banana loaf? And—'

'Slow down, Alyssa!' Rosalie chuckled. 'One thing at a time! Why don't you go and pick some of the ingredients from the fruit and vegetable patch? The non-magical plants obviously.'

Rosalie's words gave Alyssa a jolt of realisation. Of course. This would be the perfect time to harvest the banana fern for her love spell. Why hadn't she thought of that sooner? Rosalie would be too distracted by baking to notice.

'Sure thing,' Alyssa said.

She ambled past Auntie Jasmine's vegetable patch and headed instead towards the magical plants.

Out of the corner of her eye, a patch of magical viper weeds glowed invitingly. And that meant she was close to the banana ferns. Perfect.

When Alyssa returned to the kitchen with an armful of carrots, lemons, raspberries and more, Rosalie was too excited to notice the subtle scent of banana fern leaf among them. It blended with the thick green fronds of the freshly pulled carrots.

'I can't believe it worked! I just put the ingredients in the pot for Mum's pineapple upside-down cake, and look!' Rosalie said. She lifted the lid off the bronze pot and the unmistakable fragrance of warm sponge cake wafted into the air.

Alyssa peered into the pot. A picture-perfect pineapple upside-down cake sat inside it, glossy with red cherries and sticky pineapple rings.

'Amazing! What should we make next?' she asked.

Rosalie grinned. 'Literally anything you can imagine! Let's get to work.'

Alyssa loved seeing this side of Rosalie, when she was more playful than perfect. They took turns coming up with imaginary confections that turned into fully formed cakes in a matter of seconds: a seven-layer sponge filled with strawberries, a carrot cake with nutty brown-butter frosting, a delicate lemony loaf cake drizzled with raspberry icing and a tall rainbow cake among others.

The two girls were covered in flour and icing sugar, but they were having too much fun to care. Soon everything that Alyssa had harvested was used up and the kitchen counter was heaving with beautiful-looking cakes.

They decided it was too risky to take the cakes home, so they would wake up extra early and collect them first thing in the morning. They'd ask Rue and Leon to give them a hand.

'We're gonna raise so much money!' Rosalie said. 'Hemlock won't stand a chance.'

Alyssa nodded and yawned in response, the tiredness suddenly hitting her. She longed for her pillow.

'Let's get to bed,' Rosalie said, chuckling. 'We have another big day ahead.'

When Rosalie wasn't looking, Alyssa took the handful of thick green banana-fern leaves and stuffed them into a kitchen drawer. She didn't want Rosalie to smell them on the way home, so they would have to stay here until she collected them tomorrow. They put away the cakes and cleaned the kitchen in the magical way (closing their eyes and picturing a perfectly clean kitchen) before making their way out of the spell garden.

Primrose
(for finding treasure)

CHAPTER TWENTY

'When you lot said early, you weren't messing,' Leon said with a big yawn as he met them at the allotment's entrance. 'I brought a few crates from the takeaway for the cakes.'

'Thanks, Leon. Won't your mum and dad notice they're missing?' Rosalie asked.

'Are you joking? They were more than happy to help with the bake sale, no questions asked. Mum was amazed to see me out of bed this early on a Saturday,' he said, laughing. 'And I don't mind the early start if it means I don't have to sweep floors.'

'Must be nice.'

'Working at the takeaway? Yeah, the all-day food is pretty sweet.'

'Oh. I meant being around your mum and dad all day,' Alyssa said.

Leon pretended to be deep in thought. 'I can't lie. I'd take the mac 'n' cheese over Dad's terrible jokes!'

'This had better be worth getting up at the crack of dawn,' Rue grumbled.

'Oh, it will be!' Alyssa said cheerily.

She was looking forward to seeing their faces when they saw the cakes, but she was also anxious to pick up the banana ferns she'd tucked away in the drawer.

'How did you manage all this?!' Leon gasped, his jaw dropping when they opened the door to the spell-garden kitchen.

'Never mind that,' Rosalie said, carefully putting a cake into the crates. 'If anyone asks, we'll say that our mums stayed up late to help us bake.'

While everyone packed up the cakes, Alyssa sneakily opened the drawer where she'd put the banana fern and spotted the small clump of delicate green fronds in the back. She pulled them out and went to put them in her pocket, but something was wrong. The banana fern smelled ... different.

Alyssa sniffed the leaves. There was no subtle scent of banana milkshake. In its place was the grassy-green smell of something else entirely. It reminded Alyssa of Mum's salad dressing. Whatever it was, it wasn't banana fern.

'Why are you sniffing parsley?' Rosalie asked.

Parsley! That's what the smell was.

'Oh, um, it reminds me of Mum,' Alyssa muttered before dropping the wilted herbs onto the kitchen counter. She must have been so sleepy last night that she'd mixed up the banana fern with something else entirely.

If that was parsley, where was the banana fern? The other drawers were empty and the rest of the kitchen was spotless.

Alyssa began to panic. Where could it be?

'Um, Rosalie. What happened to the ingredients we didn't use last night?' Alyssa asked.

Rosalie smiled proudly. 'We used everything in the cakes, of course. Any waste went straight into the compost bin.'

Alyssa sighed. Great. She would have to come back after the bake sale and harvest some more. Right now they had work to do.

They made their way to the community hall, gingerly carrying one crate each across the road. The Hemlock kids were already setting up their tables outside while Lisa chatted to the community-hall volunteers: an elderly woman Alyssa recognised as

Sister Hortense, and an older man she didn't know. When the Hemlock kids saw Rosalie and the others setting up their own table, they began muttering to themselves. After a few moments, Kieran came over.

'What are you doing here? We were supposed to have the community hall to ourselves today,' Kieran protested.

Rosalie crossed her arms. 'Go on, tell Lisa! I'm sure she would love to know how you tampered with our fundraising yesterday. Valerian-infused crux-water, was it?'

Kieran looked confused. 'What are you talking about? We were too busy organising our bake sale to worry about your silly dog walks.'

'Of course you were,' Rosalie said sarcastically.

Lisa approached, a steely look in her eyes. 'Everything all right, gang? Because if it isn't, we can cancel the fundraiser and go back to the spell garden.'

Kieran nodded reluctantly. 'We're fine.'

'Fabulous. I won't be around to manage the bake sale because I need to watch the shop. Miss Jasmine has taken a turn for the worse, so she's staying in bed.'

Alyssa's stomach gave a lurch. Auntie Jasmine's bedroom door had been shut this morning when they'd left, but Alyssa had assumed she would have gone to the shop by now, like she usually did. Something was seriously wrong if she was too ill to even get out of bed.

'Thankfully the community-hall volunteers, Sister Hortense and Mr Erdogan, have offered to watch you, in exchange for free cake,' Lisa continued, smiling brightly.

'Um, Lisa!' Rosalie called. 'Can I ask about the water levels? You know, in the spell garden,' she added in a low voice. 'You checked the levels, right?'

Lisa smiled, but this time it didn't reach her eyes. She was definitely worried. 'Ah. Yes, I checked. I'm afraid it's not looking good.'

The kids groaned.

'Do you have any idea what's causing it?' Kieran asked.

Lisa looked at Alyssa. 'Well, we're not sure. But... we did have a wonderful surprise when Alyssa joined us for the summer. It took her a little time to get used to her powers, and there were some ... magical mishaps, shall we say.'

Alyssa felt sick.

Seeing her expression, Lisa smiled gently at her. 'No one is blaming you for anything, Alyssa,' she said, squeezing her shoulder reassuringly. 'Don't worry. We'll figure this out.'

Alyssa was comforted by Lisa's confidence, but she couldn't shake the thought that this was all her fault. She would try to make up for it by fundraising extra hard today.

'Right, I must return to the shop,' Lisa said. 'Best of luck today, guys!'

Kieran skulked back to the Hemlock table to tell an annoyed-looking group of Hemlock kids that they would be sharing the venue.

'I have to admit, their food looks good,' Alyssa said as she eyed the frosted fairy cakes, cookies and gooey brownies. 'They must have worked really hard.'

'As if!' Rosalie said, pointing across the road. A small van labelled *Byrne Family Bakery* was parked outside the community hall while the Hemlock kids unloaded crate after crate of sweet treats. 'They're getting donations from the Byrne place down the road.'

'Wow, really?' Leon exclaimed. 'I love their gingerbread men!'

'And their sprinkle cakes!' Rue chirped. 'It's where Auntie Jasmine gets our birthday treats from.'

'I guess we don't have to feel bad about not baking our own cakes,' Alyssa muttered. 'Hemlock clearly didn't!'

'Why is the bakery giving away food? Something isn't right,' Rosalie muttered. She walked over to the small van to investigate for herself.

More Silverleaf and Hemlock kids poured into the area outside the community hall, each group being careful to stick to their own side. As Alyssa marvelled at the cakes lining the table, she felt excited to show off the creations she had had a hand in making – even if it was with magical assistance.

Leon rubbed his hands together. 'If they taste half as good as they look, we're gonna be rollin' in it!'

Rosalie returned from her brief chat with the bakers. 'I don't believe this! They're giving away food to Hemlock because they're closing down. They said the rent increases have made it impossible to stay,' she said sadly.

'They're only a few doors down from our takeaway,' Leon said. 'Mum and Dad won't talk about the rent thing with me, but I know they're worried.'

While they were chatting, Rue sneakily reached for a slice of carrot cake.

'Oi! No freebies,' Rosalie said.

Rue rolled their eyes. 'You mean I can't even taste? Think of it as quality control!'

'We can't afford to waste a single slice. That's money down the drain!' Rosalie leaned in and lowered her voice. 'Besides, we already know that food from the spell-garden kitchen tastes incredible.'

'Good morning, children!' Sister Hortense exclaimed. 'I am mightily impressed by this spread. What talented bakers you are. You certainly don't get it from Jasmine,' she added with a chuckle.

The kids laughed along.

'What can we get you, Sister Hortense?' Rosalie asked.

'None for me, darlin'. I have a tooth operation this week and my dentist would have a fit if he saw me eating cake,' Sister Hortense said.

Despite the delicious-looking cakes, the morning got off to a sluggish start. No one seemed to want a giant wedge of icing-covered cake first thing in the morning, which Alyssa couldn't understand. When she became a grown-up, she planned on having cake for breakfast at least three times a week.

Luckily for Hemlock, their dried fruit flapjacks and oat cookies seemed to count as a breakfast food for the residents of Holloway. They sold dozens to people waiting at the nearby bus stop. Meanwhile Silverleaf's elaborate cakes were beginning to wilt in the mid-morning heat.

'If we don't get some customers soon, then our food is gonna go to waste,' Rosalie groaned as she fanned the seven-layer strawberry-cream sponge to keep it cool. 'These cakes might have been prepared magically, but that won't stop them going off.'

As lunchtime approached, more people trickled into the small park next to the community hall. Alyssa watched as some of the locals read the 'Pay to Play' sign with varying levels of disbelief. Judging by the shock on their faces, tapping a card to enter a public park was outrageous even in London. A few people paid until someone had the bright idea of using a large rock to prop open the gate. The park soon filled up and felt a bit more like normal.

'If we don't get more customers, then can I at least get a slice of raspberry-lemon drizzle?' Rue asked with a heavy sigh.

'Ow!' Rosalie shrieked.

Rue looked taken aback. 'Chill out, Rosalie, it was just a question!'

'No, it wasn't you. Something just hit the back of my neck. Hard,' Rosalie said, rubbing a sore spot.

Alyssa heard a faint cracking sound, like tiny pebbles hitting the ground. A few cold specks landed on her scalp.

'I felt it too!' Alyssa yelled.

They all looked up. A few light clouds drifted across the bright blue sky. Where was it coming from?

Suddenly there was a great flash of lightning, followed by a deafening crash of thunder. One minute, Alyssa was looking at a clear blue sky, the next a grey pallor had fallen over it, as though a giant blanket was blocking out the sun. A smoking black slash in the grass was the only indication that lightning had struck.

A few people lounging in the park grabbed their food and made for the nearest exit, while some took out their phones to record the evidence of this weather phenomenon.

The tiny pebbles fell harder and faster, small white beads gathering on the ground.

'It's hail!' Leon yelled.

'Save the cakes!' Rosalie screamed. They dived towards the table and grabbed what they could, before rushing into the community hall.

Everyone else had the same idea. The Hemlock kids ran inside clutching their wares, closely followed by people in the park looking for shelter.

A young woman tapped Rosalie on the shoulder. 'Excuse me, how much for a slice of carrot cake?'

A few other grown-ups followed suit, casting their eyes over the tables in the hall in search of a sweet treat.

'This is amazing!' Leon whispered to Alyssa. 'We have a captive audience.'

Soon, all the newcomers to the hall had a paper plate with a slice of Silverleaf's cake, whether it was banana bread or a towering wedge of rainbow-striped sponge. If the strange weather was an effect of the crux-water shortage, at least it was working to their advantage today, Alyssa thought, as she served another slice of cake.

'This is so unfair,' Alyssa heard Eniola groan from across the hall. 'We put the hard work into making the flyers and getting people to come, and they're stealing our customers!'

The young woman with the carrot cake ate it in three seconds flat and licked the cream-cheese frosting from the paper plate. 'Best. Cake. Ever!'

Alyssa smiled. Yes, the cakes had been made with magical assistance, but she still felt proud. 'Thanks! Would you like another slice?'

The young woman didn't seem to be listening, though. In fact, she did something so strange that Alyssa didn't quite believe what she was seeing. She kicked off her shiny black heels, cartwheeled out of the front door and danced barefoot in the hailstorm.

'Guys, did you see—' Alyssa began. She stopped. **Several other adults were doing the same.**

The kids rushed to the window and watched in awe as the hysterical adults danced delightedly to a music only they seemed to hear. No one seemed bothered by the hailstones falling from the sky, or the wind that was whipping the air into a frenzy.

'Our cakes aren't that good ... are they?' Leon asked, bewildered.

'Only one way to find out!' Rue said quietly. With Rosalie distracted by the adults shimmying in the hailstorm, they backed away and reached out for a secret slice of cake.

Alyssa's tummy rumbled. She hadn't eaten since breakfast and that was hours ago. Surely one slice of cake wouldn't eat into their funds?

'*Psst*, Rue!' Alyssa hissed. 'Wanna split a slice of raspberry-lemon drizzle?'

Rue nodded and took the last slice of sticky cake for them to share.

'Not so fast!' It was crotchety Mr Erdogan. 'I've had my eye on that all morning.'

Rue and Alyssa exchanged glances.

'Enjoy, Mr Erdogan!' Rue said brightly as they handed over the paper plate.

Meanwhile, the storm-soaked adults were still outside dancing. They'd joined hands and spun round in a circle, giggling like toddlers.

'Alyssa, check it out! This is too weird.' Rue chuckled, gazing out of the window.

'Weird is the word,' Rosalie whispered. ' I wonder if it's magic-related … If Hemlock laced our dog water yesterday, I wouldn't put anything past them.'

'When would they have had the chance?' Leon asked. 'We haven't left the cakes alone for a single second.'

Rosalie nodded. 'You're right. But this—' She waved her hands at the adults dancing in the hailstorm. 'It isn't normal! Our neighbourhood is friendly, but not *this* friendly.'

'*Wheeeeeee!*'

Everyone in the hall turned towards the sound. It was Mr Erdogan, his lips smeared with cake crumbs and a look of wide-eyed delight on his face.

'Wait for meeeee!' he yelled, rushing out of the hall to dance with the others.

'Mehmet, what the devil has got into you?' Sister Hortense called after Mr Erdogan.

Kieran stared at the Silverleaf bunch with daggers in his eyes. 'You lot are such hypocrites! I can't believe you enchanted your cakes.'

'What are you talking about?' Rosalie yelled.

'First you make up some lie about us using magic to ruin your dog walk. Then you go ahead and use magic yourself to give yourself a head start!' Kieran snapped.

'Hey, at least we made them ourselves!' Rue said.

'Come off it,' Eniola said. 'That's a love spell in action, even if it's a clumsy one.'

The Hemlock and Silverleaf kids continued to argue, but Alyssa wasn't listening. She had a horrible sinking feeling in her tummy. Suddenly she realised what must have happened to the banana ferns last night.

Alyssa pulled Rosalie to one side. 'Um, I think we have a problem. Last night I might have accidentally harvested some banana ferns and they got mixed with some other ingredients . . . I think it's in the cake.'

Rosalie's face fell. 'Why were you harvesting— Never mind! Which cake? Do you remember which cake?!'

'I don't know. It might even be in all of them. I just don't know!' Alyssa said.

'I hate to admit it but Hemlock are right. Those people out there are under the influence of some weird spell,' Rosalie muttered.

Alyssa glanced outside. Mr Erdogan was sniffing the rose bush with an expression of sheer bliss on his face. 'I thought banana fern was meant to make people fall in love?'

'A small amount of banana fern in a tea, sure,' Rosalie said. 'But the freshly picked ingredient is way too unpredictable if it's consumed any other way!'

Before Alyssa could answer, the hall doors slammed open. The shivering – though still blissfully happy – grown-ups skipped inside and marched straight to the Silverleaf cake stand.

'I'll have the rest of that carrot cake, please!' said one lady, grinning.

'Um, sorry, madam, but we can't sell any more cake,' Rosalie began. 'It's ... contaminated. I sneezed on it!'

'Nonsense!' the woman yelled. She took out her purse and tipped the contents onto the table. Several banknotes and coins fell out. 'Have it all,' she said.

Before anyone could stop her, she grabbed the remains of the carrot cake and ran out of the hall, shrieking with laughter.

'Did that just happen?' Rosalie asked, counting up the cash. 'She paid more than fifty quid for half a carrot cake!'

The other adults in the room seemed to become antsy when they saw the cake supplies dwindling.

'How much for the rainbow sponge? I'll pay whatever you want!' one man called out.

'I'm sorry,' Rosalie said. 'We can't sell any more cakes.'

'Hold on,' Alyssa whispered. 'They have already eaten a bit of banana fern so the damage is done. Why not use it to our advantage?'

Rosalie nodded. 'We *do* need the money...'

She paused, thinking. Then she spun round to face the crowd. 'I'm afraid we have limited stock, so the cakes will go to the highest bidder. The bidding for this rainbow sponge will start at thirty-five pounds. Do I hear forty?'

Leon guffawed. 'She can't be serious.'

But the adults in the room began to bid. The Hemlock kids watched stone-faced while the value of the cakes crept up and up. By the time the hailstorm ended, Silverleaf were clean out of stock. Not a single crumb remained.

They had made *triple* their goal for the bake sale.

'You know what this means, right?' Kieran said as they packed up their unsold baked goods.

'That we're the superior school in every way?' Rosalie replied tartly.

He shook his head and uttered one word: '*War.*'

Pimento
(for passion)

CHAPTER TWENTY-ONE

Alyssa, Rosalie and Rue handed over the cash raised to Lisa for safekeeping. She was impressed and said they'd reach their goal in no time. But when they got home and told Auntie Jasmine about all the money they had raised, she was barely listening.

'That's nice, dears. Did you see that hailstorm this afternoon?' Auntie Jasmine asked as she watered the plants on the balcony. 'They nearly ruined my little mango plant.'

'Yeah, the weather has been so weird lately,' Rue mused.

Auntie Jasmine shook her head and coughed. 'It's more than weird, I'm afraid. It's a further sign that **our protection spells are fading.**'

Alyssa had been so excited about the success of the bake sale that she'd almost forgotten about the strangeness of the storm and what that might mean. Poor Auntie Jasmine seemed really upset.

But they were so close to raising the money to save the shop. After that, everything would get better, wouldn't it?

Right now she needed to concentrate on her magical tea blend. After seeing the effect of fresh banana fern, Alyssa decided that she might be better using the dried stuff from the store cupboard for her spell. Otherwise, she might have two parents who spent all their time giggling and cartwheeling. Still, it would be better than arguing, she supposed.

She would have to be more careful next time. Rosalie seemed to have forgotten to ask her any more about the banana fern, thanks to the cake chaos.

*

Silverleaf's next fundraising event, planned for Monday, was a car wash. Simran's dad, Mr Hossein, was a mechanic and he'd said that they could clean his customers' cars in exchange for donations. After the pace of the last few days, it felt like a break to Alyssa.

'Remember what Kieran said,' Rosalie said as they

walked to the garage. 'They mean war. We need to be on our guard, okay?'

'I don't suppose Miss Jasmine has sorted things out with the landlord, has she?' Leon asked hopefully.

'I don't think so,' Rosalie said. 'She still seems pretty stressed.'

They walked to a quieter side street away from the main road. Withered leaves crunched underfoot, papering the pavement. The trees were completely bare.

'Something feels strange,' Rue said.

'I swear these trees had leaves yesterday,' Leon muttered.

'Guys, we need to focus,' Rosalie interrupted. 'We have to raise even more money than we did on Saturday. Otherwise, we can't save the spell garden.'

Thankfully, the day got off to a good – and uneventful – start. They had a steady stream of customers who were delighted to donate to a good cause and get their cars cleaned at the same time.

The problems came after lunch when a funny-looking car pulled into the garage. It was a sensible dark-blue colour, apart from the streaks of what looked like neon-yellow paint all over it.

'Whoa, what happened?' Leon whispered to Alyssa.

'It looks like a clown car!' she replied, chuckling.

The driver of the car stepped out and Alyssa stopped laughing. 'Wait, didn't we wash that woman's car a couple of hours ago?' she asked.

'What kind of prank do you call this? You've ruined my car!' the woman shrieked.

As Mr Hossein tried to calm down the angry customer, Rosalie told everyone to stop washing the cars until they figured out what the problem was.

'We didn't do anything wrong!' Rue said. 'Check the soap for yourself.'

'It's from a bottle. It's the same soap my dad uses on cars all the time,' Simran said.

But when several other cars they'd washed drove up to the garage with the same problem, they had to admit that something was amiss.

'It was fine for the first hour, then – *poof!* – bright blue streaks appeared on the paintwork out of nowhere,' another customer said.

'I want a refund!' someone else said – their cherry-red sports car now had bright green splodges all over it.

'I'm sorry, sir. Let us fix it,' Rosalie said in her calmest voice.

'There's no way I'm allowing you kids near my car again!' the sports-car driver yelled.

Another car drove by and pulled to a stop. 'There's another car wash down the road,' shouted the driver. 'They sorted my Volvo out in minutes after these kids ruined it! Don't waste a second here.'

The angry drivers got into their cars and drove off.

'Did you guys know about the other car wash?' Leon asked.

Alyssa and the rest of Silverleaf dropped their sponges and ran down the road. Hiding behind a parked car, they watched Hemlock kids merrily wash the neon paint off the cars with ease.

Rosalie closed her eyes as the truth sank in. 'Enchanted soap. Of *course*,' she groaned.

'What do you mean?' Alyssa asked. 'I thought most grown-ups couldn't see magic.'

'Non-believers can't see magic in action, but they can certainly feel the effects of it,' Rosalie said. 'Look how the banana fern in the cake affected them on Saturday.'

Simran was shaking her head. 'There's no way they enchanted our soap. I saw Dad open the soap bottles himself from a new shipment. They were sealed!'

Alyssa thought for a second. 'What about the sponges? Or the water?'

'She's right. It doesn't have to be the soap that's

enchanted. It could have been any of our equipment,' Rosalie said.

'And now they have the antidote, it seems,' Leon said.

The neon paint rinsed off the cars with ease, leaving them sparkly clean. The customers were overjoyed.

'We're not going to have a single customer for the rest of the day!' Rosalie said. 'We might as well cancel and come up with a new idea. We're still way behind on our goal.'

'I'm so mad!' Simran huffed. 'Those customers are never going to come back to Dad's garage now. I bet he'll lose money.'

'And with all the refunds we had to give, we've lost money too,' Rue said sadly.

'This is typical Hemlock,' Rosalie said. 'They don't think about anyone but themselves. First it's putting those dogs under a sleeping spell, now this!'

'We have to get our own back,' Rue said.

'Let's focus on our next fundraising idea,' Leon said. 'We can't let Forsythe take away the spell garden. We're meant to be working together, remember?'

'Tell Hemlock that,' Rosalie snorted. 'What's the point of coming up with another idea if *they* are gonna sabotage it? We need to show them we can't be messed with. Once and for all.'

'How do we do that?' Alyssa said.

'Well, I hate to give Hemlock any credit but their paint prank was clever,' Rosalie said. 'It didn't look like magic, even though it blatantly was. We need to do the same!'

Alyssa was surprised. 'Are you encouraging us to break the rules, Rosalie?'

She sighed. 'I think we can bend them a little. It's the only way we're going to win – I mean, save the spell garden.'

'If we hurry, we can go back to the spell garden and whip up a spell. How about we get them to drink viper-weed tea and give them a case of perma-tickles?' Simran said. 'They can't wash cars if they're feeling ticklish!'

'Great idea!' Alyssa said. If they went back to the spell garden, she could peel away to get the banana fern.

Rosalie shook her head. 'It would be impossible to get them to drink tea from us. We need something more subtle.'

'We can see you, you know!' yelled a voice from across the road. It was Kieran.

The Silverleaf kids rose from behind the parked

car. There was no point in hiding any more.

'Shouldn't you lot be planning your next fundraiser? You're lousy at car washing, that's for sure,' he said, smirking.

'You know what you did,' Rosalie said with a steely stare.

Kieran shrugged. 'Dunno what you're talking about. Looks to me like you mixed up the soap with the paint restorer. Easily done when you can't read.'

The Silverleaf kids gasped. Rosalie stepped forward. 'What did you say?'

'You heard me,' Kieran sneered. 'Once a loser, always a loser.'

'You take that back!' Rue yelled furiously.

'Forget it, Rue. He's not worth it,' Rosalie said calmly. But the hurt on her face was plain to see.

Kieran laughed and went back to washing cars while a few Hemlock kids sniggered at Rosalie's humiliation. They were enjoying this.

Alyssa hated to see her cousin upset. The Hemlock kids needed to be taught a lesson.

All of a sudden, she felt a familiar fizziness in her fingertips. Alyssa closed her eyes and concentrated. She allowed herself to explore her worst fears. The sort that had her waking up in the middle of the night, breathless and sweaty.

Walking into secondary school with your skirt tucked into your pants.

Being picked on by a nasty maths teacher for not knowing the answer.

Alyssa felt her heart rate pick up. This was a good start, but she needed more.

Mum and Dad arguing at the supermarket while Becky and her perfect family overheard.

This was a memory from a few months back. It startled Alyssa to realise that she'd tucked it away into the recesses of her mind. She couldn't remember what Mum and Dad had been arguing about, but sharp whispers had soon turned to raised voices in the cereal aisle.

Alyssa had stood away from them, keeping her eyes on the cornflakes and hoping that no one else could see her parents having what they later called a 'disagreement'. But when she'd bumped into Becky and her family in the next aisle afterwards, she could tell that they had overheard everything.

Alyssa's face grew hot just thinking about it.

Her fingers tingled, warmth spreading through her body. The magic was working! She just had to concentrate and hold this feeling for a little while longer.

Even if the thought made her want to cry.

Alyssa opened her eyes and looked down. Her hands radiated rainbow waves.

Perfect.

She focused her energy and emotions on the bucket of soapy water Kieran was hauling between cars.

Quick as a flash, the bucket tipped backwards, splashing Kieran from the waist down.

'Aargh!' he yelled, his face recoiling in shock.

Alyssa wasted no time. Before Kieran could recover, she forced the soapy sponge in his hand towards his face.

'*Yeuch!*' he exclaimed, taking in a mouthful of foam.

'Kieran, what's the matter with you?' one of the Hemlock kids asked.

'N-n-nothing!' he stuttered.

Kieran wiped his eyes and picked up the bucket, but Alyssa was one step ahead. She focused on his shoelaces, which unlooped and caused him to trip, spilling the rest of the bucket of water inside the open car door.

'My interiors are ruined!' a customer yelled angrily as Kieran tried his best to sop up the mess.

Next, Alyssa spied the thick green water hose that lay on the ground. She made it wriggle uncontrollably on the ground and spray water in all directions, soaking the Hemlock kids and their customers.

'Whoa! Alyssa, is that you?!' Rosalie said incredulously.

Alyssa was concentrating too hard to do anything but nod.

The Hemlock kids rushed towards the green hose and tried to tame it, but it flipped and flopped, soaking them all in the process. Within a matter of minutes, the car-washing area was slick with water and white soap foam. It looked like a flood had just washed its way through the street.

'Alyssa, move!' Leon hissed.

Before she could react, he ran forward and shoved them both onto the road with the other Silverleaf kids.

'What are you doing?!' Alyssa demanded.

CRASH!

A giant branch from a nearby tree thundered to the ground, splintering into dry wooden shards.

'Just saving your life!' Leon said.

Alyssa and Leon struggled to their feet, then stepped forward to inspect the branch and the tree. The branch looked desiccated.

'All the leaves ... They're dead,' Rue said quietly.

'In the middle of summer? This must be related to the crux-water levels,' Rosalie said.

Alyssa was suddenly overcome with guilt. Seeing Kieran get his comeuppance had been satisfying, but was it worth using her magic when she knew it exhausted crux-water?

She remembered what Lisa had said about how the time-reversal spell to fix the shop had used a lot of crux-water. She'd tried to push the thought away, but it was hard to ignore when things kept getting worse.

'What if it's all my fault?' Alyssa said, tears in her eyes. What if her magical disturbances could put her new friends in danger?

'It isn't!' Rosalie said soothingly. 'You were looking out for me.'

'I shouldn't have used so much power to punish Kieran,' she said. 'I should be using it to save the spell garden.'

Rosalie nodded. 'I hear you. We can't lose the spell garden.' She paused for a moment, thinking. Then she marched across the road towards Kieran, who looked too shocked to say anything. Rosalie whispered something in his ear and pointed to the fallen tree branch. Kieran nodded.

'What did you say to him, Rosalie?' Rue asked.

'We're meeting in the spell garden in an hour,' Rosalie said. 'We're going to make this right.'

Rowan
(for success)

CHAPTER TWENTY-TWO

If there had been tension between Hemlock and Silverleaf in the past, it didn't compare to the deathly silence that fell now, when the two schools found themselves face to face in the spell garden's central enclosure.

'This'd better not be a waste of time. You said the spell garden was in trouble; that there was something we didn't know,' Kieran said, arms folded.

Rosalie nodded. 'It is. There's a crux-water shortage, and—'

'We know *that*!' Eniola interrupted.

Rue shook their head. 'It's worse than we thought. You know the scary weather? It means Auntie Jasmine's protection spells are fading.'

Kieran rolled his eyes, but he seemed upset. 'Why didn't you tell us sooner? We deserve to know too!'

Rosalie sighed. 'I'm sorry. I guess we got too caught up with our competition.'

Eniola and a few of the other Hemlock kids looked anxious.

'I don't know what we'd do without our spell-garden lessons every summer,' Eniola sniffed.

'Same. I haven't been here long, but I couldn't imagine this neighbourhood without it,' Leon said.

Alyssa knew how they felt. In just a couple of weeks, the spell garden had bewitched her completely.

At the back of her mind, a little voice reminded her: *And don't forget about the love spell.* Her tummy twinged with guilt. How could she think about herself when the entire fate of the spell garden was at stake?

'So we can all agree: saving the spell garden is more important than our little competition, yes?' Rosalie announced.

Everyone nodded.

'It's not just the spell garden,' Alyssa added. 'The neighbourhood is changing too. The local shops are disappearing overnight, pay gates at the park, and the trees collapsing? It's bigger than just our garden.'

'What do we do?' Kieran asked.

'We need to seriously focus on getting the landlord off our backs,' Rosalie said. 'Auntie Jasmine is making herself ill with worry, and Lisa and Auntie Debbie don't seem to know what to do about the crux-water. We've got to work together to find a way to pay the rent advance, otherwise we'll lose the spell garden. But we need more money. The eighteenth is *this Friday.*'

'Dog walking and car washing is off the cards,' Rue said drily.

Eniola smiled. 'Yeah, we suck at that.'

'What would Auntie Jasmine do?' Alyssa asked.

Rosalie shrugged. 'She always puts the community first, I guess.'

'So let's do that!' Alyssa said. 'What do you think the neighbourhood needs right now? How can we put it first?'

The two schools sat down and bounced around ideas. Even though Rosalie was still angry at Kieran, they managed to put aside their differences to come up with a plan.

By the time dusk was drawing in, they had made a decision: on Wednesday, they would throw a fundraiser party at the community hall. They had two days to prepare.

'Auntie Jasmine, are you sure you feel well enough to come?' Rosalie asked.

Their great-aunt sat on the sofa and shivered despite the sweltering afternoon heat in the flat.

'Miss the biggest party this neighbourhood has ever seen? Not a chance!' Auntie Jasmine said. 'One more cup of your delicious healing tea, and I'll be right as rain.'

Alyssa smiled. She'd noticed that their healing tea wasn't having quite the same effect on Auntie Jasmine any more, but she didn't say anything.

Over the past few days, Auntie Jasmine had seemed to grow weaker and weaker. Lisa was looking after the shop and helping Debbie in the spell garden whenever she could, so she hadn't been able to help with organising the party very much. Luckily there had been no shortage of volunteers.

Organising it was easier than Alyssa, Rosalie and Rue had thought, especially when they joined forces with Hemlock. All the kids called on their parents, older siblings and neighbours to plan the party: every local business (the ones that remained, anyway) donated prizes for the raffle, neighbours helped to set up the decorations in the hall, and Leon's parents set up a BBQ selling fragrant jerk chicken outside the hall.

'I'm so nervous,' Rosalie said as they walked to the community hall. 'What if no one turns up?'

'Then we get to eat fifty patties each!' Rue said cheerfully. 'Don't be silly – of course people will turn up. We must have put posters on every lamp post on Holloway Road yesterday.'

The party was set to start at five o'clock, giving the kids a few hours to make the hall look worthy of a celebration. They saw an embarrassed Mr Erdogan give a shy wave across the community hall. No doubt the memory of him cartwheeling out into the park was still fresh in his mind. Alyssa bit back a guilty giggle when she thought about it.

'I still feel a bit bad about what happened with the cakes,' Alyssa whispered as they hung up paper streamers from the window.

'It happens to the best of us,' Rosalie said. 'When all this is over, remind me to tell you about the time I tried to enchant my English teacher's vision so he'd ignore the spelling mistakes in my homework.'

Alyssa gasped. 'No way! You used magic in school?'

'It was a disaster. I spiked his coffee with tea leaves, but all I managed to do was give him blurry vision for the day. The poor guy kept bumping into chairs all lesson,' Rosalie said. 'I'd never seen Auntie

Jasmine so angry. Not because I'd messed up the spell, but because I used magic for personal gain.'

'Yeah, I can imagine,' Alyssa said. She couldn't help feeling guilty. She knew the love spell she was planning wasn't exactly for the good of the community. But what choice did she have? She only had a few more days left of her stay here, but she'd need her mum and dad forever. Dad was picking her up on Sunday, which gave her four days to create her magic tea blend.

They had barely hung the last decoration when a queue began to form outside the community hall. The guests were arriving! A couple of Hemlock and Silverleaf kids worked together to sell tickets at the door and the hall soon filled with excited people of all ages.

Alyssa had volunteered for raffle duty, selling tickets for prizes donated by local businesses: one month's worth of free lattes from the coffee shop, a Jamaican cookery lesson from Leon's mum, Gloria, a fruit basket from the greengrocer's, a psychic reading from Debbie, and other random but lovely prizes. The clink of coins in their money bucket was like music to Alyssa's ears.

An hour passed and Auntie Jasmine was still nowhere to be seen. Finally, Alyssa heard the packed hall break into rapturous applause, and she looked up to see her great-aunt walking through the doors, arm in arm with Auntie Dahlia. She looked even more tired than earlier that day, but her face was a picture of joy. She seemed so happy to see the many familiar faces.

The guests spilled out of the community hall and into the small park outside, lured by the fragrance of BBQ food. Auntie Jasmine sat on a chair in the hall while Auntie Dahlia fetched her cool drinks and people walked by to chat. Not for the first time, Alyssa realised how much she would miss this little community when she went back to Milton Keynes. As excited as she was to see Mum and Dad, there was nothing like this back home.

The hours flew by. Hundreds of raffle tickets later, it was time to announce the winners. The small community hall didn't have anything as fancy as a stage or a microphone, so Debbie stood on a chair and cleared her throat.

'QUIET, PLEASE!' she yelled. 'Thank you. Before we announce the raffle winners, I'd like to thank you all for reaching deep into your pockets, and your hearts, to keep my dear friend Jasmine's shop going. Jasmine's Teas is more than a shop; it's the beating heart of this community. Whether it's a cup of tea or soothing words, Jasmine is always there for us. Now we must be there for her!'

The crowd whooped and cheered. Alyssa watched as Auntie Jasmine dabbed a hankie delicately under her eye.

'But we also wish to acknowledge that many much-loved local shops are under threat. We hope that today's event helps you to drum up some extra cash and raise awareness,' continued Debbie. 'Now, time to announce the raffle winners. The winning ticket of this delightful fruit basket is ...'

'*Psst*, Alyssa!' Rosalie said, thrusting a bucket into her arms. 'Help me get some more donations, will you?'

As the two girls passed the money bucket around the hall in a last-bid effort to get more donations, Debbie announced the raffle winners. Everyone was having so much fun, even if they didn't win anything. When the raffle was over, Auntie Jasmine slipped out quietly with Auntie Dahlia. The party had lifted her mood, but she still looked exhausted.

At the end of the night, the Hemlock and Silverleaf kids and their parents stayed late to help Debbie, Sister Hortense and Mr Erdogan tidy the hall.

'You children should be very proud of yourselves,' Sister Hortense said as they stacked chairs, separated the rubbish for recycling and swept the floor. 'Today, you really showed us the true meaning of community.'

'It was a team effort,' Rosalie said proudly. 'We couldn't have done it alone.'

'Listen, Rosalie,' Kieran said, pulling her aside. 'I'm really sorry for making fun of you at the car wash. I was just embarrassed that I made a mess of myself with the water.'

Alyssa cringed. She was going to have to own up. 'That was because of me,' she said. 'When you were nasty to Rosalie, it kind of . . . triggered my magic.'

'You can't take all the blame,' Rosalie said. 'We egged you on!'

Kieran looked shocked. '*You* did that? With the hose and the water and the bucket?! What are they teaching you at Silverleaf?'

Alyssa, Rosalie and Rue giggled.

'Apology accepted, Kieran,' Rosalie said.

'What a fabulous party!' Lisa trilled as she came through the hall door. Alyssa realised she hadn't seen her all day.

'You missed it! We didn't see you!' Rue said.

'I wouldn't have missed this for the world,' Lisa said. 'You didn't see me because the hall was so full.'

'Lisa, can we count the money in the shop tonight?

We need to know if we've hit our goal,' Rosalie said. 'I won't be able to sleep otherwise.'

'I'm not sure about that ...' said Lisa. 'It's getting late.'

'Lisa's had a long day, children,' Debbie said. 'She's had to do the work of two people this week. Lisa, allow me to take the children to the shop and I'll lock up. I'm sure Jasmine wouldn't mind.'

Lisa sighed. 'That's okay, Debbie. I can do it. I'm sure the young ones will be quick,' she said pointedly.

Rosalie and Alyssa punched the air, while Rue jumped for joy and said, 'We will, don't worry!'

While Sister Hortense and Mr Erdogan locked up the hall and the rest of the kids went home, Alyssa and her two cousins walked with Lisa to the shop, with buckets of loose change clinking in their hands.

'We're going to be here all night counting this lot,' Lisa grumbled as she unlocked the shop door and let them in.

It didn't exactly take them all night, but night had well and truly fallen by the time they finished sorting the change into money bags. Then the moment of truth arrived. Lisa opened the safe and laid the stacks of banknotes on the counter.

'Whoa!' Rue said.

'I can't believe we raised all *that*,' Alyssa said.

'Let's not get too excited,' Rosalie warned. 'It might not be enough and the deadline is on Friday.'

'What are you waiting for? Get counting!' said Rue.

Rosalie took a deep breath and began counting the cash, separating it into piles of one hundred pounds. There was total silence in the small shop apart from the clock ticking.

Rosalie stopped counting. 'Oh. My. Gosh,' she said.

'What's the matter? How much are we off by?' Rue asked. 'Because I can always sell my Xbox!'

'I don't believe it,' Rosalie said, shaking her head. 'We've exceeded our goal!'

'What?!' Lisa sputtered.

'Unbelievable!' Alyssa yelled.

The three cousins bundled into a giant group hug and yelped for joy.

'We did it!' Rue yelled.

'I can't wait to tell Auntie Jasmine,' Rosalie said.

'Well done, guys,' Lisa said. 'Just in the nick of time!'

Rose (for relaxation)

CHAPTER TWENTY-THREE

They locked the cash back in the safe and arranged to meet Lisa at the bank first thing in the morning: the seventeenth, the day before their deadline. There, they'd deposit the money and send it straight to the landlord a day early!

The cousins were so excited that they barely slept. Auntie Dahlia stayed the night on the sofa to keep an eye on Auntie Jasmine. She'd been staying more often since Auntie Jasmine became unwell.

When Alyssa and her cousins woke bright and early, Auntie Jasmine was still sleeping. They met Lisa outside the bank at nine o'clock sharp, as she carried the cash from the shop in her rucksack.

The moment they'd deposited the money bags on

the bank counter, Alyssa had never felt prouder. The money was a physical symbol of their hard work and ingenuity. Maybe one day she'd be able to tell Mum and Dad about this very special week.

'It's going to take a while for the bank teller to count this up,' Lisa said. 'Don't feel like you have to stay.'

Alyssa and her cousins didn't need telling twice. It was too hot in the bank, so they were relieved to leave Lisa to finish the paperwork.

'Now that we've sorted the rent, we can focus on this crux-water shortage,' Rosalie said as they walked back home.

'Chill!' Rue said. 'Let's celebrate our win first. I've got a packet of Skittles under my pillow that I'd be more than happy to share.'

'So that's why I always hear crunching in the night!' Alyssa laughed. 'Do you think normal Silverleaf lessons will start again, now that we've paid the rent?'

'Nerd alert!' Rosalie teased.

'Well, I haven't got much longer. Dad's picking me up on Sunday, and I want to learn what I can,' Alyssa said. She was super-keen to pick up her tea spell and finish what she'd started.

'Oh, look! There's Leon,' Rue said, pointing to their

friend in the distance. 'He's outside the takeaway. They don't usually open this early.'

The cousins picked up their pace, excited to share the good news with their friend. But one look at Leon's dismal expression told them that their news would have to wait.

'Leon, what's going on?' Rosalie asked.

Alyssa peered inside the takeaway and saw cardboard boxes being stacked on the tables and floor by Leon's parents. The street was lined with skips filled with rubbish – there was practically one outside every shop.

'We've been evicted,' he said sadly. 'The landlord demanded this ridiculous rent advance yesterday. Mum and Dad didn't want to worry me so they kept it secret until after the party. They've been trying all night to negotiate, but the landlord isn't having any of it.'

'But the deadline's tomorrow!' Alyssa said.

Leon shook his head. 'Not for us it wasn't. They sent round the bailiffs this morning.'

Rosalie gulped. 'We only paid the rent increase this morning. Do you think we'll be okay?'

'As long as those thieves get their cash, I don't think they'll mind,' Leon said bitterly.

'Why is it so quiet?' Alyssa asked suddenly.

It was a Thursday morning. Usually this area was heaving with shoppers, cars and double-decker buses. Alyssa had been in such a good mood about depositing the rent money at the bank that she hadn't noticed how eerily quiet the high street was. Pretty much every business was closed.

Not just closed. Boarded up or shuttered, with a sheet of white paper taped to each door.

'Anyway, I have to help Mum and Dad finish packing,' Leon said. His mind was too obviously full of worry to notice that no one else was around.

Alyssa and her cousins swapped numbers with Leon and promised to stay in touch. When they walked further down the high street, Rosalie paused outside the closed greengrocer's shop and read the white paper on the door.

'It's from the landlord! They've evicted the greengrocer for non-payment of rent, which was due yesterday,' she said.

'That's the same as Leon's takeaway. It's lucky that Auntie Jasmine's deadline was tomorrow,' added Rue.

Alyssa suddenly had a twisty feeling in her stomach. Something wasn't right.

Her cousins clearly felt the same. Without saying

a word, they ran down the empty high street and didn't stop until they reached Jasmine's Teas.

It took Alyssa a few seconds to notice what had changed. A heavy grey padlock was fastened to the front-door handle and a white letter from the landlord was taped to the glass window.

Rosalie gasped. 'It's the same letter. Our deadline *was* Wednesday!'

'That's impossible,' Rue said. 'Auntie Jasmine told us it was the eighteenth! That's tomorrow.'

Rue yanked at the door handle, but it didn't budge. Alyssa felt like crying. All their hard work had been for nothing.

'Maybe she made a mistake,' Alyssa said quietly.

Rosalie shook her head, tears building in her eyes. 'Auntie Jasmine never makes mistakes when it comes to the spell garden.'

'We're not going to get anywhere standing in the street. Let's go home. Auntie Jasmine and Lisa will know what to do. Maybe the landlord will change their mind now that we've paid the money,' Alyssa said.

But she sounded a lot more confident than she felt.

Rosewood
(for anxiety)

CHAPTER TWENTY-FOUR

'Mum!' Rue yelled. 'There's something wrong with the shop.'

The flat was quiet. The kitchen and the living room looked untouched, just as they'd left them that morning. The kids burst into each room in search of a grown-up. They found Auntie Dahlia in Auntie Jasmine's room.

The curtains were drawn and an electric fan hummed gently in the background. Even though it was dark, the space around the bed glowed electric blue, thanks to the lamps surrounding it.

When Alyssa stepped closer, though, she realised the light wasn't coming from lamps. It was coming from Auntie Jasmine. The air surrounding her was an electric blue haze that crackled and glowed. Underneath the haze, Auntie Jasmine lay completely still.

Rue gasped. Alyssa felt the urge to cry but held it back. Auntie Jasmine looked so small and frail.

'Is she . . . sleeping?' Rosalie whispered.

'There's no need to whisper,' Auntie Dahlia said. 'We think Auntie Jasmine is in a . . . magical coma of sorts. There's no noise on earth that could wake her.'

'When did this happen? She was fine this morning,' Rue said. 'We left her breakfast,' they said, motioning to the untouched tea and toast on the bedside table.

'Well, she wasn't completely fine,' Alyssa remembered. 'She looked tired. And she hasn't been herself since she got the letter from the landlord.'

'It must have happened later this morning,' Auntie Dahlia said. 'I found her like this. I've never seen anything like it.'

Alyssa stroked Auntie Jasmine's hand. Her skin was warm and soft, though her washed-out, serious face looked nothing like the Auntie Jasmine she had grown to love. Was this really because of the crux-water shortage? Was this because of . . . *her*? Auntie Jasmine had said herself that they'd never had problems like this in the spell garden before – not until Alyssa showed up.

'What can we do to fix it?' she said, trying to be brave.

'I'm working on it,' Auntie Dahlia said. 'The truth is that I don't know how to revive someone in a magical coma. The only person who does is Auntie Jasmine. My mother may know, but she's not answering her phone right now. She's even worse with technology than Auntie Jasmine,' she said, and chuckled without humour.

Rue's gentle sobs broke the heavy silence. Auntie Dahlia hugged them close.

'Come on,' she said. 'Let's give Auntie Jasmine some peace.'

In the living room, they opened the curtains and windows. The bright sunlight only emphasised how drab the plants looked.

Auntie Dahlia sighed and tried to force a smile. 'What an eventful summer this has been for you all. Especially you, Alyssa. I'm sorry your time in the spell garden has been cut short by all the problems about the rent. Hopefully you can come back to play with Rosalie and Rue next summer.'

'Alyssa has done more than play, Mum,' Rosalie said. 'She can really do some damage!'

Auntie Dahlia looked at Alyssa with a slight smile on her face. 'Well, you and your mother have that in common.'

'Are you talking about the fire?' Alyssa asked.

'Don't pretend like you don't know this time!' Rue pleaded.

'Yeah! We know there's this big family secret. What are you keeping from us?' Rosalie asked.

'If Violet wants you to know, she can tell you,' said Auntie Dahlia.

'It's so unfair!' said Alyssa. 'All these secrets ... They make me feel like I'm not really part of this family. I deserve to know my own history, don't I?'

Auntie Dahlia paused. She looked as though she was mulling it over. Alyssa waited with bated breath. Then Auntie Dahlia seemed to decide something. She shook her head, and finally said, 'It was your mum who started the fire.'

'W-what?' Alyssa stuttered.

It didn't make sense. Her calm, sensible mum started a *fire*?

'It was an accident, of course,' Auntie Dahlia continued. 'Years ago, when we were teenagers, Violet and I had an argument. Don't ask me what it was about because I don't remember.'

Alyssa sat down cross-legged on the rug. All eyes were on Auntie Dahlia as her story unfolded.

'What I do remember is this: Violet got so angry that it unleashed her magic. It collided with the gas stove and the kitchen went up in flames.'

That bit sounded familiar to Alyssa – it had only been a few weeks and she'd made her fair share of magical mess. But the girl Auntie Dahlia described sounded nothing like her controlled mum.

'It's not like Mum to lose her temper,' Alyssa said.

'It was a terrible accident.'

'What happened after?' Alyssa asked.

'Luckily no one was hurt, but we did have to move house. After that, Violet shut down. She went from being excited about magic to never wanting to speak or think of it ever again. I believe she feared causing another fire.'

How was Mum going to accept that Alyssa was a Keeper-in-Training when she hated magic?

No, Alyssa realised. *Mum doesn't hate magic. She's* terrified *of it.*

'That's why Auntie Jasmine established Silverleaf. So we had a place to train and practise our magic in safety. But Violet went to university and wanted nothing to do with it. Over the years, we stopped seeing each other. Our relationship fizzled out.

When our parents moved back to Jamaica, we lost touch,' Auntie Dahlia said.

Alyssa remembered the first time her magic exploded at the tea shop and suppressed a shudder. 'That must have been so scary for you guys,' she said. 'But why didn't Mum want to learn more about her magic? That way she could try to control it.'

'I couldn't tell you, Alyssa. But I do know that Violet avoids things she can't control. Whether it's difficult feelings or magical outbursts, I think she'd rather pretend they didn't happen,' said Auntie Dahlia.

Alyssa nodded. That was Mum all over.

'I really hope Mum changes her mind about magic,' she said to her aunt. 'I want to come back to Silverleaf every summer.'

Auntie Dahlia smiled sadly. 'I hope there's a Silverleaf for you to return to.'

*

The rest of the day passed in a blur. Debbie came round and tried to revive Auntie Jasmine with magical smelling salts, a potent blend that did nothing but make the entire flat stink of menthol. Auntie Debbie tried to get hold of Lisa but she wasn't answering her phone.

Alyssa had something else on her mind. Later that evening, she got a text message from Dad saying

that he would pick her up on Sunday as planned. It reminded Alyssa that she had just a few days to make her magical tea blend. The thought of leaving when everything was so awful made her heart feel heavy. But if one good thing came out of this mess, she thought, maybe it could be getting Mum and Dad back together.

Alyssa packed her rucksack carefully that evening: she plucked a fistful of rose petals from the balcony, pinched a wrinkled passionfruit from the fruit bowl and triple-checked that she still had the root of mandrake from last week.

At the crack of dawn, she snuck out of bed and made her way to the spell garden. She jogged down the eerily quiet high street. As Alyssa approached Jasmine's Teas, she stopped in her tracks.

How was she going to get into the spell garden when Jasmine's Teas was padlocked shut?

Then she remembered. Rosalie's shortcut.

Alyssa followed the route she'd taken with Rosalie and soon found the hidden corner. She squeezed through the narrow space, her rucksack in hand, and she was in the allotment.

She looked around, surprised. It was ... different. Perhaps it was the cloudy dawn sky, but everything appeared drab and grey.

Alyssa gulped. She didn't have time to worry about the community's plants on the allotment.

She dashed towards the wooden door to the spell garden. It was easier to find now that the hedge was missing a few leaves. Well, more than a few. It was practically bare.

She pushed open the wooden door with ease. A little too much ease.

The door swung off its hinges, smashing against the wall. The wood was crumbling and rotten.

'Oops!' She fixed the door back into place but it was wonky.

She stepped onto the gravel path. Something was wrong. Very wrong.

Alyssa looked down. The path was littered with tiny scraps of paper – or were they dried leaves? She bent down for a closer look.

She gasped.

Flicker-bees!

They were everywhere. But not the shiny, lively creatures she remembered. They were dull and droopy. Some of them crawled on the ground, while others could barely hover above Alyssa's knees.

'They're fading,' she muttered. It made her heart break to see it.

What had Auntie Jasmine said about the

flicker-bees? They pollinated the magical plants so they could grow, just like non-magical bees did. *They're nearly as important as the crux-water to the health of the spell garden.*

Alyssa trudged down the path, the sound of her footsteps piercing the awful quiet. The garden's background noise, the thrum of life that had seemed ever present, was gone. For the first time since she'd discovered it, she wanted to be out of the spell garden as quickly as possible.

There was no time to waste, though. She ran to the store cupboard and found a dusty jar of dried banana-fern leaf on the shelf. She grabbed the entire jar.

Working fast, she tumbled the ingredients into the centre of the giant bronze bowl one by one, guessing the ratio: the root of mandrake, banana fern, passionfruit and rose.

'One of leaf, two of fruit, three of flower, four of root ...' Alyssa muttered the formula to herself.

With the ingredients in the bowl, the next thing she needed was crux-water. She turned the bronze tap but nothing came out, not even a dribble.

Alyssa was on the verge of tears. She was *so* close.

Fighting back a sob, Alyssa took a deep breath. There was no point hanging around when she couldn't cast the spell. She had to get back before Rue realised she was missing. She couldn't believe she'd failed at the last hurdle. Anger and frustration pulsed through her.

The dim silver-blue glow of the plants illuminated her path. She hadn't noticed it earlier because she'd been too upset about the flicker-bees. It was like the time Alyssa had visited the spell garden with Rosalie, except not quite as bright. The crux-water glowed in the dark, turning every plant into a night-light.

Wait a second...

Alyssa stopped walking. If the crux-water glowed in the dark, and the plants around her were illuminated, that could only mean one thing.

There was still some crux-water inside the plants! Maybe even enough to power her spell.

She roamed the spell garden looking for the brightest plant with the thickest stem. It didn't take long. There, at the edge of the spell garden, a large tree glowed the brightest. Effie's tree.

Alyssa ran towards the tree and tugged at a low-hanging branch. Supple and green, it twisted easily in her hand. The core dripped precious silvery crux-water.

'Yes!' she yelled.

Alyssa held the branch and ran to the enclosure. She headed towards the giant bronze dish and found the table that was loaded with bronze tools. She used her hands to carefully squeeze the plant's hidden nectar into a small jug.

It wasn't much, but there was enough.

An aeroplane flew overhead, the sound of its engines roaring dully in the distance. Alyssa looked up at the sky. The familiar magical haze protecting the spell garden was no more. It seemed so exposed.

The noise of the engine faded but left something else in its place. Was that the sound of conversation drifting over from the allotment?

Alyssa walked towards the wall and crouched low beside the wooden door. Who else would be in the allotment at dawn?

'Thank you for organising this at such short notice, madam,' a man's voice said. It reminded Alyssa of her head teacher.

'Our company has had our eye on this prime piece of land for some time,' another voice said. It sounded like a woman. 'We were thrilled when you contacted us.'

'Absolutely,' said the man. 'Tell me, what changed your mind? We've been contacting the tenant of Jasmine's Teas for years.'

Alyssa held her breath. She knew that Auntie Jasmine would never leave her beloved shop or put the spell garden in danger.

'Let's just say we had a change of heart,' a familiar voice replied.

Lisa?

But that was impossible. Jasmine's Teas wasn't Lisa's shop. It belonged to Auntie Jasmine.

There had to be a mistake.

'The timing couldn't be better,' the woman said. 'We've just completed negotiations for the rest of the high street.'

The empty shops. The awful quiet. The skips lining the road.

The entire high street was being wiped out.

'It's so exciting. I've been saying for years that the neighbourhood needs a fresh start.'

Alyssa's heart plummeted. There was no mistaking it. That was Lisa's voice.

'We're not wasting any time,' the man said. 'Our demolition team will be here around lunchtime. In a few hours, this entire space will be unrecognisable.'

'All this mess will be gone. It'll be the perfect spot for London's first fully automated high street!' the **woman said excitedly.**

An automated high street? Like vending machines? They were going to replace the family bakery, Leon's takeaway and Mr Brown's fruit stall with a bunch of machines!

Lisa was helping to destroy a magical spell garden for *that*?

The voices drifted away as the grown-ups toured the grounds. But it didn't matter. Alyssa had heard everything she needed to know.

In a couple of hours, the spell garden would be demolished. Auntie Jasmine had been betrayed by her own apprentice. And there was nothing Alyssa could do to stop it.

Or was there?

Perhaps if she finished the spell at lightning speed then ran home, she could alert Auntie Dahlia? The sun was only just rising, so they had a good couple of hours before seven a.m. She could save her family *and* the spell garden.

Alyssa turned away from the wall and crept towards the tree.

CRUNCH.

The gravel made a telltale sound beneath her feet.

The wooden door slammed open, falling off its hinges completely.

'I thought I heard a pest,' Lisa said coldly.

Sea Fennel
(for vitality.)

CHAPTER TWENTY-FIVE

'Lisa! What are you doing here so early?' Alyssa asked, trying desperately to sound normal.

'I could ask you the same thing,' Lisa said. 'How long have you been here?'

'I just arrived,' Alyssa lied. She needed to get out of here; she needed to run home. 'I came here early because ... because ...'

Lisa rolled her eyes. 'You're a terrible liar. You might as well tell me what you heard.' She stood at the spell garden's entrance, blocking the way out. 'You're not going anywhere until you do.'

Alyssa gulped. 'I heard ... I heard about how you betrayed Auntie Jasmine.'

Lisa smirked. 'I didn't betray anyone. All I did

was give your great-aunt the wrong date for the rent deadline.'

'H-how?' Alyssa stammered. 'The letter said it was the eighteenth! Unless . . . you faked the letter?' She knew she was right as she said it. It would have been easy for Lisa to do that. Auntie Jasmine wouldn't have known the difference.

'Your great-aunt is a silly old woman who doesn't understand how the real world works. She's sitting on a gold mine!'

'You know how special this place is,' Alyssa said. 'How can the spell garden help anyone when it's covered in concrete?'

Lisa looked around the dusty, dry spell garden. She raised one eyebrow and said, 'Face it, Alyssa. The spell garden isn't helping anyone right now.'

'That's because we have a crux-water shortage!' Alyssa protested. Then it hit her. 'Was . . . was that you as well?'

Lisa sighed and pulled something out of her pocket. It was a grey stone. 'Listen. I didn't want to steal anything. But I did what needed to be done.'

'You stole crux-pebbles!'

'I wish you would understand. I had to make it easier for Miss Jasmine to give up the land. So I took the crux-pebbles one by one.'

'Where are the others?' Alyssa demanded.

'Don't worry about that,' Lisa said. 'I thought that if the spell garden became barren and dry, Miss Jasmine would be more willing to sell up.'

'But it didn't work,' Alyssa retorted.

Lisa's mouth twisted into a cruel smile. 'In the end, I didn't have to persuade her. You see, Miss Jasmine had the good sense to leave all the paperwork to me. It was easy to arrange a meeting with the developers without her knowing. And when her little niece came to stay for the very first time, she was too distracted to pay me any mind.'

Alyssa's stomach twisted with guilt.

'The timing couldn't have been more perfect,' Lisa continued.

Then Alyssa remembered Lisa telling her how much crux-water fixing the shop had required. She gasped. 'You let me think it was my fault! But all this time you were stealing the crux-pebbles.'

'Can you blame me? Your magical outbursts were messy, costly and the ideal distraction. And the fact that you kids were busy trying to sabotage Hemlock last week? I couldn't have planned it better myself,' Lisa said. 'I put the dogs to sleep and you didn't even consider it was anyone but them.'

Alyssa felt sick. While the two magic schools were

arguing between themselves, the threat had been right under their nose the entire time.

Lisa took a few steps forward, though she still blocked the gravel path leading to the doorway. 'You know I can't allow you to leave, don't you, Alyssa? You'll run home and spoil my plans. No, you'll stay here until the demolition crew arrives. Then it'll be too late for you to stop them.'

There was no way Alyssa could escape. Although... if she stalled long enough, maybe someone would come looking for her.

Maybe.

'So, what do you get out of this?' Alyssa snapped.

Lisa folded her arms. 'I could ask the same thing of you. Don't tell me you're here because you like the scenery. Why have *you* come so early?'

Alyssa straightened up. 'I asked first.'

This completely different side of Lisa was scary, but Alyssa couldn't let her see that. She had to stand up to her.

'I worked with Forsythe to get Jasmine out and, in exchange, they will reward me with a modest commission,' Lisa said.

'You betrayed Auntie Jasmine for ... money?'

Lisa looked offended. 'It's not like I'm buying a designer handbag! The money will be used wisely. Working in Jasmine's Teas was meant to be temporary until I started a business of my own. But that didn't happen. Getting a business loan isn't easy, especially if you're from a neighbourhood like this.'

'How is that Auntie Jasmine's fault?' Alyssa asked.

Lisa shrugged. 'It's not. But I can't work another day in this rundown shop knowing how much better things could be. I'll use the crux-pebbles to start a spell garden that actually makes money *and* helps people. I've already spotted the perfect factory space that can mass-produce magical tea for all!'

Alyssa could hardly believe Lisa's plan. 'You're only getting away with this because Auntie Jasmine's sick. If she wasn't in a magical coma—'

'I didn't mean for Jasmine to get sick,' Lisa said. 'But she will recover soon enough.'

Alyssa's eyes filled with tears. Seeing Lisa like this, so cold and mean, was chilling. 'What if she doesn't?'

'It's too late – it's already done,' Lisa said with a shrug.

Alyssa felt a familiar tingling in her fingertips. *Her magic!* Could she muster the energy to push Lisa away and escape? But as soon as the tingling started, it stopped.

The crux-water, Alyssa realised. There wasn't

enough in the garden to fuel her magic. She would have to escape the old-fashioned way.

Without hesitation, Alyssa leapt past Lisa, towards the open door. But in a matter of seconds thick branches rose from the ground and grew in front of it, blocking her way. She was trapped.

Lisa stood behind her, arms raised as she magically manipulated the surrounding plants, summoning the last drops of crux-water from the spell garden.

'How—' Alyssa uttered in amazement.

'Your little tricks might impress the other kids,' Lisa sneered, 'but I've been studying spell work since before you were born. I can't have you running off and ruining my plan. So tell me. Why are you here?' she demanded.

Before she could stop herself, Alyssa's eyes flicked to the bronze bowl, and Lisa quickly understood. She marched down the gravel path and up to the giant bronze bowl.

'What do we have here? This is advanced spell work for a Keeper-in-Training.'

Alyssa's cheeks flushed as she ran after Lisa. 'That's none of your business!'

'Hey, I'm not judging. What's the point of having magical powers if you can't get what you want?'

Alyssa didn't know what to say. She couldn't argue with that. A part of her kind of agreed with Lisa. That was why she was here, after all.

Lisa made a show of examining what was in the bowl. 'I see banana fern and rose . . . I take it this is a love spell. For Mum and Dad, I assume?'

Alyssa's eyes filled with tears. She nodded.

'It can be our little secret.' Then Lisa checked her watch. 'The demolition team will be here soon. Looks like you have just enough crux-water for the one spell. Use it wisely.'

Alyssa's thoughts swirled in her head like a cyclone. Casting this spell could give Alyssa her family back. No more arguing. No more fights. She wouldn't have to split her life between two homes.

But if she allowed Lisa to get away with this, what kind of person did that make her? She'd only been part of this community for a few weeks, yet it felt like her second home.

And it wasn't just the spell garden – it was the entire community. Leon's takeaway, the Byrne family bakery, Mr Brown and his strawberries – their fates hung in the balance.

The quote behind the till in the tea shop lingered in her mind. *We are each other's harvest.* Finally, Alyssa understood what it meant.

She depended on the spell garden. Now, the spell garden was depending on her.

I have to do something.

Lisa handed her the small bronze jug of crux-water and stepped back.

But I can't do it alone.

Silently, Alyssa took the small jug of crux-water. She thought about the spell garden and everyone who helped to nurture it: her cousins, her aunties, her friends and fellow Keepers-in-Training. Then, instead of pouring it over the magical plants in the bronze bowl, she tipped the silvery liquid into her open hand.

WHOOSH!

The second the liquid met Alyssa's fingers, she felt a tingle and the crux-water turned into a silvery plume of cool flame.

'What are you playing at?!' Lisa yelled.

Alyssa looked up in wonder. The silver flame shot past the spell garden's walls and into the air, exploding like fireworks against the early morning sky.

It was a warning flare. Every Keeper and Keeper-in-Training in the neighbourhood would see it and come running.

'It's too late!' Lisa snarled. 'The contract's already

signed. The bulldozers are on the way. You wasted the last bit of crux-water for this?'

Alyssa couldn't answer. The silvery fireworks had drained every bit of effort in her body and mind. She had to save the spell garden, if it was the last thing she did.

That was her final thought before everything went dark.

Sorrel
(for strength)

CHAPTER TWENTY-SIX

'Alyssa, wake up!'

Alyssa blinked her eyes open. She felt totally drained.

'Oh, thank goodness! She's not dead,' Rue said.

'Which means I can kill her myself for being so reckless!' Rosalie said. 'Why on earth did you sneak out?'

Alyssa sat bolt upright. She was no longer in the spell garden but in the allotment. Someone must have carried her. Concerned faces looked down at her. Faces from Silverleaf, plus Auntie Dahlia, Debbie and a load of kids from Hemlock. She felt completely drained. Was it too late? Had she wasted the last of the crux-water?

'Where's Lisa? We have to stop her!' she yelled, scrambling to her feet.

'Lisa? Why? What are you talking about?' Rue asked.

'I summoned you here for a reason!' Alyssa said.

'Wait, that incredible explosion of magic was you?' Rosalie asked. 'We felt it and came running!'

Alyssa nodded. 'Listen! We don't have much time.'

She told the small crowd everything. Lisa's betrayal. The disappearance of the crux-water. And the fact that, at any moment now, bulldozers would be destroying their land.

'I can't believe this. We've known Lisa our entire lives,' Rue said quietly.

Rosalie shook her head. 'Why would she do this?'

'Let's save the questions for later, my loves,' Auntie Dahlia said gently. 'We need a plan.'

'What can we do? Is it too late?' Kieran yelled.

'As the most advanced Keeper here, I can cast a protection spell,' Debbie said.

Everyone watched while Debbie closed her eyes and focused on her spell.

But it didn't feel right.

Nothing happened.

'Every drop of crux-water is really gone,' Rosalie whispered.

'How do we protect the spell garden without magic?' Rue asked.

'I bet Auntie Jasmine would know,' Rosalie said.

Over the past three weeks, Alyssa had seen the power of the community. Auntie Jasmine loved her neighbours and they loved her back.

Alyssa cleared her throat. 'I might have an idea,' she said.

She told the small crowd to round up as many people in the community as possible and to tell them that Jasmine's Teas was in trouble. If enough people showed up to protect the neighbourhood, they wouldn't need magic.

Auntie Dahlia called everyone she knew. Rosalie and Rue went knocking door to door in Auntie Jasmine's block of flats, directing them to the tea shop. And a few of the older kids from Hemlock used social media to reach even more people.

With every minute that passed, more and more people gathered on the pavement outside Jasmine's Teas. A couple even turned up in dressing gowns. Alyssa couldn't believe the turnout they had by midday.

'Alyssa, what's going on? I got Rosalie's message!' It was Leon, pushing his way through the crowd, closely followed by his parents.

'The spell garden is going to be torn down any minute!' Alyssa replied urgently.

Before she could say more, a loud beeping sound, like a lorry reversing, pierced the air.

'*Demolition will begin in fifteen minutes. Please depart!*' a crackly voice boomed through speakers.

On the other side of the high street, over the top of the crowd, Alyssa saw something that made her blood run cold.

An army of bulldozers trundled slowly and surely down the road. It was clear they meant business.

Auntie Dahlia's eyes flashed, the only clue to her real emotions, while her voice and face stayed calm. 'Kids, I want you to go home. I can't let you get hurt.'

'We're not going anywhere!' someone in the crowd yelled.

'That's right!' It was Sister Hortense, a silk scarf covering her roller-clad hair. 'This neighbourhood would be nothing without Jasmine.'

As people walked by and asked what was happening, more of them joined the swelling crowd. Murmurs of '*We can't stand by and let this happen*' rang through the crowd.

'What can we do?' asked Mr Begum.

'We form a human chain!' Debbie yelled. 'Everyone, link arms and block the entrance!'

The community assembled, filling the pavement with a crowd several people deep. Rosalie and Rue joined them, breathless.

'Wow! Are all these people here for Jasmine's Teas?' Rue asked.

Alyssa and Leon made their way to the front of the group, followed by Auntie Dahlia.

'Well done, kids,' Auntie Dahlia said. 'Half of the estate are here.'

'And there're more on the way,' Rosalie said. 'Everyone wants to help Auntie Jasmine!'

'Kids, it really would be much safer for you at home,' said Auntie Dahlia.

'But we need everyone we can get!' Alyssa protested.

Auntie Dahlia sighed. 'Okay. Just ... keep close to me, all right?'

The roaring of the bulldozers grew louder.

Demolition is scheduled for five minutes. Please depart!' The warning crackled through the megaphones again.

'Link arms!' Auntie Dahlia said.

Alyssa, Rosalie, Rue and Leon obeyed. They shuffled into the front of the crowd, arms linked.

'Stay strong, everyone!' Debbie shouted.

'Alyssa!' a familiar voice yelled. A woman jumped

out of a car across the road and ran towards the crowd.

'Mum!' Alyssa exclaimed. 'What are you doing here?'

She broke the chain to give her mum a massive hug. She realised how much she had missed the sound of her voice, her familiar cocoa-butter scent.

'I had a feeling something was wrong. A terrible dream woke me up and I knew I had to find you,' Mum said frantically. She turned to look at the bulldozers rolling towards them, the worry in her eyes changing to confusion. 'What's going on? Surely this isn't legal?'

'It's a long story, Mum,' Alyssa said.

'You can explain in the car. Let's go,' Mum said to her.

'Violet, wait!' Auntie Dahlia said urgently. 'The bulldozers are coming for Jasmine's Teas, but we can't let them destroy the spell garden. We aren't going anywhere. Please – join us.'

Mum hesitated. 'It—it's too dangerous! I need to keep Alyssa safe from all this.'

'I have to help, Mum!' cried Alyssa. '*We* have to help. Otherwise the community will be destroyed. And losing the spell garden will break Auntie Jasmine's heart.'

'Are you with us, Violet?' Auntie Dahlia said.

Mum paused, then nodded. She squeezed between Alyssa and Auntie Dahlia, and they all joined the chain. It stretched the length of the high street, an impenetrable line of people chanting and raising their voices.

Alyssa had never felt stronger in her life. The excitement and power of the community surged through her. She looked down.

Rainbow waves danced around her fingers. Her magic was back! The power of community was a magic of its own, greater than Alyssa could have ever imagined.

Now, though, the bulldozers were right outside the shop. Alyssa counted three of them, plus a shiny car with blacked-out windows leading the way. The car pulled up outside the shop and two people in sharp suits stepped out – a man and a woman.

The man had a megaphone in his hand. 'You are obstructing a legal demolition!' he said through it.

Alyssa recognised the voice right away. It was the man who had been talking to Lisa in the allotment several hours earlier.

'How can it be legal?' Auntie Dahlia yelled over the bulldozer's engines. 'The real owner of Jasmine's Teas never agreed to any of this.'

'She's right! I demand to see the paperwork,' Mum said in her most assertive voice.

The man smirked. 'Our lawyers say otherwise. Besides, we have paid far more than what this land is worth. These establishments are an eyesore!'

The crowd gasped and yelled.

'How dare you!' Alyssa shouted. She was furious.

'It's time for a fresh start for the neighbourhood. Don't you want a shiny high street instead of this dump?' he said through the megaphone.

'No! I want an allotment!' Mr Begum yelled.

'Our family has lived in this neighbourhood for three generations!' Auntie Dahlia said. 'We're not moving any time soon.'

'Yeah!' all the kids shouted in unison.

The sharp-suited woman took the megaphone. 'I must insist that any complaints be put in writing. Our lawyers will deal with them within twenty-eight working days. Until then, you must move aside.'

'*Hell, no! We won't go!*' the crowd chanted over and over. Alyssa's throat was sore from shouting.

'You have one minute to move. Otherwise, I will be forced to contact law enforcement and have you all arrested,' the man said through the megaphone, and the front bulldozer revved its engines.

Alyssa felt Mum and Auntie Dahlia hold on to her even tighter. She wished she could wipe the smirk off that awful man's face.

Anger rose within her. Electricity zipped through her veins and pulsed beneath the surface of her skin. She flexed her fingers as her hands crackled with magical energy.

It was time for her magic to do the talking.

Alyssa clenched her fist, channelling her fury into the tips of her fingers. She focused her gaze on the bulldozer at the front.

Suddenly the bulldozer spun round so hard it nearly threw out its driver. The crowd gasped and stepped back.

'It's working!' Alyssa said to herself.

The bulldozer now faced the opposite side of the road.

'Oi! You're meant to be facing *that* way!' the man yelled through the megaphone.

'I'm not touching it!' the bulldozer driver shouted back. 'It's malfunctioning!'

Without warning, the other two bulldozers did the same. They spun round, jerking forward and crashing into a shopfront repeatedly.

Glass windows shattered and a metal sign for *WÜF* fell to the ground.

'They're destroying the snobby guy's shop!' Rosalie cried with delight.

Alyssa watched as the three bulldozers smashed the horrible shiny doggy ice-cream parlour that had replaced Mr Rasheed's corner shop.

Then, just as Alyssa was running out of energy, all three bulldozers stopped mid-destruction. The three drivers climbed out, knees wobbling.

'What are you doing?' the developer man yelled. 'Get back in those bulldozers, this instant!'

'No way. The machines are a liability!' said one of the drivers.

'We have a demolition scheduled!' snarled the developer man.

'Not today, boss.' With that, the drivers all marched away.

The developer man turned to the crowd. 'This isn't over!' he shouted, and he and his colleague got back into their car and sped away.

The crowd erupted into cheers.

'We did it!' Alyssa yelled, hugging her cousins. She wanted to jump in the air, she could have cried with relief and joy. She couldn't wait to tell Auntie Jasmine—

Then, out of the corner of her eye, Alyssa saw Auntie Dahlia and Mum in a heated conversation.

Uh-oh, this doesn't look good, she thought, and ran over to them.

'I can't believe Alyssa was involved in this mess,' Mum was saying. 'I trusted Auntie Jasmine to look after her, to keep her safe. What were you *thinking*, allowing her to be part of this?'

Before Auntie Dahlia could answer, Alyssa interrupted. 'Mum, I chose magic! Or magic chose me – I'm not sure which. My powers appeared and I had to learn more about them.'

'But ... it's not safe!' Mum said, tears filling her eyes. 'Magic is too dangerous.'

'We kept her safe, Violet,' Auntie Dahlia said softly. 'You never let us protect you. You ran away and shut us out. Let us protect Alyssa now. She's family.'

Mum sniffed. For a moment, Alyssa wasn't sure whether she was going to cry or start shouting. Then she said, 'How's Auntie Jasmine? I missed her so much. I missed you all.'

Auntie Dahlia leaned forward and embraced Mum in a hug. 'I'll take you to her now. We've got a lot of catching up to do.'

woodruff
(for victory.)

CHAPTER TWENTY-SEVEN

'Who knew that today would turn out to be so exciting?' Rue said.

'Did you see the bulldozers mash up that shop? Wish I'd filmed it,' Leon said delightedly.

Rosalie folded her arms and stared at Alyssa. 'Why do I think you were behind this?'

Alyssa smiled. She still couldn't quite believe her plan worked, but she was so happy it had. 'I just gave the bulldozers a helping hand.'

They all laughed.

'Well, I'm pleased you did,' Rosalie said. 'Don't get me wrong. I love Jasmine's Teas, but I wasn't about to throw myself in front of a bulldozer.'

'If Alyssa's magic is back, does that mean . . .' Leon trailed off.

'The spell garden!' Alyssa cried. 'This morning it was all shrivelled and dry. Maybe it's healing?'

They dashed through the shop – the padlock having been removed by Mr Begum with a wrench – and out to the allotment. It already looked brighter and greener than it had earlier that morning.

Alyssa held back tears of joy. 'It's returning to life,' she said softly. *But . . . how?* she wondered. Was it what they'd done, because of the way they'd brought everyone together to stop the bulldozers? But how could there be a spell garden with no crux-pebbles?

The kids pushed through the spell-garden door. Alyssa ran up the grassy hill, wildflowers tickling her ankles, and didn't stop until she reached the crux well.

She cranked the handle, lowering the bucket.

'Is there crux-water?' Rosalie asked breathlessly.

'Can't tell yet!' Alyssa said.

The faintest sound of splashing came from inside the well. The two girls peered into the well.

There, at the very end of a dark, deep hole, was a glint of silver.

'It's back!' Alyssa yelled. She pulled the bucket back up. It was half full with crux-water. They couldn't have been happier to see it. 'But this doesn't make any sense ... Lisa stole the crux-pebbles. That's why we had a shortage in the first place ...'

'How can we have crux-water without the pebbles?' Rue asked.

'I think that's a question for when Auntie Jasmine wakes up,' Rosalie said quietly.

Alyssa's heart lurched. If the spell garden was healing, would that help Auntie Jasmine? She hoped more than anything that it would.

From the top of the hill, Alyssa saw the spell garden fill with kids from Silverleaf and Hemlock.

'We have some crux-water!' Rosalie yelled. 'It might just be enough to get this garden back in shape.'

The kids and grown-ups formed a line stretching from the crux well to the foot of the hill. Alyssa and Rosalie filled buckets and jars with crux-water, which were passed down the line.

Even though the crux-water pipe would be slowly sending water around the garden, the kids didn't want to wait. At the bottom of the hill, everyone got to work. Plants, trees, bushes and shrubs were watered with precious crux-water.

The transformation happened before their eyes. The plants grew plumper, the petals turned brighter and even the grass felt springier beneath Alyssa's feet.

But something still didn't feel quite right. *Auntie Jasmine should be here to see this*, Alyssa thought.

'Um, guys?' Alyssa said to her cousins. 'Maybe we should go and check on Auntie Jasmine.'

It was like she'd cast a spell – their reaction was so quick. Rue and Rosalie dropped their buckets and they all ran.

Alyssa's heart raced as they jogged to Auntie Jasmine's flat. Rosalie unlocked the front door. The flat felt deathly silent.

Rue walked ahead to Auntie Jasmine's bedroom and pushed through the door. 'Hey, come quick!'

Alyssa and Rosalie rushed into the bedroom. The bed was covered in cushions and sheets. But Auntie Jasmine wasn't there. Alyssa's heart thumped painfully. Had the worst happened? Had they been too late to save Auntie Jasmine?

Suddenly they heard a humming sound. It was coming from the kitchen. They rushed to see Auntie Jasmine standing on the balcony, holding a watering can. She was watering her plants, while Mum and Auntie Dahlia sat on the small metal chairs.

Auntie Jasmine turned and smiled at them through the open door. She didn't quite have her usual glow, but the important thing was that she was awake. Alyssa thought she might cry. This was turning out to be the best day ever.

'You're not in a coma!' Rosalie gasped.

'Excellent skills of deduction, my dear,' Auntie Jasmine said. 'I woke up an hour ago feeling better than ever. But I was disappointed to see so many thirsty plants ...'

'How did you wake up?!' Rue asked.

Auntie Jasmine set down her watering can. 'I've been tending that spell garden for decades now,' she said. 'We are more entwined than I realised. When the garden thrives, so do I. And when it doesn't ... Well, you all saw that for yourselves.'

'Auntie Jasmine, you won't believe what just happened. And it's all Lisa's fault!' Alyssa said.

Auntie Jasmine stepped into the kitchen and sat down. She sighed heavily. 'I had a feeling that Lisa might have something to do with it. But I didn't want to believe it. Tell me all about it, sweetness.'

Alyssa recounted everything she knew about Lisa's betrayal: the fake deadline on the letter from the landlord and her plans to start a new profitable spell garden with the crux-pebbles.

'What we don't understand is how the crux-water was restored if Lisa stole the crux-pebbles,' Rosalie said. 'There wasn't much, but there was enough to revive the spell garden.'

'The crux-pebbles are buried quite deep into the well,' Auntie Jasmine said. 'I guess there must have been a small shard of pebble that Lisa overlooked when she climbed down there.'

'Just one tiny pebble?' Alyssa said. 'Will that be enough to draw up crux-water for the entire spell garden?'

Auntie Jasmine sighed. 'I don't know, sweetheart. I'm just grateful we have that.'

Rue had peered down the well earlier. 'Lisa really *climbed* down there? Gross,' they said.

Auntie Jasmine chuckled. 'If you look carefully, the well has little footholds in the inner wall. It's the only way in or out.' She paused. 'Children, I think that the community spirit you witnessed was enough to revive the well – there's nothing our magic loves more than community.'

Alyssa was puzzled. 'But there's been community spirit for a while now,' she said. 'Why didn't the crux-water level revive when we did the bake sale or the community party?'

'It's an awful thought,' replied Auntie Jasmine, 'but I suspect that Lisa was siphoning the crux-water to make sure the levels stayed low. She could have taken it when she went down the well and pinched the crux-pebbles.'

'I can't believe she tricked us,' Rosalie said sadly.

Auntie Jasmine squeezed Rosalie's shoulder. 'Let's focus on the positives. It sounds like you all pulled together today.'

'Gathering the community was Alyssa's idea,' Rosalie said with a smile.

Auntie Jasmine beamed at Alyssa. 'You should be proud, sweetness. You should all be proud.'

Rosalie looked at the floor. 'I suppose our competition with Hemlock didn't help matters either,' she mumbled.

Auntie Jasmine's eyes lit up. 'A competition, you say? What exactly did I miss?'

*

With many shops on the high street closed and Auntie Jasmine's fridge practically empty, they weren't sure what to make for lunch.

'Well, we have enough flour and eggs for pancakes,' Alyssa's mum said, after rummaging through the fridge and cupboards.

'Now, what would be lovely is if you could cook for us, Violet. It's been years since I've had one of your Jamaican breakfasts,' Auntie Jasmine said.

'But it's lunchtime,' said Rue.

Auntie Jasmine shrugged. 'It's my first meal in days, so I make it breakfast.'

'Breakfast it is. I need ripe plantain, ackee, saltfish ...' Mum said.

Auntie Jasmine sent Alyssa and her cousins to the newly revived spell garden to see what they could forage from the kitchen and vegetable patch. They returned with bags of fresh produce, the non-magical kind – although the ripe avocado, perfectly blackened plantain, ackee fruit and lush-green callaloo leaves had been grown with magical assistance.

As Alyssa pushed open the kitchen door, she paused. Mum and Auntie Dahlia were in the middle of an intense conversation.

Mum sighed. 'It's hard to explain ... The magic terrified me. I thought if I just had space away from my family, I wouldn't have to deal with it.'

'But the fire wasn't your fault, Violet. Mum should have trained us from a young age, like I did with my two,' Auntie Dahlia said.

'I still think about that day. I nearly killed us, all because I lost my temper,' Mum said. 'You know I haven't so much as raised my voice since, Dahlia? Joseph thinks I don't have any feelings.'

'So the divorce is happening?'

Mum nodded. 'Yes. Neither of us thought it would come to this but—'

Alyssa felt a stab of ice in her heart. She dropped the bag of plantain.

'Who's there?' Auntie Dahlia called.

Alyssa picked up the plantain and walked through into the kitchen. 'Just me. We have the food now.'

'Did you hear our conversation, Alyssa?' Mum asked.

Alyssa nodded, her gut twisting with anxiety. She knew she'd done the right thing by choosing to save the spell garden, but now she had to face the reality of Mum and Dad breaking up. Her heart splintered. Things would never be the same.

'I'll give you two a minute,' Auntie Dahlia said, leaving the room.

Mum reached for Alyssa's hands and clasped them in hers. 'I know this is difficult for you to understand, my love. But we tried so hard to make it work. The truth is that your father and I are so much happier apart. And that means we can be better parents to you.'

Alyssa sniffed, holding back tears. 'Couldn't you have both tried harder?'

Mum smiled sadly. 'I'm so sorry. We really didn't want it to come to this.'

'I just want everything to go back to normal. I want us all to be happy,' said Alyssa.

Mum pulled her into a giant hug, patting her braids softly. 'You make me and your dad happy every single day, my darling. Never forget that. We love you so much.'

Alyssa hugged her mum back tighter.

'Your dad is back from his work trip now. He's coming here later. How about the three of us go for ice cream tonight? We can talk more about our plans. Things will change a little. But what won't change is how much we love you.'

Alyssa felt the loss of a weight she didn't know she was carrying. She realised that she didn't need a love spell to restore Mum and Dad's happiness, or to feel like her family was whole again. They had never left her.

'I'd like that. But does it have to be tonight?' she asked. 'It's just that ... we only just got the spell garden back. I'm a Keeper-in-Training now, Mum. Auntie Jasmine says I've got talent.'

Mum gave her a small smile. 'If that's what you want. Can you give me a hand with the meal first?'

Once the spell garden's produce had been brought to the kitchen, Alyssa cut the firm plantain into diagonal slices for Mum to fry in hot oil. They had a little production line going.

'Perfectly sliced plantain, Alyssa,' said Mum.

'Mum,' Alyssa asked after a while, 'how come we never eat like this at home?'

Mum paused. Then she said, 'Honestly? It's because I didn't want to think about anything that reminded me of my childhood. Of my heritage. Of *our* heritage. I thought my magic was dangerous. Dahlia said she'd told you about the fire.'

Alyssa nodded.

'I guess I've had trouble dealing with my emotions. Emotions are tied to magic. And magic was tied to my Jamaican heritage and family. Instead of working through the knotty issues, I put the whole lot in a big box in my mind, then hid that box in a dusty corner.'

Alyssa was quiet for a moment. 'I think I get that. But sometimes it's good to tell people what you're feeling. They might understand.'

Mum smiled. 'Wise words, sweetheart.' She sliced the avocados and fanned them out onto a platter.

'Do you still have magical powers, Mum?' Alyssa asked.

'I imagine I'm very rusty. But I don't think powers ever disappear completely. After all, something alerted me that you were in trouble. I dreamt that you were in terrible danger,' said Mum. 'But I knew it was more than just a dream – call it mother's intuition.'

They continued cooking in a steady rhythm. Mum mixed flour, water and salt in a giant metal bowl. She showed Alyssa how to roll the dough into round balls with a dimple in the middle. As Alyssa quietly rolled the dough into balls, Mum fried the dumplin's until they were crisp and golden. Cooking with Mum felt just like old times.

'I'm soooo hungry!' Alyssa heard Rue's voice from the living room.

'Won't be long!' Mum called, her voice lighter and breezier than Alyssa had heard in a long time.

Alyssa looked up at her mum and saw something else she hadn't seen in a while: a smile. A real smile. It warmed Alyssa down to her toes.

Rosalie poked her head through the kitchen door. 'Is there anything I can do to help?' It was her polite code for: *How much longer is this going to take?*

'You can lay the table,' Mum suggested. 'The food will be ready in five minutes.'

Alyssa helped her mum to bring platters of food to the table: golden fried plantain, ripe avocado slices, fried dumplin's, and fragrant ackee and saltfish.

'Violet, what's your secret? You always did make the lightest dumplin's,' Auntie Dahlia said, as they sat down to eat.

'I use cake flour,' Mum replied, beaming at the compliment. 'Luckily Auntie Jasmine had some lurking in the back cupboard.'

'I use cake flour too,' Auntie Dahlia said. 'Must have left that here from the last time I made breakfast.'

'I hope they're all right. It's been such a long time since I've made them,' Mum said.

Auntie Jasmine looked like she was about to cry with happiness. 'What an incredible treat this is! It's been years . . .' She trailed off.

'Years since what, Auntie?' Alyssa asked.

'Since I've seen my two favourite girls look so happy,' she said quietly.

Alyssa followed her eyes across the table, where Auntie Dahlia and Mum were smiling at each other.

When Alyssa had tried to come up with a love spell, she'd only wanted to heal the bond between her mum and dad. That might not have worked, but she couldn't help glowing at the fact that something else wonderful had happened this summer. As she looked around the table at her family, she knew this was a meal she'd never forget.

wild Petunia
(for beauty)

CHAPTER TWENTY-EIGHT

'This is one thing I definitely don't miss about London,' Mum said as the car ground to a halt. They were in bumper-to-bumper traffic. 'Know any spells to get us out of a traffic jam?'

Alyssa giggled. 'Nope! Sorry.'

She and Mum were on their way to the spell garden for the first time in weeks. In the end, she had got to spend the rest of the summer with her cousins before Dad took her to the seaside on the weekend before school.

Alyssa was now getting used to splitting her time between her house and Dad's new flat. Dad's place was literally two minutes from her new school, which made early-morning starts much easier. In fact, secondary school had turned out to be a lot less scary than Alyssa had thought. Learning that she could make new friends in the spell garden made it easier for her to make friends at school, like Leah and Zohra who happened to share Alyssa's love of fantasy novels. Alyssa realised that if she could face a bulldozer, she could handle talking to a new person at lunch.

Mum and Alyssa had made the decision to tell Dad about the magic school. No more secrets. He'd taken the news better than Alyssa expected. There were no spells allowed in the house without Mum's supervision, but he approved of Alyssa's newfound passion for gardening. Especially when the sunflowers in his garden shot up several centimetres overnight.

Although Alyssa hadn't really believed her, Mum was right. The divorce made them better parents. Mum and Dad both spent less time working, and in the evenings Alyssa had their undivided attention. She still felt a bit wistful when Dad dropped her home and went back to his place, but deep down she knew that a magical tea wouldn't have fixed her parents. It was weird to think that the split had made her family whole again.

After what felt like hours of sitting in traffic, they finally made it to Holloway. Alyssa looked out of the window and took in the familiar sights. She never had made it to the London Eye or any other world-famous landmarks. But she wouldn't have swapped being in this neighbourhood for anywhere else.

It was late September, but the skies were blue and the sun was warm. The high street seemed busier than ever when they pulled up outside Jasmine's Teas. The shop was shut, and a sign taped to the door read:

Closed Early for Holloway Park
Grand Reopening

Mum and Alyssa made their way to the small park across the road. They walked down the gravel path, past the sports field and dog walkers, following the sound of music and laughter.

'It looks so different,' Alyssa said.

The last time she had been in this park was for Auntie Jasmine's fundraiser party. That was over a month ago, and it had transformed.

Before, there was a rickety playground, a scrubby patch of grass and the dreaded pay gates. But now? The lawn was lush and green, wildflowers were everywhere she turned, and there was a pond teeming with shimmery fish.

After seeing what had happened with the developers, Auntie Jasmine's landlord returned the rent advance because they didn't want the bad publicity. She decided that as the community had raised it, it ought to go back to them. And everyone agreed to spend it on making the park a really nice space.

'Is that a vegetable patch?' Mum said, bending down to inspect a raised wooden bed filled with soil and greenery.

'Mum, if you'd seen this place last month . . . Now, it's just like the spell garden,' Alyssa said.

She'd never seen the neighbourhood look this good. The crux-water must be positively overflowing.

'You're here, finally!' said a voice behind them. Alyssa spun round to see some familiar faces. It was Rosalie and Rue, with Leon just behind them.

Rosalie and Rue gave Alyssa a massive hug. 'We missed you.'

'I missed you too,' Alyssa said. She pulled back and took in the sight of her cousins. 'Is that a new badge?'

Rue's yellow, white, purple and black striped non-binary badge glimmered in the sunlight. 'Yup!' they said proudly.

'Hey, Alyssa!' Leon said. 'It's been a while.'

She grinned. 'It's good to see you! How are you enjoying being back home?'

'I'm loving it,' he replied. 'The landlord was practically begging for Mum and Dad to return. They even slashed the rent. When the developers left, loads of the new shops went with them – they didn't want to open in a neighbourhood where there were protests.'

'I don't believe we've met,' Mum said to Leon. 'But tell your parents that they should contact me if they have any more landlord trouble,' she said, handing over her business card. 'I helped Auntie Jasmine sort out her contract.'

'Hi, Auntie Violet,' Rosalie said. 'Mum and Auntie Jasmine are by the picnic benches.'

Mum turned round to give them a wave. 'If you need me, sweetheart, I'll be over there,' she said to Alyssa.

Rosalie, Rue and Leon pulled Alyssa over to the BBQ so she could get some food.

'I told Auntie Jasmine to make sure we had non-spicy chicken wings for you,' Rue said proudly (and a little too loudly, for Alyssa's liking).

Alyssa blushed. 'Thanks, Rue,' she said. 'But the whole park doesn't need to know I can't handle spicy food.'

As they queued for the BBQ, Alyssa took in the

crowd. All the usual Silverleaf and Hemlock kids were there, along with their families. She saw Auntie Jasmine's neighbours from the estate and a few of the local shopkeepers too. She and her cousins took their paper plates of food and sat in a corner of the park shaded by a large tree.

'So what have I missed? Spill!' Alyssa said, before digging into her food.

'Auntie Jasmine has decided to expand the spell garden,' Rosalie said. 'Since we banished the developers, the crux well is producing more crux-water than ever.'

'Sweet!' said Alyssa. 'Any news from Lisa?'

'You mean Auntie Jasmine never told you?' said Rue.

'Told me what?' Alyssa asked.

'About a week after you left, we spotted Lisa trying to break out of the spell garden with an armful of magical plants! She had enough crux-pebbles to start her own spell garden, but she was too impatient to wait for her magical plants to grow,' Rosalie said. 'It turns out she knew about my secret entrance.'

'Little did she know, Auntie Jasmine had cast a protection spell that would trap Lisa in the spell garden if she returned,' Rue added. 'When we came in for lessons the next day, Lisa had been stuck in the garden all night!'

'No way!' Alyssa said.

'Auntie Jasmine wouldn't let her leave until she told her where the crux-pebbles were. She was also stripped of her title as Keeper's Apprentice and banished from the spell garden forever,' Rosalie said.

'So the crux-pebbles are back! That explains why the garden looks so lush in September,' Alyssa said.

'Yep,' Rosalie said proudly. 'Greener than ever!'

Suddenly the music drifting over from the sound speakers paused. Auntie Jasmine stood up and cleared her throat. It was time for a speech.

'C'mon, let's get closer,' Alyssa said. They stood up and moved towards the front of the small crowd sitting on picnic benches and blankets.

Auntie Jasmine saw Alyssa in the crowd and winked at her. She had a paper cup with a logo in her hands.

'Is Auntie Jasmine drinking … a latte?!' Alyssa whispered to Rosalie.

Rosalie smirked. 'Yep! She decided that change wasn't all bad, and now she's addicted to the matcha lattes from the new place across the road.'

'Thank you for coming to the grand reopening of Holloway Park!' she said. 'Now, I can't take any credit for the beauty you see before you. This happened because every single person here contributed in some way. Magical things happen when people pull together.'

The crowd clapped and cheered.

'She's being modest,' Rosalie whispered. 'Auntie Jasmine had a whole lot to do with reclaiming the park.'

'There's still work to do,' Auntie Jasmine continued. 'Like all community projects, the park will need to be maintained. This will rely on the skills of every single person here. Every one of you has something to offer. I hope that, when I come back in a few months' time, the park is just as busy and loved as it is now.'

'Come back? From where?' Alyssa whispered.

'For those of you that don't know, I'm going to visit my sister in Jamaica for the winter,' Auntie Jasmine said, as if she had heard Alyssa's whispers from several metres away.

'A well-deserved break!' someone yelled.

Auntie Jasmine chuckled. 'Precisely! But I know that I'm leaving the neighbourhood in a pair of safe hands. Several of them, in fact.'

When her speech finished, the music returned and the crowd started chatting again, Alyssa made her way to Auntie Jasmine.

'I didn't know you were going away!' she blurted out.

'Hello to you too, Alyssa,' Auntie Jasmine said. 'Come and give me a hug. I've missed you!'

'I missed you too,' Alyssa said. She had missed Auntie Jasmine's kaftans and the humming when she watered her plants. She missed her rose-oil scent and her unusually warm hands. 'I thought I could come back and see you over half-term.'

'I'm afraid the spell garden will be hibernating this winter, and I'll be in Jamaica sipping tea on my sister Hyacinth's veranda, my dear,' Auntie Jasmine said. 'It'll be my first time back since I was a child. And my first time leaving the spell garden.'

'I'm glad you're having a break, Auntie,' Alyssa said.

'It's long overdue. I've protected this community for so long, it never occurred to me that I could ask them to look after me. I know the neighbourhood will be in safe hands. When I'm back from Jamaica, you can come and visit us any time,' Auntie Jasmine said with a smile.

Alyssa sighed with relief. 'It's going to be weird spending half-term in Milton Keynes, now.'

'I'm sure there are other things you could do over

the school holiday,' Auntie Jasmine said. She looked pointedly at Rosalie, Rue and Leon. 'Ask them,' she whispered.

Alyssa didn't ask Auntie Jasmine how she knew this question had been on her mind. She learned that there were some things you didn't ask. She approached her cousins and Leon, who were sitting on the lawn chatting. Just a couple of months ago, approaching the people who had become her best friends had filled her with anxiety. Now she couldn't imagine her life without them.

'Auntie Jasmine said the spell garden is hibernating over half-term,' Alyssa said.

'Yep! Every winter,' Rue said.

'It's so annoying. It means I have to practise spell work at home and it just isn't the same,' Rosalie said. 'In secret, of course.'

'If the spell garden is closed ... do you guys want to visit me in Milton Keynes? There's no magic but Mum and Dad have promised to take time off work for fun stuff.'

'Yes, please!' Rue yelled.

'Seriously? I'd love that,' Rosalie said. 'As long as I can get some homework in, yeah?'

'You're a lifesaver! I'd have to work in the takeaway otherwise,' Leon beamed.

Alyssa couldn't help but smile. 'Milton Keynes isn't as exciting as London, but I'm sure we'll have a good time.'

'Of course we will,' Rosalie said, grinning.

Although she would miss the magic and wonder of the spell garden, Alyssa realised that the true magic lay in her new friendships. What a wonder it was to have people who could laugh with you. Who you felt safe with. Who truly got you. She wouldn't swap that for all the magic tea in the world.

'We always have fun when we're together,' Alyssa nodded. Then she sat down on the grass beside her friends as they planned their next adventure.

ACKNOWLEDGEMENTS

I am so deeply grateful to everyone who has shaped this story and supported me during the writing of this book. I'm living my dream.

Thank you to my agent Lauren Gardner and the team at Bell Lomax Moreton for their support over the last few years. I'm especially grateful to Lauren for her patience and wisdom as she guided me through several redrafts of the novel before we struck gold.

Thank you to the truly wonderful team at Faber, particularly my editor Natasha Brown. I'm so proud to be supported by such a brilliant bunch of people and it's been an absolute joy working with each and every one of you. Thank you to my copy editors Jenny Glencross and Wendy Shakespeare for making the book sparkle. I'm also very grateful to Bex Glendining for their incredible book cover – thank you for your talent and for bringing the spell garden world to life.

Thank you to my creative writing support group for patiently and lovingly giving me feedback on drafts of this novel going back to 2019. This book wouldn't be the same without your excellent, sharp critique.

Finally, thank you to my friends and family for showing up for me at every turn. You don't know how much it means to be enveloped in your love, support and encouragement. Thank you, thank you, thank you.

Watch out for
Alyssa's next adventure,
coming soon . . .